MILLIE'S SE

The Town of Pearl 4

Dixie Lynn Dwyer

LOVEXTREME FOREVER

Siren Publishing, Inc.
www.SirenPublishing.com

A SIREN PUBLISHING BOOK
IMPRINT: LoveXtreme Forever

MILLIE'S SECOND CHANCE
Copyright © 2012 by Dixie Lynn Dwyer

ISBN: 978-1-62242-082-7

First Printing: November 2012

Cover design by Harris Channing
All art and logo copyright © 2012 by Siren Publishing, Inc.

ALL RIGHTS RESERVED: This literary work may not be reproduced or transmitted in any form or by any means, including electronic or photographic reproduction, in whole or in part, without express written permission.

All characters and events in this book are fictitious. Any resemblance to actual persons living or dead is strictly coincidental.

Printed in the U.S.A.

PUBLISHER
Siren Publishing, Inc.
www.SirenPublishing.com

DEDICATION

To my reading fans who have enjoyed the Town of Pearl series, I hope you enjoy this tale about empowerment, survival, and success. As women, we sometimes face barriers that seem overwhelming and potentially indestructible, but somehow, someway, we triumph and overcome them. The Town of Pearl is a very special place, where many women wind up in search of their second chances.

May you enjoy Millie's journey and the development of an organization in Pearl that represents those women who have succeeded in achieving their second chance while they wait with open arms for those who are still searching.

Live by the saying…"I am woman…Hear me roar!"

Hugs!
~Dixie~

MILLIE'S SECOND CHANCE

The Town of Pearl 4

DIXIE LYNN DWYER
Copyright © 2012

Prologue

Millie laughed as Stacy stared after Mickey Sullivan.

"He has a really nice butt," Stacy whispered, and Anna gave Stacy a light smack on her arm.

"Lower your voice, Stacy! He might hear and come back this way."

Stacy placed her hands on her hips and stared at Anna.

"Like that would be so terrible?"

Millie shook her head as she grabbed the notebook from Stacy's hand.

"Is that who you've been writing about in your diary?" she teased.

"Give that back, Millie!" Stacy demanded.

Anna remained quiet and Millie stopped a moment to look at her as she handed Stacy her book.

She worried about Anna. She was always so quiet and reserved all the time. Lately she'd been extra quiet and she was sporting another new bruise on her upper arm.

Stacy caught Millie's line of sight and joined her by Anna as they sat cross-legged on the blacktop.

"Hey, whatcha thinking about, Anna?" Millie asked.

Anna sighed. "You ever think about what's out there in the world? I mean aside from city life?" Millie swallowed hard. Whenever Anna got talking about other places to live, it meant that things were bad at home.

"Sometimes I do. I remember how beautiful Texas was, but now I've gotten used to life here."

"I'm going to work in one of those tall skyscrapers one day," Stacy chimed in then stared off toward the buildings in front of her. It wasn't that they could see the tall buildings from outside their apartment complex, but they all knew what they looked like.

"I'm going to wear really fashionable suits and dresses. My high heels will be expensive and I might even snag me a rich husband." Stacy pressed her boobs together, forming a small cleavage and both Millie and Anna laughed.

"You'll need to do some growing in that department," Millie teased Stacy.

Stacy looked down at her chest. "Hey, I'm fourteen and way past training bras. I've been hiding these well."

They giggled.

"Maybe you should ask Michael if they're big enough," Millie teased and they all giggled.

"You shouldn't be talking, Millie. I've seen the way you look at Vinnie Malone. You get all goo-goo and gaga over his tan complexion and his accent."

"I do not! He's seventeen and he's a troublemaker." Millie crossed her arms in front of her chest.

"Anna, tell her it's obvious that she likes Vinny. She always goes for the dangerous bad-boy type," Stacy stated.

Millie eyed Anna and Anna's cheeks reddened.

"You do like the bad boys, Millie. Every time Vinny comes around he checks you out."

"He does not! I do not!" she was rambling on, and Stacy looked her over.

"You may be fourteen, Millie, but you have got a set on you already. You look like a mature woman."

Millie shook her head and gave both Anna and Stacy a mean look. They were her best friends. She didn't want this kind of attention from men. She was chubby and had large breasts, larger than both her friends', and she didn't like that her breast size was grabbing the attention of older men. Even if they were good-looking Italian men like Vinny Malone.

"Hey, we were just teasing you. Look at the three of us. We're known on the streets as the triplets with the great bodies and we're all virgins. I'd say if we play our cards right and we stick together, then we'll have our choice of men. Good men that will treat us like gold and get us out of the projects," Stacy stated firmly.

"Maybe you guys, but not me. I'm stuck here. It's destiny," Anna replied then looked at her watch.

"I have to go. I have to stop at the store then start dinner before Mom and Dad get home. I'll talk to you tomorrow," Anna said then hugged her two friends before leaving.

Millie watched her go then turned to Stacy.

"He hit her again," Millie whispered.

"I know. I wish we could do something, but living with her parents is better than living in some shelter or in foster care."

"One day, we'll all be happy and we'll be best friends forever." Millie closed her eyes and wished her words would come true.

Stacy covered her hand and squeezed it.

"We'll be friends forever no matter what."

Millie opened her eyes to look at Stacy but instead she saw Frank.

Millie screamed and shuffled out of bed.

Little by little, she absorbed her surroundings and realized that it had all been a dream. A childhood memory locked inside her mind. She glanced at the clock on the bedside table. Tonight was the big gala. She had dedicated many hours to the job. She made a lot of business connections, some that she hoped could help launch her homemade jewelry business. Her current job was getting too stressful, she couldn't move any higher up because family held other positions and Stewart just dumped her. He was a friend of her boss, and yesterday at work her boss mentioned budget cuts and layoffs. Well, at least she had tonight.

As she thought back on her dream, she ignored the ending and the sight of Frank. He was behind bars for at least another fourteen months. She was safe from him and would never give him the opportunity to hurt her again. She had been so foolish back then, thinking that he loved her and that every time he hit her or spoke down to her, that he did it because he loved her so much. *What were his words again? Oh yeah, "This is for your own good, baby. You need to be perfect and any woman of mine will obey me in my commands. Besides, you know I love you, don't you?"*

She swallowed hard. His disturbing and distorted view of making her into a better woman caused her to wind up tied to a bed, beaten and nearly strangled to death. She would always remember that day. More than twelve hours of sexual assault, beatings, and his constant explanation that he was cleansing her. The sick bastard had the nerve to tell her that it was her fault. He said he saw her talking to another man. Jordan was not even a friend. He had just been an acquaintance from work that she said hello and goodbye to and perhaps he would ask if she was hanging out or going to any new clubs. It was an innocent conversation viewed by her psycho boyfriend Frank as cheating, and it nearly cost her her life.

She recalled lying there, tied to her bed, her body bloody, her mind losing focus as he repeatedly struck her. She prayed for death. She accepted it, wanted it so badly she told him to just kill her. As he grabbed her throat and squeezed, the door crashed open and all hell broke loose. Millie could hardly see the figure with the baseball bat swinging and hitting Frank before the tables turned. Millie heard Stacy scream and Millie cried, fearing for her best friend's life. It felt like their battle lasted forever as Millie begged to maintain consciousness. She feared that Stacy was going to die just as members of the police department arrived. She closed her eyes and hadn't awoken until three days later as she lay all hooked up to tubes and wires in the ICU.

The tears rolled down her cheeks. Millie quickly wiped them away. She didn't want to think about him. He scared her. All her self-defense training, counseling, and achievements were accomplished because he wasn't around to hurt her or break her down. She was a different woman now, but she still hadn't learned shit about picking the right man. Stewart had been another great mistake in her life, another control freak. She stretched her arms out above her head and looked at the black dress covered in dry-cleaning plastic. Taking a deep breath, a smile formed on her face. Stewart wouldn't know what hit him.

Chapter 1

Town of Pearl
Lewis Dojo

"I think you better give up right now, Hank," Marco Lewis told his brother as Dalton Lewis circled around the mat after knocking Hank clean on his ass.

"I don't think so. This has been a long time coming and Dalton's been moping around and being grumpy for way too long," Hank replied, and Dalton gave a sidekick to Hank's knee, but Hank stepped to the side, quickly avoiding the strike.

Marco laughed. His brother, Hank, had been right. Dalton was never happy. He just worked in the MMA fighting gym training military and law enforcement officers then headed home. He never went out anymore, and forget about hooking up with some woman or women. He just wasn't interested.

"Hey, that was unfair," Hank yelled at Dalton as Dalton swept Hank's legs out from underneath him.

"Okay, you two, that's enough. I have to be at the department in thirty minutes. I'm not leaving you two here alone to battle out your differences," Marco stated.

Hank and Dalton stopped as they stood a few feet away from one another, breathing heavily.

"You should snap out of this slump you're in, bro. Come out with us tonight, or maybe hookup with Stella, Lisa, Paula, or even Melody. They want you so badly," Hank teased.

"Fuck you! I'm not into easy chicks and I sure as hell don't want to get trapped by any of those women." Dalton reached down to the floor and grabbed his Gatorade.

"Trapped? What do you mean? They just want sex," Hank replied.

"No, they want husbands and I don't trust any of them. You'd better watch your ass around those women," Dalton reprimanded and Hank looked surprised.

"Watch your dick, too. I heard through the grapevine that all four of them want to land a Lewis brother," Marco added.

"Then you're not safe either, Deputy Lewis," Hank teased Marco.

"Like I'd fall for their tricks? I am the oldest. That means I know which head to use. You should try it. The both of you," Marco replied then began to walk out of the room.

* * * *

"Hey, I was just joking with you. I was hoping to make you laugh, not anger you more," Hank told his brother Dalton. He was concerned about his seriousness lately and the fact that once he left the dojo he kept to himself. Dalton was a good man, and sure, he had a wicked scar from serving in the war and surviving his tour in Fallujah, but Hank thought it made him look tough. Despite his brother's insecurities, the women seemed attracted to that scar and the silent, brooding type. Hank chuckled to himself.

"I don't need cheering up. I'm fine and I sure as hell don't need the complications of women right now. I'm good, Hank, so cool it, okay?"

"All right. No problem. Let's get ready for the kids' class. I think I'm going to take some ibuprofen now while I can. You know, cut off the headache before I get it," Hank said and Dalton chuckled.

* * * *

Dalton was changing his shirt in the back room as he thought about his brother's tactics in teasing him. He chuckled to himself at first and then he felt that tight feeling in his chest and emptiness in his gut. Dalton was a military man and used to handling everything on his own. He didn't do gentle and didn't like meaningless sex with women. He was getting older and feeling tired. His desires for more in life were changing dramatically. Perhaps it had something to do with the conversation he had with his four brothers about finding and sharing a woman. The thought about settling down with one and starting a family scared the shit out of him. *What the fuck do I have to offer a woman? I'm ornery most of the damn time. I'm mean and I know, it even though I don't mean to be, and hell, I'm set in my ways, and I expect discipline and respect.*

He ran his hand through his hair. He had told his brothers this. They had shared their feelings, which was incredibly awkward but over a lot of beers seemed acceptable at the time. He learned that his second oldest brother Anthony, the owner of a local construction company with their other brother Jeremy, wanted to have kids. From that admittance came a nod and mumble from their oldest brother, Deputy Marco Lewis, which indicated he wanted the same thing. Then of course Hank, being Hank, sensitive, ready to talk your ear off, wanted to make immediate plans to choose a woman and start wooing her. That just made the rest of them feel completely uncomfortable and freak out. Thankfully, their youngest brother Jeremy cracked jokes about the process of finding a woman who would be interested in having sex with five men and how inspiring the process to locate her would be.

Jeremy was a total flirt and ladies' man at only twenty-five years old. Most things to him were still a joke, but Dalton knew that this wasn't a joking matter. In fact, since that night, he seemed to think about finding that special woman more and more. But just as others found their partners in Pearl and beyond, he and his brothers needed to wait it out. If they were meant to share a woman, then she would find them and maybe then he would be ready to face and embrace his emotions and desires.

"Hey, the kids are arriving. You ready?" Hank asked as he appeared in the doorway. Dalton nodded his head then took a deep breath, feeling that emptiness in the pit of his stomach. Maybe there was some woman out there that could accept him for his faults, his shitty personality and the damn scar that made him so somber inside.

* * * *

What a crazy and emotional week, Millie thought as she smoothed her hands down the silk dress she wore, being sure to straighten it on her hips. She looked into the mirror and could suddenly see all the imperfections of her body and the flaws that Stewart had pointed out to her in a fit of rage while attempting to hide his infidelity. Could she call it that? Infidelity, when they weren't even married? She exhaled then tilted her head to the side and adjusted her large breasts. She may be a good ten pounds overweight and have a little "pouch" in front from sitting at the damn computer all day, but at least she had her breasts. The "twins" were one asset she was surely going to use tonight to piss off Stewart.

She felt her inner confidence shine, then the tightness of the dress, the way that little bit of extra skin rolled over the material under her arms, seemed to outshine the twins.

"Son of a bitch! I am so sick and tired of men," she stated out loud to the mirror. Even as she cupped her breasts and lifted, that bit of extra fat pushed out. She couldn't show up to the event looking and feeling like a fat pig. She had worked hard to raise money for the women's shelter and she had saved a lot of money and put in the extra hours at the office, despite the constant rumors that people were going to be laid off after the event. Would Stewart stoop so low and talk with Mr. Arthur, her boss? Shit!

She turned a little to the right and then a little to the left. She was jiggly, as Stewart had informed her. But hey, she had been working hard, sitting for hours, and unable to attend any workout classes that kept her firmer. She could worry about exercising and losing weight tomorrow. Tonight, she wanted Stewart and his other asshole buddies to see what they would be missing. She'd never been any smaller than a size twelve. She didn't do single digits. She chuckled at her own thoughts then reapplied some lip gloss before glancing in the mirror one last time.

Millie had splurged on the salon and spa treatment to look her best for the gala. She had her hair done and placed in an updo to not hide the open back to her dress. Her ass was too big, too. She should have a beeper attached for when she backed up.

She felt her spirits disintegrate. All of Stewart's nasty insults were not so easily forgotten. He had scorned her, made her feel unworthy of his high class, his perfect physique. She couldn't spend three hours a day at the gym. Her exercise experience consisted of six months of self-defense training that she slowly fell out of the routine of going to. Even at the dojo she felt inferior despite her ability to do all the moves. Stewart had even put down her black belt status and forbid her to attend more classes. She was weeks away from achieving the belt and he destroyed that. Perhaps he was afraid that she would use the moves on him? Maybe she should have. But those classes were expensive and her job was too demanding to attend the routine classes she wanted to. She wasn't born into money. But she had dignity and it had been her work and efforts to establish the shelter. She would attend the event and be done seeing that jerk Stewart ever again.

She took a deep breath and headed out of her apartment. It took three hard pulls as she simultaneously twisted the knob and turned the key in order to lock her front door. Everyone living in the building had similar problems. It was part of living in the city. It didn't matter that this complex was considered really nice, almost upscale. She released a shaky breath and headed downstairs to the waiting taxi below.

* * * *

Just as she entered the cab and gave the address, her cell phone began to ring. The tune "Cowboy Casanova" by Carrie Underwood began and Millie smiled as she answered her cell phone and the taxi took her to the event.

"Hi, Stacy. What's going on?" Millie asked, thrilled that one of her best friends was calling her.

"Oh, Anna and I are hanging out and just wanted to wish you luck tonight. We're so proud of you and the money you raised for the battered women's shelter. It's such a good cause."

"Thank you so much. It's been a bit crazy and was a lot of work but well worth it."

"So is Stewart with you? Are you wearing that fancy black gown you texted a picture of?"

"Oh, yeah, I'm wearing it. It's a bit tight, though. I think I should have waited until last week to shop for it," Millie stated, thinking that in her state of upset being dumped by Stewart she shouldn't have indulged in that gallon of ice cream and potato chips. *Shit, I let another man fuck up my head.*

"You sound funny. Is everything okay?" Stacy asked.

Of course Stacy and Anna could always tell when something was wrong. She felt the tears reach her eyes then swallowed hard.

"Stewart dumped me," she whispered then sniffled.

"What? Why? What the hell happened?" Stacy asked, sounding shocked and upset. She was such a great friend.

"Well, let's just say a very thin and sexy blonde model."

"Oh, shit! Are you okay? When did this happen?"

"A couple of weeks ago."

"A couple of weeks ago and you're just telling us now?" Stacy asked, sounding angry.

"I was just trying to get through it, Stacy. I've had so much on my plate with trying to raise the money for the shelter and working to save up enough to start my own business. Then, of course, Stewart does this to me. I just don't seem to have luck with men."

"Aww, Millie, don't feel that way. Sometimes you have to go through a few frogs before you can find the prince."

"What?"

Stacy chuckled and so did Anna. Millie could hear Anna in the background. Suddenly, Anna was telling Stacy to give her the phone.

"Stacy? Hey, it's Anna. Listen, you should think about visiting us, or perhaps coming out here for good. The town is growing in leaps and bounds. It would be great to see you. You could probably sell your handmade jewelry in the boutique in town. Plus Stacy, Lena, and I have been working on the new shelter and grounds. You should see the place. Construction is going excellent. We already have five women living out here. Word is traveling fast."

Millie took a deep breath. She wasn't feeling like herself at all. She felt depressed, unsure what direction her life was going in, and she just wanted to get through tonight.

"I'll see. I'm happy that it is going so well. There are a lot of women out there in need. I'm sure word will spread fast. Listen, the taxi just pulled up at the event. I need to go, but I'll call you guys tomorrow and we'll talk some more."

"Okay. Good luck, and remember that you are gorgeous. Do not let that stuck-up, snobby, rich cheater make you feel inferior. If he brings the model, just ignore them and work what your mamma gave ya!"

"Thanks, Anna. I'll talk to you tomorrow."

Millie hung up the phone and felt a little better after talking to the girls. She wasn't ready to face plans for the future yet, but hoped that an idea would emerge and she could focus on that and forget about Stewart and all men for a while.

* * * *

The venue was extraordinary. She should have expected only the best from Mr. Arthur. It was very glamorous and upscale and completely paid for by one of many contributors to Mr. Arthur's company. There had to be several hundred in attendance, and most were decked out in fine gowns and tuxedos. Millie was now glad that she splurged on the black dress. She had already received numerous compliments, which perked her earlier misconceptions of her appearance. Dressed like this in a place so fancy made her feel beautiful and successful. The award she received about a half hour ago also perked her confidence. She was on a high right now as she sipped her champagne. Although she was only a fundraising coordinator making a mere thirty thousand dollars a year before taxes, she felt pretty good right now. Monday, when pink slips were handed out, she may feel differently. Why ruin it?

She absorbed everything she could. She wanted to remember this good feeling she had and the accomplishment she had been part of. Many women coming from abuse, neglect, or persecution would now have an opportunity for a better life. There were tables set up auctioning off various items to raise even more money for the organization. She felt proud that she had been part of it, and the fatigue from the long work hours was a distant memory.

Millie stood near a few women she knew from other local organizations. They were all dressed nicely and had complimented her on her dress, her hair, and even stated that she looked stunning this evening. She was feeling pretty good from the boost to her confidence, smiling so much that her cheeks began to ache, when she glanced around the room and caught sight of Stewart. The blonde hanging on his arm was a freaking Amazon compared to Millie.

Stewart wasn't close to six feet tall, and the blonde would have been way taller than him even if she weren't sporting the Jimmy Choo six-inch stilettos. They made an odd-looking couple. Her purple dress was shimmering and hugged the bitch's model figure. However, when she turned right or left, her breasts, probably taped in with some of that fancy clear stuff, nearly caused her nipples to show. The men around her looked as if they all needed bibs.

"Hey, don't even bother looking at her. He's an ass for dumping you," Clare whispered. Her friend from the office sipped at a seltzer with lemon. Her black square glasses were designer, but the rest of her was thrift shop. Clare was an odd mix of modern-day hippie and a fashion diva. She danced to the beat of her own drum and Millie didn't mind one bit.

Millie pulled her eyes away from the scene and took a sip of her glass of white wine. *Don't let him ruin your time. Don't let seeing him with someone else affect you.*

"Hey, you look gorgeous and classy. Don't let it bother you. There are lots of hot single guys around here. You'll have your choice."

"I know I shouldn't bother to look. She's got everyone's attention," Millie whispered as she looked at Clare.

"That's because they're waiting to see which tit pops out first, the right or the left. I'm betting on the right. I can almost see part of the areola from here." Millie nearly choked on the sip of wine she took.

She stared at her coworker, shocked by her words but tickled by the description.

"Come on, Millie. Get real, will ya? We're not at work and you have succeeded in helping to establish a great women's shelter. You should be celebrating."

"I am celebrating." Millie lifted her half-empty glass and then took another sip of wine.

"Your breasts are better than hers. You should be working that sexy figure you have."

"Sexy?"

"Oh, please. Do not tell me that you think you don't have a great figure." Clare placed her hand on her hip and gave Millie a sideways glance. "Woman, you are the Marilyn Monroe of the joint. Perfect round ass, great hips, and big, gorgeous blue eyes. Shit, I wish I had your figure instead of this pencil-thin mess of skin and bones. No matter what I eat it doesn't seem to land on my body. I want hips and ass," Clare stated a little loudly, and Millie shook her head and laughed.

"I hate my hips and ass, and as they say, 'through the lips and onto the hips.'"

"Millie, may I have a moment please?" Stewart interrupted them and Millie felt her cheeks redden and her face go flush. *Shit, I hope he didn't hear me.*

Clare gave Stewart the once-over as if he was dog turd and Millie stifled her laugh. Who would have thought that the quiet, cuckoo secretary had such a grand personality?

"What do you want, Stewart?" He took her elbow and led her toward the side hallway away from the crowd of guests. He probably didn't want to be seen with her. She felt nothing for him, and that fact made her feel stronger instead of intimidated.

He looked down at her and she was grateful that she wore the heels. Her designer shoes now made her stand at about five feet seven, and he was only an inch or so taller.

He stared at the cleavage of her dress and she was glad the twins were large and perky. His date's were the complete opposite.

"Why are you wearing something like this?" he scolded and she was shocked. Was he seriously going to reprimand her choice of dress? He had no right.

"Excuse me?"

"You're too…heavy to wear something like this. It's demeaning."

She was shocked but also stricken to her heart by his words. When she had feelings for someone she gave it her all. That had been her downfall with Frank as well as with Stewart. She wasted her love, her energy on one bad man after the next. Anger flared, but she couldn't seem to get her mouth to function. But then he reached up and ran his index finger from her throat over her breasts as if he owned her and could have her at any time. Instead of the touch turning her on, it made her feel nauseous.

"Are you jealous because your date is lacking in the same category?" she spat at him. Obviously, the wine she had gave her some confidence. She had never talked back to Stewart. That was part of the problem and she knew it. She was not an assertive woman when it came to men. She wanted a man that she could trust enough to lead her, especially in the bedroom, but so far all she met were control freaks and womanizers. Stewart was almost as evil and manipulative as Frank had been. The only difference was that Frank actually abused her and nearly killed her, where Stewart verbally abused her and feared confrontation. At least with the same sex he did. Women he could push around and control, but when a man confronted Stewart, he was such a wuss.

Stewart raised his eyebrows at her as his finger remained on the bodice of her dress. She turned slightly right so that his finger fell away from her. But then she felt the wall against her back .

He stared at her with eyes filled with disgust and anger. She swallowed hard. He loathed her and she waited in silence for his verbal attack.

"She's a model and has to watch what she eats. She cares about her body, unlike you." There it was, another strike with his tongue, and damn it, she felt it again in her heart and her confidence.

"Well, then, it's good that you're going home with her. She's more your type."

"More my type? What is that supposed to mean?"

"She's vain just like you, and so you two deserve one another. Now if you'll excuse me." She began to walk away when he grabbed her upper arm and shoved her hard against the wall. She looked around and there wasn't a soul in sight.

His teeth were clenched and his fingers dug into her skin.

"No man will ever want you for anything but a quick fuck. If they tell you otherwise, then they're lying so you'll spread your legs. You're nothing, Millie. You were a meaningless fuck and no man will ever take you as more than that."

His words tore at her heart and her body shook at his abusive grip. It reminded her of Frank and she fell speechless. Perhaps all men were like this. There was no other explanation. Why was she always getting involved with men that wanted to hurt her and treat her so badly?

"Leave, Millie. You disgust me."

He shoved her as he released her arm and she felt the tears sting her eyes and the pain collide against her flesh.

This evening couldn't get any worse than right now.

She wanted to leave. Stewart was right. She was nothing and obviously meant nothing to him.

She hurried toward the door, her purse in hand, and out to a waiting cab. Once inside, she leaned her head back and willed the tears away. She left her award back at the table and hoped that Clare would pick it up for her. Millie felt like crap and she wondered what she was going to do with her life. She felt as if she were at a crossroads. The circle she was in would always bring her to events like these and around people like Stewart. Why couldn't she find love and happiness? Was she meant to be alone without a partner in this world?

She gave the cab driver her address and she noticed the way he looked over her breasts in the rearview mirror. She cleared her throat and unsuccessfully crossed her arms over her chest. It was useless. She had always been big up top. Just like she always had that soft swell over her belly and a stocky figure. She was strong, too. She swallowed hard as Stewart's words came crashing back to her mind, and then the cab stopped in front of her apartment complex. She dug out the fare for the ride and exited the car. It was only nine in the evening, an earlier night than she had expected and worse results than she had imagined.

Millie entered the elevator and began to think about the city and her life there when her cell phone rang. The elevator chimed and the doors opened as she dug out her keys and the phone.

Fumbling with her keys and unlocking the door, she answered her cell phone.

"Hello."

"I've missed you, Mill. God, your voice sounds great."

Millie closed the door and dropped her bag on the floor. She froze in place and felt the blood drain from her body.

"What? You're not happy to hear from me? I've done nothing but think about you while I was rotting behind bars, serving my time."

Millie swallowed hard. *Frank.*

"I really don't have anything to say to you, Frank."

"Ahh, baby, come on. Don't tell me you're still upset with me for what happened?"

"Of course I am, Frank. You nearly killed me and I spent weeks in the hospital."

Her voice was shaking. Her entire body was. She should just hang up. But then she wondered why he was calling and where from. Could he be in the city? Was he outside of the complex? Fear gripped her hard.

"What do you want?" she asked as the tears rolled down her cheeks.

"What I've always wanted…You."

Millie hung up the phone then paced her apartment. Frank hadn't changed a bit. He was still an abusive psycho out to hurt her. Was he out of jail? But how? Didn't he have another year to serve?

Shit!

Her phone began to ring again and she picked it up and saw the unknown number on the caller ID.

She answered it.

"Hello."

"I'm coming for you, Millie. You're what kept me sane in there. You're my everything and I'm coming to take you back. I can't wait to touch you and hold you in my arms."

"No, Frank. I'm not yours and I'm not interested."

"You will be mine again."

"No, Frank. I'm going to call the police."

"Call them and then you die."

He hung up the phone this time and she was totally freaking out. She had to leave. She needed to get out of town for a while until he gave up on her. She should call the police right now, but she didn't know anything about where Frank was. They wouldn't do anything, just like they waited two years ago to help her. It had nearly been too late. Stacy had saved her life. *Stacy. I need to call Stacy. She'll know what to do.*

She picked up the phone and paused a moment. Frank was messing with her. He wasn't due to be released from prison for another fourteen months. She should call Detective Flynn.

Scrolling through her cell phone contacts list with shaking fingers, she passed his name twice before finally getting her fingers steady enough to stop at his number. She hit call and waited as the phone continued to ring.

"Hello?" a gruff voice answered, and she swallowed hard, remembering what Detective Flynn looked like. He was in his late forties, salt-and-pepper hair, stocky, and a man with years of experience in the NYPD.

"Detective Flynn, it's Millie Donovan."

"Millie? Hey, how are you, honey? Is everything okay?" he asked, immediately seeming to know that something was up.

"Not really. I...I wasn't sure who to call. I don't know if it is a trick or something. Well, I mean, I just didn't know what to do," Millie rambled on. When it came to Frank, she was weak and scared shitless. He had nearly killed her and she would never forget how evil, manipulating, and abusive he was.

"Millie, calm down, honey, and tell me what's wrong."

She took a deep breath.

"I just came home from an event and my phone rang. It was Frank. He said that he missed me and that he was coming for me." There, she said it, and a bit of relief in confiding in Detective Flynn made her feel a bit better instantly.

"Really? That is strange, considering that he's not due to be released for another fourteen months. Let me make a phone call and see what I can find out. What else did he say?"

"That I was going to be his again. He said he was coming for me." The tears hit her eyes and her voice hitched. She sniffled, trying to fight off the panicky feelings growing stronger.

"It will be okay, Millie. Let me make a few calls. In the meantime, lock your doors and stay put. I'll call you soon."

"Thank you." She hung up the phone.

Millie paced her apartment. She looked around, suddenly feeling like Frank had been there, but knowing that it was most likely her imagination. He still had the power to scare her even from such a distance. He was behind bars, rotting for his crimes. This was just some extra added crap to her already incredibly crappy evening.

Chapter 2

Doctor Sheila Perkins watched Frank as he walked toward the bathroom. His ass was hard as steel just like the rest of him. He did things to her. Made her want things she shouldn't want. He was sexy, wild, untamed, and manly. He was everything she wished for in a man but never caught the attention of. He served his time and was a changed man, thanks to her and their therapy sessions. She had not only learned a lot about Frank but also about herself and her inner desires.

She took a deep breath and closed her eyes. It had been years since a man shared her bed. She ran her hands along the empty sheets where Frank had lain only moments ago. It smelled like fancy cologne. She imagined his bulging muscles and the way he took her so wildly and ravaged her body. Sure, it may have had something to do with his lack of having real sex for years, but part of her wanted to believe that it was her that brought it out in him.

She heard the shower running and debated about joining him. He was still somewhat reserved in his emotions. Sure, they had sex, but he still didn't like to be touched unless he was the one who touched first.

They would work on that. She smiled to herself then slowly rolled out of bed. *Why not start right now?*

Dr. Perkins stood in the doorway and absorbed the sight of Frank's body as he washed the shampoo out of his hair. It was long, to his neck, and silky brown. She watched the water dripping down the dips and crevices of his perfectly muscular body. He was a work of art and he was all hers to enjoy. She felt her pussy clench and her nipples harden. He did that to her. He aroused her, turned her on like no other man ever had before. Brazenly, she walked closer to the shower. He abruptly turned toward her.

"I'll be done in a minute," he told her firmly and even his tone turned her on.

"No rush. I'm going to join you," she whispered then reached toward him, anticipating the feel of stone beneath her fingertips. Her eyes darted toward his cock. He was a very large man in all aspects.

"Don't!" Frank raised his voice and she immediately dropped her hand, shocked by his abrupt tone of voice. She looked up at him, suddenly feeling intimidated by his six-foot frame and the evil look in his gray eyes. This was not the same man that had made love to her or courted her in the months she spent as his therapist while he was in prison.

"Frank, I want to be with you. It's okay. I would never hurt you."

He turned off the water in the shower and chuckled at her. Turning to face her, he stepped out of the shower and glared at her. Instinctively, she took a step back. A tinge of fear hit her belly. She watched him carefully as he dried his body with the towel.

"I know you would never hurt me, Sheila. You couldn't even if you wanted to."

She didn't like that comment. What exactly did he mean by that? Again her gut instincts kicked in and warned her to be cautious.

Then he smiled, and that intense-looking gray of his eyes now appeared brighter.

"Don't push me so hard, Sheila. It was a lot for me to stay here with you and make love. Every step I take is difficult," he admitted, but her focus was on his words. He had said "make love," not "have sex" or even "fuck." It was a step in a positive direction. She smiled then lowered her eyes. He was domineering and sexy.

"I'll try not to, Frank. This is all new to me as well. You have come to mean so much to me. I just want you to feel confident and know how perfect you are. The past is behind you."

He stepped closer and cupped her face between his hands.

"You are the reason I am free, Sheila. You are my new beginning."

He kissed her deeply, covering her mouth with his own, making all her reservations and fears disintegrate with each stroke of his tongue. When he released her lips she felt faint and satisfied.

"The shower's all yours. I'm getting dressed and going out."

She watched him leave and she smiled. He was her beginning, too.

* * * *

Frank walked into the bedroom and grabbed his clothes. Sheila had brought him a lot of stuff. He smiled then looked toward the bathroom where he heard the shower running.

Too bad I can't keep her around. She is a pretty good fuck, but nothing compared to Millie. My plan is in motion and the fun is about to begin.

* * * *

Millie was pacing her apartment waiting for Detective Flynn to call. An hour later, her phone rang.

"Hello?" she answered.

"Hi, Millie. It's Detective Flynn. I made some calls and it looks like he was released on early parole."

"What? How the hell can that happen? I mean, I wasn't even informed. I would have gone there and fought that tooth and nail."

"I know, Millie, and I would have been there, too. Apparently, his therapist fought for his release, claiming he was cured and was a new man. The jails are overcrowded, and if no one shows to fight and give good reason to force them to make the prisoner finish his sentence time, the parole board has no choice but to release him. He probably worked in there, too, and proved his changed behavior. I'm going to get a copy of the minutes from that meeting. I'm sorry, Millie, but there's nothing we can do at this point in time."

"He's going to come after me. He already called and threatened me, Detective Flynn."

"If he comes around, you call the police immediately. I can't do anything until he's made a move."

"Yeah, well, if he does, it will be too late. I've been in this position before, detective. He wants me dead and he won't be happy until he gets me, has his fun, then kills me. By then it will be too late."

"I wish there was more I could do. Is there someplace safe you can go? Perhaps take a leave of absence from work and hide out for a few weeks?"

"I have to work. I need the money. I don't know what I'm going to do."

"Call me if he calls you again or if he shows up. We'll get an order of protection. In the meantime, I'm going to track him down and find out where's he's staying. He's on parole. He can't go far and has to report in to his parole officer. I'll find out who that is and see if I can make him aware of the current situation. There's not much more I can do unless he makes a move and commits a crime."

"I appreciate anything you can do. Thank you, Detective Flynn."

"You're welcome. Now make sure the place is locked up. When you go out be sure to be aware of your surroundings and never go anywhere alone, especially at night, Millie. Got it?"

"Yes. Thanks."

"I'll call you tomorrow."

"Okay. Goodnight."

Millie hung up the phone and fell to the couch. She covered her eyes with her hands and immediately saw images of Frank. He wanted her. He was free and out there, ready to come after her. She swallowed hard then began to cry.

Her life couldn't get any worse.

* * * *

Millie felt like shit when she woke up to the sound of her alarm clock going off. The weekend brought her little sleep and constant panic. There had been no sign of Frank and she had decided not to venture out of her apartment after all. Clare had called her to tell her that she had her award and would give it to her at work. As Millie got dressed, she wished she could call in sick and not have to leave her apartment. She was scared and she was completely alone. A few minutes before preparing to leave, her cell phone rang. Glancing at the caller ID, she saw that it was her boss, Vincent Arthur.

"Hello?"

"Miss Donovan, it's Vincent Arthur. Are you planning on coming into work today?" he asked, and she wondered why he would be calling to ask her this.

"Yes, sir, I'm on my way now."

He cleared his throat. "I'm sorry to inform you, Millie, but as you know, the company is making cuts and unfortunately, the first place we need to look is the fundraising department. There are two of you doing the same job, and Layla has been with the company longer. I need to release you."

"What? You can't be serious? I just brought in millions of dollars for the operation. You were there Saturday night congratulating me on a job well done. We spoke about upcoming events and I've worked my rear off all these months. Layla didn't accomplish this and she has only been working for the company two months longer than I have." The tears stung her eyes. Instantly, she thought about Stewart. *That lousy bastard. He did this.* He was a golf buddy of Arthur's.

"I'm sorry, Millie, but I have no choice in the matter. If it's any consolation, you'll be greatly missed and I'll even provide severance pay so you can handle things for a while until you get another job. I wouldn't have any problems with giving you a recommendation on another job elsewhere."

Millie was shocked. "I'll have to come in and gather my things from my desk."

"Of course. Once again, I'm sorry." He hung up and Millie growled as she stomped her feet and felt the anger nearly come to boiling point.

Stewart is a piece of shit!

Millie was very upset as she walked into the kitchen and poured herself another cup of coffee. Now what? She was jobless, she had a psycho after her, and her ex-boyfriend just ruined her life.

She heard her phone ringing and picked it up off the counter without even looking at the caller ID.

"Hello?" she answered with attitude.

"Hello, Millie. How are you this morning?" Stewart asked, and Millie swallowed hard.

"How the hell do you think I'm doing, Stewart? I can't believe that you would stoop so low and get me fired."

"Fired? Oh, dear, you mean Vincent chose Layla over you? Well, she is a lot better looking and has a lot more class."

Millie wanted to rip his head off. She was so damn angry. "You are such an asshole, Stewart. I can't believe that you did this. All I ever did was care for you and be the perfect girlfriend for you to show off."

"You bore me, Millie. You may have a great ass and big tits, but you're timid and weak. I needed a real woman. You flaunting your body last night was disgraceful. Just remember to never fuck with me. Have a nice life."

"Go to hell, Stewart. And by the way, you may have a lot of money and be on some power trip, but your dick will always be small!"

She hung up the phone and growled in anger.

"Asshole, asshole, asshole!" she yelled.

Just then her phone rang again.

"What do you want now?" she yelled.

"Now is that any way to greet your man?" Frank asked, and Millie grabbed ahold of the counter with her free hand.

"Ahhh, now that's more like it. There's my submissive little angel. I missed talking with you. I can't wait to see you, Millie."

"I don't want to see you. You belong behind bars," she stated, filled with anger. She shouldn't antagonize him. But she was in a mood. Her entire life was falling apart.

"How can you say that? You're the only woman I ever loved, Millie. My life isn't complete until I have you again."

"That's not going to happen, Frank. I don't know how you connived that therapist to get you out early, but you're not going to get away with this. I called the police. They're watching you."

She stood up and began to pace.

"No one is watching me, Millie. No one can keep me from you."

Her heart began to pound against her chest. She recognized that tone of his. She knew he meant business and she wouldn't survive another one of Frank's beatings. She ran the palm of her hand across her waist then down to her groin where the scar was.

She glanced around her apartment, frantic.

"Your silence is telling me that you know there's nowhere to turn. We belong together, you and me. We're a team, Millie, don't you forget that."

"We're not a team, Frank. You nearly killed me."

She hurried toward her bedroom and packed her suitcase. Detective Flynn had told her to get out of town for a while. Perhaps for good was a better idea.

"I'm going to make that up to you, baby. I had a lot of time to think things through. I know what I need to do."

"Stop it, Frank! Just stop it now!" she yelled at him.

"Sounds like my baby needs a little discipline. You know I'm the man to do it."

She hung up on him. Her hands were shaking, the tears streaming down her cheeks.

She recalled his beatings—his so-called disciplinary actions when she was "out of line," as he liked to call it. A smack there, an unexpected jab to her stomach. All in the name of his authority and control. She realized too late that he was abusive, and she was stuck, too embarrassed to tell her friends or get the help she needed. She was scared of him, more scared than anything, including death itself. When she was dying, because that was surely how she felt two years ago, she had given up on life when Stacy showed up and saved her.

Stacy? Oh my God, Stacy and Anna could help. They're building that new women's shelter. I would be safe in Pearl.

Chapter 3

Stacy and Anna stood side by side as Jeremy Lewis went over the plans for the set of cottages to be built near the recreational center. Lena was speaking with Anthony, his brother, about the computer images they had worked on.

"I think this will be the best spot. It's not too far from the ranch and we can tie in the electrical, well water, and so forth pretty easily, Stacy," Jeremy stated, and she nodded her head but then glanced at her watch. She was worried about Millie, and so was Anna. That's when she felt the hand on her elbow.

"She'll be fine. She called before she boarded the plane. She should be here shortly. Wyatt picked her up so we know she's safe and nearby," Anna told her.

"Who's that?" Jeremy asked.

"Our good friend from New York is moving back here. Do you remember Millie Donovan, Marie Lamorte's niece?" Anna asked Jeremy.

"I don't think I do. You said Marie is her aunt?" Jeremy asked.

"Yes. She practically raised her."

"Great. Well, I'm sure she'll love being back home."

"Yep." Anna then continued to go over the designs and construction information with the Lewis brothers.

Anna looked around the property. The shelter was complete. The cottages were still being built, but six were finished and the space for the rec center was established. Eventually, the original workers' quarters, which were just as large as the main house, would be redesigned and turned into a bed-and-breakfast. They already had other members of the community asking about employment opportunities.

She took a deep and unsteady breath. She would feel better once Millie arrived safe and sound.

* * * *

"You're mine, and we belong together."

Breaking into the apartment had been easy. Millie was still so conservative and reserved. She didn't flaunt her achievements or the money she made. It was obvious by the apartment complex she lived in. The security was a joke and the only surveillance cameras were the ones outside the front door, and since they didn't have a full view, he was able to keep his head turned to the left and remain undetected. He looked around the living room. Something wasn't right. Through further investigation he entered her bedroom, and the sweet smell of her perfume filled his nostrils. He closed his eyes and adjusted his cock.

"Fuck, baby, I wish you were here right now. We'd make good use of that bed." He moved closer, picking up what appeared to be a nightshirt. It was pink and frilly and smelled like her. He inhaled against the soft fabric and it tickled his nose. He wanted Millie so badly. His breathing grew rapid as he stared at the bedposts. He would tie her up against the posts of her bed and spread her legs wide for him to have his way with. He closed his eyes, imagining the feel of her soft skin against the rough palms of his hands. His hands were calloused from lifting weights and mopping floors. He did it all for her. He had waited too long and had planned every moment. But where was she? He knew his call would surely arouse her, but what game was she playing now? He enjoyed the chase as much as the capture. She knew that. Perhaps she was still a little frightened. He did nearly kill her. But it was only because he wanted her so badly. He wanted to brand her as his own. He wanted to know that she belonged to no other man than him ever again. The thought made him clench his teeth and growl. Where could she be? *Who would make her leave me when Millie knew I was coming for her?* Millie knew the rules.

Stacy. That bitch intervened. The anger caused him to clench the material in his hands. Then he controlled that temper of his just like the prison psychiatrist taught him. That ugly bitch thought she had healed Frank.

Dr. Sheila Perkins would die, too, that cunt. Sheila fell for his lies. She actually thought that he was in love with her, as she surely was with him. He played his role well and got what he wanted, an early parole. Thanks to the good doctor, he was released on good behavior under her continued care and her professional recommendation. Little did the warden or the parole board know, he had manipulated his own fate and used the kind doctor. But hey, it was her fault. Sheila was supposed to be a professional. But she was weak and needed the firm hand of a strong male to guide her. He was that man and there was no weakness around women.

She made his time last longer and drag on until he realized that Sheila was attracted to him. He had worked out vigorously because there wasn't anything better to do. He even worked odd jobs around the prison to strengthen his case before the parole board. That, too, had been the good doctor's advice. Well, he was nearly done with her anyway. He had his eyes on the grand prize. He wanted Millie.

Frank felt himself losing the edge and fighting the need to hurt someone. But he had a plan, a dream that had kept him somewhat sane when he was locked up. His sweet, beautiful Millie. She was so soft, petite, and voluptuous. She had natural beauty and she was reserved, never showing off her figure. She kept herself for him. She listened to him and accepted his control. There was no other, just him. He was aroused at the thought. He had taken her virginity. She was branded his woman from that very first moment.

His eye caught sight of an album on the dresser. He walked closer, noticing the jewelry stand was knocked over and no jewelry remained. It bothered him, but he was compelled to open the album. He lifted the leather book and opened the first page. His breathing hitched at the sight. He focused on her and not the man standing beside her who looked smug and narcissistic. He turned the page and then the next page. They were filled with pictures of his Millie with some sort of snotty bastard.

"Bitch!" he blurted out then threw the album against the wall.

He pulled open the dresser drawers. They were empty. He reached for another and found the same thing. Emptiness.

He walked toward the closet and pulled open the doors.

She ran.

His heart began to pound and a mix of anger and exhilaration filled him. This was going to be fun. She wanted him to chase her. Millie knew how much it turned him on when she ran from him. They played that game often. She would cry and beg for him to stop hitting her and would run only for him to chase her down, toss her onto the bed, and fuck her the way she liked it.

He began to search for clues as to where she might have headed. She didn't have any family that he knew of except for Stacy and Anna.

He smiled then looked around the room for more clues. An address, a phone number, anything that would help him find her quickly so they could join their bodies once again.

He was in his glory and lived for moments like this. He was a hunter and Millie was his prey.

"Game on, baby."

Chapter 4

Being back in Pearl already made Millie feel much better. She was miles and miles away from all her troubles and heartache. She had to admit that having a man as large and intimidating as Sheriff Wyatt Cantrell as her personal escort made her feel safer. Anna was one lucky woman.

"You look really good, Millie. Very sophisticated and grown up." Wyatt winked as he looked forward again, being sure to keep his eyes on the road.

Millie laughed. She and Wyatt had grown up together until Millie's mother had dragged her out of Pearl and to Connecticut when she was eleven. They had moved to New York City two months later. Her mother hadn't realized how expensive it would be to rent a house and they wound up in the projects instead. But that was how she met Anna and Stacy.

"Thanks for the compliment. So how's my girl Anna doing?" Millie asked.

"Keeping busy with the new shelter, the design and plans for the bed and breakfast, and the construction. Both Stacy and Anna want to be the first to share everything about it with you."

"Sounds interesting. I can't wait to see them. It's been too long. I understand that word is spreading already and they have a few women there now." They approached the stretch of road before the Cantrell ranch.

"They have five so far. I think it's going to be great and I have more deputies on duty to provide extra security, too."

He winked and she smiled.

"Well, I guess I'm number six then, huh?" she whispered and her throat closed up for a moment as the urge to cry nearly overtook her.

Wyatt reached over and squeezed her clasped hands that were on her lap.

"It's going to work out fine, Millie. You're strong, you know how the business operates, and you've got all of us here to protect and support you. I've already been in touch with Detective Flynn. He'll keep us posted on any changes."

"I appreciate that, Wyatt. I was so scared. I think coming back home to Pearl was my only option."

"We'll stop by the ranch to see the women and then I'll give you a ride over to your aunt's place."

"My aunt's? I thought that she and Ron were on a cruise?"

"They are. Anna and Stacy fixed up the cottage for you last night." He smiled. She shook her head.

"The same cottage that Stacy stayed in when she met your cousins?"

"Yep. They even stocked the refrigerator for you. Although I doubt you'll have much alone time with those two. Stacy can't wait for you to see Hope."

Millie smiled. She hadn't had a chance to leave New York and visit when Stacy's baby was born.

"I can't wait to see her."

"She's beautiful, Millie." Millie could hear the sincerity in his voice. The Cantrells were very close and Millie was certain that Wyatt, Ben, and Charlie looked at Hope as if she was their own daughter. She was envious as the lonely feelings of inadequacy and isolation trickled inside of her. Those were foolish thoughts because she knew she had Anna and Stacy. They were her family just like Aunt Marie.

"So when are you, Ben, Anna, and Charlie going to start a family?" Millie asked with a wink.

Wyatt sighed as if she had hit a sensitive subject. She was suddenly concerned.

"What's wrong? Things are okay between you three and Anna, right?"

"Oh, yeah. Of course they are. We love her so much, Millie. It's just that she's still recovering from her injuries. She gets headaches still and sometimes gets a little dizzy."

"Well, the doctors said that was normal and it could take a while. Especially since her concussion was pretty serious."

"I know. She gets upset every now and then about it. I see how she watches Stacy with Hope, Eric, and Max. She wants to start a family as much as we do, but we need to wait just a little longer."

"Well, there's plenty of time to start a family. I'm sure she'll be free and clear from those headaches in no time. So how is the crime around Pearl? Still maintaining the peace?" she teased, wanting to change the subject.

"You'd be surprised what types of things happen around town. Nothing serious, of course, but we do get a few stragglers from outside of Pearl that come in for the shops and to dine at Francine's. Anna still insists on working some hours there. Jack and Mary Boslow love her and of course Francine up and opened another restaurant in Turbank. She's mostly there."

"Wow! Well, Anna is a great cook. I wouldn't blame Jack and Mary for keeping her working steady."

Just then, they approached the front gates to the Triple C Ranch. It was even more beautiful than she recalled.

"Oh, God, Wyatt, the ranch looks so amazing. It's been so long since I've been back in Texas. I missed this so much."

Wyatt smiled as he parked the truck. He pulled right alongside Anthony Lewis's construction truck.

* * * *

Anna and Stacy nearly ran toward the truck as Wyatt pulled up with Millie.

"Excuse us, Anthony, our best friend is here," Anna stated, and they took off for the truck. The moment Anna and Stacy saw Millie, the three women screamed then hugged one another as they danced in a circle.

"Oh, God, I'm so glad you're here, Millie!" Stacy exclaimed and then Anna agreed.

"Damn, woman, you look good!" Eric exclaimed as he approached with Charlie and Ben.

Anna giggled as Eric lifted Millie up in the air and twirled her around.

"Oh, God, Eric, you haven't changed a bit," Millie stated.

* * * *

Glancing around at the small crowd that had formed, Millie felt incredibly happy and relieved to be with her family. She wasn't alone. She was back home in Pearl where she belonged.

As the others greeted her, she caught sight of two very tall cowboys standing near a truck that said "Lewis Construction" on it in in bold, uppercase black lettering. One cowboy was holding a clipboard with papers and the other was chewing on a straw, staring at her. She felt his gaze through the crowd and she was perplexed by the mixed emotions. She felt her cheeks warm. He had that look that could make even the most experienced woman blush. She looked at Stacy, who raised her eyebrows as if indicating how hot the two men were. Millie tried not to laugh. That was so Stacy.

"Millie, let us introduce you to Anthony and Jeremy Lewis. They own the construction company we hired to start the project," Stacy stated as if she sensed the men staring at Millie.

Millie smiled as Jeremy offered his hand first.

"Nice to meet you, Millie. Stacy and Anna were worried about you. Glad you made it to Pearl in one piece." As she touched his hand, she felt a tingling sensation travel past her wrist as his words sunk in.

She pulled her hand away quickly and gave a scolding look to Stacy. Stacy cleared her throat and shook her head. Did that mean that Stacy hadn't informed the strangers about her situation in New York? Damn, she hoped not.

"I'm Anthony," the other man stated, and she turned back to him. She shook his hand as not to be rude and she noticed that his hair was crew cut short as opposed to Jeremy's who had his tied back neatly. Looking back at Jeremy as she released Anthony's hand Jeremy winked at her with chocolate eyes. He was a flirt, she could tell immediately, and damn if her body didn't react instantly to it.

"Nice to meet you both. So what is this secret project you two have been hiding from me?" Millie asked.

"No secret, just something we think that you'll be interested in helping out with and being part of." Anna winked at Stacy.

"What is it?"

"Jeremy, can you show Millie the blueprints of the construction site and the main page?" Stacy asked.

"Sure. It would be my pleasure." Jeremy smiled at Millie as he looked her over again. When he and Anthony turned away, Anna gave her a nudge in her shoulder and a wink. She shook her head at her friend. Millie was done with men, especially the flirtatious kind. Plus, she was doing her best right now not to break down and cry. She had no idea what would come of her leaving New York and losing her job so suddenly. For all she knew, Frank wasn't even in New York and was just messing with her like always. But he had sounded so confident. She had done what Stacy and Anna told her to do and what Detective Flynn suggested and left town. She had contacted Detective Flynn and given him Wyatt's number at the Sheriff's Department as well. Wyatt was also the detective that arrested Frank and helped

Stacy save Millie's life. Although he had no grounds to locate Frank and arrest him, he suggested that she take Frank's threats seriously and take a vacation. She swallowed hard as she tried her hardest to submerge her emotions.

* * * *

Jeremy opened up the blueprint on the hood of his truck and then realized that Millie was too petite to see that high. His truck was an extra-wide load and very big, just like him and his brothers. He and Anthony were tall, stocky, and muscular, while his brothers, Dalton, Hank, and Marco, were trim and fit, keeping their military physiques like true martial artists.

"Grab the other end, Anthony, so she can see it better."

Millie slowly moved closer and he noticed she kept her hands clasped in front of her as if she were afraid to get too close to either of them. Jeremy smiled. She was a mighty fine-looking woman, with brown hair tied up in a ponytail and dark blue eyes that almost looked too large for her smaller features. They were the first thing he noticed about her. Then, of course, he noticed her hourglass figure. She was a knockout and dressed very conservatively in a black, sleeveless one-piece dress and a white sweater. She looked sweet.

"Is this a new development you're putting in on Cantrell's land next to the shelter?" Millie asked.

"This is something we've talked about in the past but with no real direction. Your ideas and accomplishments in New York kind of helped us zero in on our idea, Millie. As you know, we built the women's shelter so that women in trouble or on their own with no place to go can come here and have a new start," Anna stated, and Millie smiled. Jeremy watched as the tears hit her eyes and she lost coloring in her face.

"We want you to be part of this, Millie. We have a new friend, Lena, who has some really great ideas as well. She's had to deal with so much on her own, just like Anna and me and, of course, you, too. The four of us will organize and run the place. We were thinking about making a series of specialty shops. Maybe a place where you can sell the jewelry you make and other women can sell things they've made as well," Stacy added.

"Yeah, we're going to have small cottages, some single and some multifamily, so that women can share or so that women with children can live there while they work. We'll have child care services and we're even thinking about other forms of income for the women so they can eventually support themselves," Anna added.

"I've been in contact with some government agencies offering education grants and scholarship programs we can do online. Plus, with your background as a fundraising coordinator and financial coordinator, we could maybe use your connections to help us expand and really help these women out," Stacy stated.

Jeremy remained, watching Millie. She looked shocked, but he saw something else in her eyes, something that made him feel like she knew how the women felt and perhaps had been in need at one time herself, or maybe she was just touched by the idea Anna and Stacy had.

"This is amazing. This is exactly what I've been wanting to create in New York." As she said the words she covered her mouth and began to turn away. Anna and Stacy were immediately by her side.

"It will be okay, Millie. He can't get to you here," Stacy whispered, but Jeremy heard her. Immediately, he felt as if a fist tightened around his heart. Was this beautiful, sophisticated-looking woman in some kind of trouble?

He looked at his brother, Anthony, who held the same concerned expression. Anthony was a control freak. He ran their business and he ran it well. If he were concerned over Millie, he would get the answers he was looking for. Jeremy hoped that his brother remained quiet.

"Why don't you guys call it a day? I'm sure Stacy and Anna picked your brain all afternoon about the construction." Wyatt placed his hand on Jeremy's shoulder as he watched the ladies head toward the house.

"Is she all right, Wyatt? I mean, is she in some kind of trouble?" Anthony asked and Wyatt looked at Jeremy then Anthony before he glanced toward the women as they headed for the porch.

"It's not my place to say, but thanks for your concern."

"She seems real nice and Anna and Stacy talk about her a lot," Anthony added.

"Yeah, they've been friends for many years. All three of them went through a lot of hard times back in New York."

"Well, Pearl is an amazing place. You let us know if you need anything. We'd get here in a flash, Wyatt," Anthony offered, and Wyatt smiled.

"Thanks."

Jeremy folded up the blueprints and got into the truck as Anthony got behind the wheel and they headed out of the Triple C.

They were quiet as Anthony drove the truck.

"She was real pretty wasn't she, Anthony?" Jeremy asked as he looked out across the open land and wondered about Millie.

"She sure was. Seemed real sweet and timid, though."

Jeremy nodded his head in agreement.

"Did you hear what Anna and Stacy said to her back there? The part about him not finding her here?" Anthony asked.

"Sure did. Kind of makes me wonder if she's running from trouble."

"Well, if she is, there's no safer place than Pearl. Not with so many deputies and cowboys looking out for women and children."

Just then, they passed by Marie Lamorte's place.

"At least she's staying with Anna and Stacy," Anthony stated.

"She's not staying with them. She's staying in that cottage on Marie's ranch."

Anthony turned toward his brother with a scowl on his face.

"All alone? Marie and Ron are away, right?"

"Yep."

"Well, maybe we'll be sure to stop in and see Millie just to make sure she's okay."

Jeremy smiled. He was all for that. Any chance to get another gander at Millie would make his day.

Chapter 5

"So let me understand this correctly, Millie. Detective Flynn said he couldn't do anything and that it might be wise to take the vacation while he checks things out unofficially?" Wyatt asked as they all sat around the porch. It was Anna, Stacy, Wyatt, Ben, Charlie, Eric, and Max.

Millie nodded.

"I got the phone call on my way home from the awards dinner. He sounded so close by. It gave me the chills and my gut instinct was to run, but I didn't. I called Flynn and he said he would check things out. He confirmed that Frank was released early on good behavior and under the personal recommendation of his therapist. I waited out the weekend and then…"

Millie took a deep breath and tried to control her emotions. The thought that Stewart made her boss fire her still irked her.

"Then what? What happened?" Anna asked.

"I got fired Monday morning over the phone."

"What?" Stacy and Anna asked simultaneously.

"Stewart's doing."

"What a loser!" Stacy stated with a scowl on her face and Millie smirked then chuckled.

"He is a loser. I guess I really know how to pick them."

Anna reached over and touched Millie's knee. "Not all men are like Frank and Stew. I can't believe that Stew would stoop that low."

"Well, he did and a few minutes after that phone call I received one from Frank. That was intense."

"He said some bad things, huh?" Stacy asked and all Millie could do was nod and then rub a hand over her mouth as she took a deep breath then released it unsteadily.

"I had no choice but to leave New York. He said he was coming to get me. So I took the time to grab some things and pack, then called you and headed here."

"Is this detective going to stay in contact with you and investigate where Frank is and if in fact he's out of prison?" Ben asked.

"He called before I boarded the plane to tell me that Frank was definitely released early on good behavior and that the parole office said Frank declined the recommendation of heading toward a shelter because he had a place to stay. I think he meant my apartment." Millie took a deep breath.

Anna squeezed her hand. "We'll protect you here, Millie. You can stay here for as long as you need to."

"I don't know what I'm going to do. Things were getting crappy back in New York anyway," she admitted as she looked at her clasped hands.

"Honey, what else was going on?" Wyatt asked her. She swallowed hard and she hoped that Wyatt and the others knew it was difficult for her to talk. Maybe it was best that she talked with Anna and Stacy first. Not that she was uncomfortable in front of their men, but she was embarrassed by her stupid decisions. Things could have been worse.

"I'm going to stay in touch with Detective Flynn. I know you trust him and he seems like he's concerned over your well-being," Wyatt quickly added.

"Yes. I trust him. When Stacy stopped Frank from killing me, Detective Flynn followed minutes later. He did everything he could to get Frank the maximum sentence. That's why it's so surprising that he's out in under two years' time."

"We'll check it out and keep on top of things. You be sure to let us know if Frank tries to contact you," Ben added.

"I will, guys, and thank you for everything."

"Hey, that's what family is for," Stacy added, and Millie smiled.

* * * *

Stacy stood by the counter in the kitchen making a pot of coffee. Anna sat in a chair at the table while Millie held baby Hope in her arms.

"I think she's out cold, Stacy," Millie whispered as she smiled down at Hope.

"She is such a good baby. She hardly ever fusses." Stacy turned the coffeepot on and walked over toward Millie.

"I'm going to go put her in the crib for the night."

Millie lifted Hope up toward her mother and smiled as the tears reached her eyes.

"She's beautiful, Stacy. I can't believe you're a mamma."

"Who would have thought that Stacy would be the first one out of the three of us to start a family?" Anna asked.

"She seems to be doing all the firsts, doesn't she?" Millie whispered then smiled.

"You mean the ménage relationships?" Anna asked and Millie nodded.

Anna stared at Millie a moment and she saw the emotion in her eyes.

"Tell me what happened the other night, before the call from Frank."

Millie shook her head. It was obvious that she didn't want to talk about it. Just then, Stacy returned and walked over to the counter and turned on the baby monitor. Then she grabbed some cups and poured the coffee.

"Come on, Millie, you're very strong and have a lot of self-confidence. Look how far you've come," Anna pushed.

"You give me more credit than I deserve, Anna. I swear, my entire world seems to be crashing down around me and it all has to do with men."

"You mean Frank?" Stacy asked as she placed a cup in front of Anna and one in front of Millie before taking a seat at the table.

"Frank was the worst mistake of my life. He nearly cost me my life."

"Yeah, but you survived and he went to jail where he should still be," Stacy stated.

"You mean Stewart, don't you, Millie?" Anna asked, and Millie nodded as she placed her hands around the mug of hot coffee as if she were cold. It was a warm spring night and nearly eighty degrees.

"He was such a jerk," she whispered as the tears rolled down her cheeks.

"What did he say to you the other night at the awards ceremony? It's obvious that you saw him there. His company helped to support your fundraising, didn't it?" Stacy asked.

"He was with the blonde supermodel. She was tall and thin and her breasts were hanging out of her top. She looked glamorous."

"If you're into skin and bones, maybe," Anna added.

Millie chuckled.

"What happened between you and Stewart?" Stacy asked.

"Besides the skinny blonde, I think my lack of perfection."

"What?" both Stacy and Anna asked at once.

Millie cringed.

"He put me down all the time. He said that I was fat, and at the awards gala, when other people complimented my appearance and the dress I wore, he told me that I looked cheap and that men would just want me for an easy fuck."

"That lousy piece of shit!" Stacy exclaimed, and Millie chuckled.

"I know I'm a bit overweight. I always have been and my boobs are too big for my small frame, but they're what God gave me." Millie shook her head as she looked down at her coffee.

"Millie Marie Donovan, you are not seriously going to sit here and believe the words from some stuck-up stockbroker who only gives a shit about money and status. You are beautiful and you are far from fat. Women would kill for your Betty Boop, Marilyn Monroe body. That asshole was jealous and he was a jerk who used you and has no idea what being a real man is about."

"Betty Boop? Really?" Millie asked, and they all laughed.

"You know what I mean. You should be posing in *Playboy*. Is that a better description?" Stacy asked. Anna laughed and Millie gasped in shock then chuckled as she rolled up a napkin and threw it at Stacy.

"You have great breasts, Millie. You always have. This goes beyond the physical," Anna added.

"It sure does. I can't pick a man for shit. I fall all gaga over their charms and good looks and bam, they treat me like shit. I don't know how to fight back and I wind up smacked around or where I am now, about to self-destruct. I will never live a normal life. Not as long as I remain a magnet to mean, self-centered men."

"Not all men are self-centered and mean. There are men out there that know how to treat women," Stacy stated.

"Sure there are, and you two scooped them up. Two very lucky women, you two are. I'm so happy for both of you. Pearl has really helped you to find happiness." Millie took a sip from her cup of coffee.

"You should stay here, Millie. There are good men around the area, men that would surely treat you like gold," Stacy began to say and Millie held up her hand for her to go no further.

"Stacy, I have so much baggage right now and so much fear in me that I'm not certain which direction I'm going in. If Frank is out there and he wants to hunt me down, I sure as hell can't stick around Pearl. Not with you two here and baby Hope."

"You're safest here where there are men to protect you. There are more men in Pearl than there are women. Their duty is to protect the women and children at all costs. You are a member of the community and people will protect you," Stacy stated firmly.

"I was a member of the community, but now I'm afraid that I may have to stick to moving until Detective Flynn can catch Frank in some kind of criminal activity. I have to head back to New York to get my things. I had to pay my rent for the apartment six months in advance. I left some of my jewelry-making materials there as well and that may be my only form of income for a while. There are too many responsibilities to just jump up and move back here. I came here on impulse and out of fear," she rambled on then paused as the last words seemed to be absorbed by her friends.

"You're not going back to New York until Frank is located and watched. You're not risking your life again, Millie. You deserve better, and being in Pearl, taking some time to figure things out, will be best for you right now," Stacy added.

Millie raised her eyebrows at Stacy's commanding tone.

"You've become quite bossy, Miss Stacy," Millie teased in an attempt to lighten the atmosphere. She was terrified to return to New York and face Frank. No amount of self-defense training ensured that she could defend herself against someone like Frank.

"You should see how she runs the ranch and now the construction plans. She's the foreman, not the Lewis men." Anna covered her mouth to stifle the laugh when Stacy's mouth gaped open as if shocked by the description. Stacy shook her head.

"I have my men to support me and a baby to raise. I'm sorry if it seems I can be bossy at times. I get things done, don't I?"

Anna and Millie chuckled.

"Good for you, Stacy. Maybe some of that attitude can rub off onto me. I sure can use it," Millie added.

"You betcha, honey. So what do you think about our plans?"

"I think it's a wonderful idea. I am certain there are many women out there who will find out about it and come looking for help. Have you decided on a name yet?" Millie asked.

Anna and Stacy shook their heads.

"We still can't decide. Tomorrow you'll meet Lena and Sage. Lena's involved with the Jones brothers," Stacy added.

"You mean Kenny, Bryant, Quinn, and Blake?"

"Yep. Lena was living on the streets of Detroit before she ran from a drug dealer that wanted to kill her. It was crazy. I'm sure she'll share the story with you. She has a lot of insight into the shelters and what fears the women might have," Anna told Millie.

"Coming to Pearl saved my life and Anna's life," Stacy added.

Millie exhaled as she thought about that statement. She looked at her best friends and had the feeling that they were really hoping to convince her to stay in Pearl and live here. But who in their right mind just up and leaves their life and relocates? There were things to consider here. Would she even consider moving back to Pearl if Frank weren't looking for her? Millie knew she had some serious thinking to do.

"Do you remember when you both came to Pearl?" She stood up and brought her empty cup to the sink.

"I sure do. I was scared and I didn't know anyone but Stacy," Anna stated.

Millie faced them as she leaned against the counter.

"Stacy, you remember how pissed off you were about being tricked into coming here to relax and regroup as your boss remained in New York looking for you?"

"How could I forget?"

"Well, then, just think about how difficult this is for me. Pearl was where I was born and raised until I was forced to leave with my mom. Coming back here has brought back a lot of memories, both happy and sad. Just riding through town and seeing all the new store fronts mixed in with the original ones brought tears to my eyes. I swear when I passed by the old Benson ranch I remembered hanging out with Charlie, Sally, and their cousins and going swimming near the water hole."

"Those sound like fun times," Stacy added then smiled.

Millie lowered her head then took a deep breath before she stared out the window.

"When I passed by my aunt's place, I remembered that time my mamma came home and told me that my daddy was gone and never coming back. My life changed that day. I cried for hours and prayed that they would work things out in their marriage. But he never showed. Not a card, not a letter, not a phone call wondering how I was doing. I was his only baby girl." She ran a fingertip over the baby monitor sitting on the counter.

"Definitely some tough memories there, Millie, but you were just a child. You were innocent and your mamma had to make some tough decisions for you," Stacy stated.

"It isn't easy, Stacy. I guess I need to embrace the good with the bad while I'm here. More importantly, I'm struggling with some things right now that I need to handle. I know that you're both here for me to lean on and all, but I truly need to regroup and gain back some of the self-confidence I had after surviving Frank's attack. I need to find that woman who gained a fight inside of her that she thought could never be broken down again. I'm weak, ladies. I'm battered, not broken, but feeling beat down and headed in no specific direction."

"That's understandable, Millie, and we're glad that you're here in Pearl where there are people to keep you safe." Stacy smiled.

"It will work out, and you've been so busy this is a great time to visit and get to know Hope and, of course, our men." Anna winked.

"Speaking of men, what did you think of Jeremy and Anthony Lewis? Pretty hot stuff, huh?" Stacy teased then winked.

Millie shook her head. "I really didn't notice."

Anna made a funny-sounding noise with her mouth. "You are so full of shit, Millie. I saw your cheeks blush when Jeremy shook your hand then lowered the map so you could see. That was mighty sweet of him."

"Yeah, and Anthony looked like he was memorizing your every feature. I nearly offered him a hankie to wipe his drool," Stacy added and both she and Anna chuckled.

"You two better cut it out. I'm not planning on entertaining any men for quite some time. I've been burned and burned again and this woman needs to regroup. I'll get an update from Detective Flynn tomorrow and see what the plan is. In the interim, I'll try to help you as much as possible with the women's shelter."

Anna clapped her hands and squealed, and Stacy smiled wide then gave a fist punch in the air.

"Yes! We are going to make an awesome team. I can't wait for you to meet Lena, Millie. You're going to love her. Most importantly, the crew is back together again after years of being apart," Stacy stated, and the three of them smiled as tears filled Millie's eyes.

Chapter 6

Detective Flynn had the landlord unlock Millie's apartment for him. He entered and scanned the area, not noticing anything out of the ordinary. Millie appeared to be a neat freak. Further investigation in the bedroom initially brought him some concern. He sniffed the air and smelled both perfume and men's cologne. But he dismissed it. He knew nothing of Millie's love life and didn't want to assume the worst. He knew that Millie had left in a hurry and had packed some suitcases and jewelry. Things were knocked over, including a photo album that lay on the floor. He glanced around the room and noticed a desk in the corner. The narrow drawer was tipped over and all the contents were spread out on the rug. That didn't seem like something Millie would do as she gathered her things for a quick escape.

His gut instincts kicked in and he was in police mode as he moved closer, trying to find out if the culprit had been Frank.

He took out his handkerchief and picked up the photo album. Flipping through the pages, he noticed a torn picture and then a page that seemed to be missing a picture. She could have taken them with her instead of the entire album, but that didn't sit right with him. He would have to ask Millie.

He looked around the room and nothing really stood out, so he entered the kitchen. Detective Flynn didn't like the feeling he had. Frank Bennett was slick and conniving.

He walked into the kitchen and noticed some things on the counter. Moving closer, he saw what appeared to be a long, thick stick that had one side wrapped in thick electrical tape like a handle and the other end was narrower. There was a note on a piece of paper that said, "Pain equals submission and respect."

Detective Flynn swallowed hard. Millie was in trouble and it appeared that Frank had been in her apartment. He knew this weapon. And indeed it was a weapon. Detective Flynn recalled the scene of the attack on Millie. Frank had been beating her with a similar weapon. He had come onto the scene after a desperate call from Stacy. That woman had been incredibly brave and determined to save her friend.

The detective shook his head as he looked at the weapon. He had to find Frank before Frank located Millie.

* * * *

It was six o'clock in the morning and Millie sat on her front porch looking out toward the fields. She inhaled, smelling all the old scents of country life and the thick indicator that the horse stables were just beyond the row of large trees and her Aunt Marie's home.

She missed those scents and strangely enough, they provided some comforting feelings. She took another sip of the fresh-brewed coffee and exhaled. Last night had been fun hanging out with Stacy and Anna, but once she got back to the cottage and settled in, fear began to ride her mind hard. Both Anna and Stacy noticed her reservations and offered for her to stay at one of their houses until Millie was ready to be by herself. But she didn't want to admit to that weakness, especially with their men nearby. Millie didn't want to be that weak, fragile female she had been years ago when involved with Frank. No, things were different. She was different.

She took a shaky breath, her subconscious reminding her about her faults and about how easily Frank put fear into her. Did that make her the same weak woman from two years ago? As much as she hoped not, the reality was clear as day. Apparent in her shaky hands, her rapid heartbeat, and the anxiety that he was out there, he was looking for her and he wanted her dead.

She had had little sleep and mostly tossed and turned last night because of similar thoughts. She didn't miss the sounds of living in the city, the slight hum of traffic outside her apartment complex, and the bright city lights invading the blinds in her apartment. Surely the quiet sounds of night in the country on a ranch were more appealing and better for a good night's sleep. However, that same quietness that once brought her peace and relaxation had her anxiety levels higher. The creaking of the old porch as the wind blew and the sounds of bugs in the night had her straining to hear what she really feared—the footsteps of a man coming to get her, the crackling of leaves beneath his feet as he approached the cottage, ready to strike. Crazy thoughts like that had kept her up most of the night. She knew that she wasn't completely alone out here and that her aunt's workers were yards away in their sleeping quarters, but still, her mind played tricks on her. It became apparent that she was still deathly afraid of Frank.

She swallowed hard, feeling her heart rate increase and her throat clog up. Then she took a sip of coffee to try and alleviate the sensation.

Then came the anger. She had worked hard after surviving the attack. She never wanted to be a victim again. Now images of Stewart jumped into her mind. She shook her head and sighed. *So much for gaining back self-confidence and taking all those martial arts classes.* She had been just shy of achieving her black belt when Stewart demanded that she quit messing around and act more ladylike. She, of course, didn't stand her ground and she caved in. Her instructors were disappointed and so was she.

When will I gain a backbone and learn to stand up for myself? Where do I go from here?

She heard the horses approaching and glanced up to see two cowboys in the distance. She smiled at the sight. It appeared the men were hours into their work already and here she was sitting around feeling sorry for herself.

She shook her head as enthusiasm for the day ahead motivated her movements. Standing, she stretched, took a breath of fresh country air, and headed inside the cottage to start her day. Anna and Stacy were picking her up at nine to go into town.

Change begins within myself, and today is a first step toward that change.

Chapter 7

"Jacob Frost, is that any way to treat your brother, a fellow student?" Dalton Lewis asked his student as Jacob tripped his brother, Thomas, then sat on him. He had to hide his chuckle. They were young and quite the handful. It was tough sometimes teaching martial arts to children, but Hank and his brother loved doing it.

"Sorry, Sensei Dalton, but he's annoying," Jacob responded as he continued to sit on his five-year-old brother.

"Get up off of him now, Jacob, and get serious."

"I am not annoying. I do better front roll dan him, dat why Jacob mad at me," little Thomas replied as he attempted to wiggle his way from under Jacob.

Dalton placed his hands on his hips and eyed the two boys. Immediately, they scrambled up off the mat and got back into line with the rest of the class. The other ten children were doing kickboxing drills on the bags with Dalton's brother, Hank.

Dalton looked at the clock. It was nearly ten and class would be out soon. He had an hour before the next class started at eleven. That was a mixed martial arts class that was used as a training session for both firefighters like himself and Hank as well as deputies and law enforcement officers like their brother, Marco.

"Fall in!" he called and the children hurried to their positions.

"Attention!" Hank called the class to order and all the children lined up in order with their hands by their sides.

He looked at a few of the younger ones who were at their limit of concentration.

"Remember, when I say 'attention' you bring in your right foot to your left foot and stand tall with your hands by your sides." He nodded his head as the few who made the errors fixed themselves.

"Very good, class. I expect there to be no other problems or unnecessary outbursts during Wednesday's session," Hank began to say then looked directly at Jacob and Thomas. Dalton held a firm expression as well, even though he wanted to chuckle at the sight of fear on Jacob's and Thomas's faces. They were so little and both Dalton and Hank were over six feet tall, ex-military, and highly trained.

"Yes, Sensei!" Thomas blurted out and the other children chuckled low but held it together. Maintaining their attention for the full hour at their young ages of five through eight was difficult at times.

"Be sure to practice your moves for the test Wednesday. You are all doing great." Hank bowed his head, they did the same, and then he dismissed them.

* * * *

"Hey, what is that place over there?" Millie asked as she, Stacy, and Anna walked past Main Street.

"Oh, that's Anthony and Jeremy Lewis's brother's place. It's kind of like a mixed martial arts school, a combat training school for the law enforcement officers, firefighters, and even some military guys. Pretty cool stuff. They even offer classes to children," Stacy told Millie, and Millie was surprised. She also felt a spark of enthusiasm.

"Really?"

"Hey, didn't you do that martial arts thing for a while?" Anna asked.

"Sure did. I loved it until Stewart made me quit."

"He made you quit? What for?" Stacy asked.

"He thought it wasn't ladylike."

"*Asshole...*" Anna sang the word as she took Millie's hand and began bringing her across the street toward the dojo.

"Hey, what are you doing?" Millie asked as they crossed the street.

Anna looked over her shoulder at Stacy and winked. Stacy chuckled and Millie wondered what wasn't being said amongst the friends.

As they approached the front window, they could see the class in session.

Millie smiled at the sight of such young children enjoying the training and discipline of the sport. Then she caught sight of a very large, tall man dressed in an all-black gi. One child was sitting on top of another child.

"Oh my goodness, it looks like the Frost boys are at it again." Stacy chuckled.

Millie smiled as the Sensei defused the problem and the children returned to class. She peeked to the right and saw another man leading the group. He was very tall as well and nearly identical to the first man. They had hard expressions.

"The first one in all black is Anthony and Jeremy Lewis's brother, Dalton. The blond is their other brother, Hank," Anna offered.

"Very sexy and mysterious men," Stacy added.

"And feared, too. Not men to mess with from what the guys have talked about."

"They look like they know what they're doing. They seem to be doing great with the kids," Millie stated, not taking her eyes off the two men as she watched them prepare to dismiss the kids.

"The parents think that Hank and Dalton are great. So do our men. Those two are disciplinary and strict. They both compete in mixed martial arts competitions, too," Stacy added.

"Wow. That is impressive." Millie moved closer and looked around the gym. It was pretty big and looked like they had multiple rooms. There appeared to be military pictures on the walls, from what little she could see from outside, and then she saw the parents come out from a side room and gather their children.

"I'm going next door to the boutique," Stacy stated.

"Oh, I'll come, too, and see what new clothes Melissa and Diana got into the boutique. Why don't you check out the programs they offer, Millie? Getting back into something you love would be a step in the right direction," Anna offered. Millie looked away from the window and at her friends.

"I'm not sure. It's been a few months since I worked out and did the moves. I'm not even sure they'll have the same programs."

"Check it out. The blond with the green eyes is Dalton and the other blond with the blue eyes is Hank." Anna began to walk away toward the boutique.

Millie waited as the children filed out.

* * * *

Hank watched from the mats as the parents and children left the building. He immediately noticed a young woman looking through the front window along with Anna and Stacy. He wondered who she might be.

"Okay, next time you take the lead with that class. I've been heading up the last few weeks and I'm not sure what to do with Jacob and Thomas." Dalton undid his jacket and tossed it onto the chair.

The bell above the door jingled and the young woman Hank had noticed entered.

When she did, she bowed her head in respect, clearly familiar with the ritual of honoring the dojo, then smiled as she approached.

She reached her hand out to them.

"Hi, I'm Millie, friend of Stacy and Anna. I was just reacquainting myself with the town when I noticed your place. What kinds of programs do you offer?" she asked, and Hank shook her hand first.

"Hi, Millie. I'm Hank Lewis and this is my brother, Dalton. Welcome to Pearl."

"Thank you. Well, to be honest with you, I grew up in Pearl on Marie Lamorte's place, but then my mom moved us to Connecticut. I've been living in New York for a few years and just moved back here for a bit."

Dalton shook her hand next and he held her gaze. Hank wondered if he felt what he was feeling right now. Millie was gorgeous and had a beautiful smile. He actually felt a funny sensation in his gut.

Caught staring at her, he cleared his throat and tried to gather his thoughts. That had never happened to him before.

"Well, come on in, Millie, let's show you around and tell you about our programs," Hank began as he motioned with his hand for her to enter the main area.

Dalton's deep voice made her immediately stop and look up toward his face.

"Do you have any martial arts training?"

She nodded her head but seemed to be caught off guard by his authoritative tone and height. Or maybe it was the large scar from shoulder to ear. The crazy bastard was nearly killed by insurgents in Fallujah and the scar was noticeable.

"Well, what kind?" he asked.

"Self-defense," she replied rather abruptly then turned away from his brother. Hank wondered if Dalton had scared her. She seemed real friendly when she entered, but Dalton seemed to put her on the defensive.

Without meaning to, both he and Dalton blocked her only exit from the main dojo and she suddenly appeared concerned. They both towered over her, so Hank took a step back, but Dalton crossed his arms in front of his chest and stared at Millie.

"Do you have a flier or something? Maybe times and types of classes that you offer?" she asked as if she were in a hurry. But she did look at Dalton and her cheeks appeared pinker. Was she attracted to his brother?

She had a great body. She looked solid, muscular, and sexy. Her hourglass figure was perfection, but her eyes, deep, dark, and blue, looked like a deer caught in headlights right now. Sometimes he forgot how intimidating he and his brothers could appear.

"Sure, let me grab you our latest flier. It contains our upcoming schedule and payment plans." Hank walked back toward the front desk.

* * * *

Dalton cleared his throat and eyed her from head to toe. She was stunning, but he didn't like the way his body instantly reacted to her. His heart actually felt as if the beat increased, and damn it, she smelled really good, too. He wondered if she was just like some of the other single women who came in to the dojo claiming to need self-defense training or wanting to get stronger and learn to fight, but really, they were after one of the brothers. The Lewis brothers were pretty well-known around Pearl and Turbank. They had each established good businesses and came from large families, wealthy from striking oil. Though he and his brothers chose different paths, their cousins continued in the oil business and were doing very well.

"So what specifically did your sensei teach you?" He pushed for more information even though he really didn't care. She was just like the other women. She was probably single and looking to land a husband or two. Well, he wasn't going to fall for it. Then she stared right back up at him with such annoyance he nearly faltered a moment. But like most women, she was probably turned off by his scar and wouldn't like to see the other more defined ones across his chest and back.

"Karate, jujitsu, tae kwon do."

"He didn't stick to one teaching?"

"No. Like I said, it was kind of a self-defense class that I enjoyed and continued to participate in. He wanted to keep me interested so he threw in various things. I liked it."

"You sound like it was in the past. How long has it been since you worked out?"

Her mouth opened wide and she lowered her head a moment. She pulled at the loose-fitting black T-shirt she wore as if he was insulting her. Then it hit him. *She thinks I'm calling her fat.*

"I didn't mean that you need to work out. I just meant if it's been a while, you may have forgotten a lot of the moves," he rambled on as his brother, Hank, gave him a dirty look.

"I had to quit. But that was before and this is now," she told him. Dalton couldn't help but sense some upset in her comment. Perhaps someone told her to quit, or maybe she got lazy. It didn't seem like a possibility.

"Here you go, Millie. Just stop in or call me if you have any questions." Hank handed Millie a few fliers with class schedules. "We have two programs starting tomorrow. One is at nine in the morning and is for self-defense and kickboxing."

She looked at the paper.

"What's this one at seven in the morning? Mixed martial arts and grappling?" she asked.

"Oh, that's for the more advanced students. We usually have law enforcement in there and black belts, people training for deployment," Dalton told her as he walked past her and leaned against the desk. He crossed his arms in front of his chest and stared at her.

"Oh, well that sounds like a good workout," she replied with an attitude back.

Hank watched as Dalton looked Millie over.

"It's for experienced fighters and martial artists. You said you did self-defense classes." He sounded like he was interrogating her and Millie stepped back.

Hank interrupted.

"We would test you first, Millie, to see how much you know and then we can place you in the right program. If we don't have something for you, we offer one-on-one training, too, and not at a higher price."

"Why not?" she asked.

"It's a small town and we're here for the people. We help to train the deputies in the latest techniques as well as military getting ready for new deployment or ex-military like my brothers and I who want to stay in shape and love to train."

"Sound good. I'll think about it and let you know."

She began to leave.

"Come back tomorrow at nine and we'll see what you remember. There'll be a few other women and men here. They're beginners, too," Dalton added then got up from the desk and began to walk toward the water cooler.

Millie followed him with her eyes then looked at Hank.

She smiled.

"Thank you, Hank. I'll see you tomorrow morning at nine."

* * * *

"What the hell is wrong with you?" Hank asked Dalton after he watched Millie cross the street and head into the boutique.

"Nothing's wrong with me, why?" Dalton asked.

"You were all over that girl. Shit, Dalton, I know it's been a while since you had a woman, but don't you remember how not to bite their heads off or make them run for the hills?"

Hank knew exactly what was up with his brother. Dalton had been immediately attracted to Millie just as he was, but Dalton thought that Millie was another one of the many single women walking into the dojo looking to land a man or mess around. They had had their share of women and Hank knew women well. Millie was different and he couldn't wait to see her tomorrow.

"She doesn't know shit about martial arts, karate, jujitsu, or whatever."

"Oh, yeah, that was really nice how you interrogated her. Made her feel like she didn't look like she worked out. Did you notice the definition in her thighs and on her arms? She works out and she's strong, too. Definitely not like some of the skinny weaklings that come in here acting like damsels in distress."

Dalton turned and gave Hank a dirty look.

Then Hank challenged him.

"You still aren't over Sylvia, are you? Man, you didn't even sleep with that bitch and she had your emotions all twisted up in knots. She was a conniving bitch and used you to piss off that dirtbag boyfriend of hers, Larry."

"Enough, Hank. I don't need to talk about that woman. I didn't see what you and the brothers saw. I truly thought she wanted to break up with Larry."

"Whatever. Just don't be so quick to judge people before you even know them. She seemed sweet."

"Sylvia?"

"No, you idiot! Millie. She seemed really nice and had that New York accent."

"Whatever." Dalton walked out of the room. Hank looked out the window just as Stacy, Anna, and Millie exited the boutique. Millie was smiling as Stacy and Anna seemed to be introducing her to some of the other residents of Pearl. Then Lena and Bryant showed up. That was a young woman who was tough as nails. He was happy for the Jones brothers. They landed them all a fine woman.

* * * *

"Lena, Bryant, this is Millie," Stacy said. Bryant remembered Millie from elementary school.

Millie kept looking toward the MMA fighting place across the street. Dalton was a fierce-looking man and a mean one to boot. Hank seemed really friendly and was very attractive. She wondered why she kept thinking about them. She needed to give herself a mental kick as a reminder about her track record with men. Not that she had a chance with men as gorgeous as the Lewis brothers she met so far.

"Hi, Lena, it's so nice to meet you. Stacy and Anna have told me so much about you."

"And they told me lots about you, too. I'm glad you're here. We could use all the help we can get with the new shelter and community center. I saw you going into the MMA fighting place. Do you know karate?"

"I do, but I've been out of it for a few months. Long story, but I'm motivated to get back into it. I could use the boost of empowerment."

"Yeah, I take the beginners' course there in the morning at nine along with Sage. She loves the kickboxing part."

"It's a great workout."

"It sure is. I was thinking about asking Dalton and Hank if they would be willing to run a class once or twice a week at a discounted price over at the new rec center. I'm sure the women would love it and want to feel empowered, too. Plus they might not feel comfortable heading into town."

"That sounds like a great idea, Lena," Stacy chimed in.

"Millie and you should go ask them about it," Anna suggested then winked at Millie.

Why did it seem like Anna and Stacy were pushing her toward one or more of the Lewis brothers? They were out of their minds.

"I think their next class is going to start up. That's an intense one, too. My leg is still giving me problems, but Dalton tries to rearrange the program so I can handle it," Bryant stated.

"How is the therapy going, Bryant?" Stacy asked.

"It's going well."

"He's a pain and gives me hell every day about it," Lena replied and Bryant snagged her around the waist and hoisted her up against his side.

They all laughed.

"Well, we're headed back to the site now. I think Anthony and Jeremy are working with their crews on finishing the rec center. We're supposed to have our paint picked out by tomorrow," Stacy stated.

"Well, let's head over to the hardware store now. That way Anthony and Jeremy will be set and on schedule as usual," Lena added and they headed toward the middle of town.

Chapter 8

Clare stood outside of Millie's apartment after work. She had been so busy the last two days, with Millie being fired for no damn good reason other than that asshole ex of hers, Stewart. She had been holding on to her award from the gala and wanted to see Millie.

No one answered when she knocked on the door, so she pulled out her cell phone to text her. Maybe Millie would be back soon and Clare thought she could wait for her.

Just as she finished texting and was about to leave, the door to Millie's apartment opened.

Clare was stunned to see the tall, very muscular man answer her door. She swallowed hard and instantly picked up on the man's sex appeal and bright smile. *Looks like Millie is on the rebound and in the right direction.* This guy was all muscles.

"Can I help you?" he asked in a very scratchy, deep voice that made her toes curl.

Millie, you lucky lady. Good for you.

"I'm looking for Millie."

"And you are?" he asked in a tone that demanded an answer yet was sweet, too. Man, this guy was lethal.

"I'm Clare, a friend of hers from work. Well, her old job, anyway. I wanted to drop off her award from the ceremony over the weekend."

He raised his eyebrows as if he hadn't a clue about the awards ceremony. She rolled her eyes and shook her head.

"She didn't tell you, did she? That's Millie for you. She never boasts about her success and her caring ways. She helped to get major funding for the new women's shelter downtown."

"No, she didn't tell me. I'm kind of here to surprise her. We used to date and things didn't work out because I had to go out of town for business for a while. I was hoping to win her love back."

"Oh, how sweet. Well, I'm sure she'll be home soon. She never goes out, really. Kind of a workaholic. What was your name?"

He smiled at her then gestured for her to come inside.

"Why don't you come in and join me? The name's Frank," he told her as she walked into Millie's apartment, hoping to find out more about the hunk with all the tattoos and big muscles.

* * * *

Millie headed into the dojo a few minutes before nine o'clock. She acknowledged Hank and then the other men and women in the class along with Lena and Sage.

She had met Sage yesterday back on the Triple C when they arrived with paint colors and ideas for the gardening around the building. That was when she met Anthony and Jeremy Lewis again. They were very good-looking men and she could see the resemblances between them and both Hank and Dalton. Jeremy had been a huge flirt and Anthony seemed very businesslike and in command. He liked to be in charge just as it appeared Dalton did. She wondered when she would meet the fifth brother, Marco.

Millie took position behind Lena and Sage. From her position, she could see Hank clearly and also had a view of the larger room where Dalton worked with a group of six men. They were grappling and working on maneuvers with hand-to-hand combat. It looked intense.

"Okay, class, let's begin."

"Attention!" Hank declared and half the people lined up straight, bringing their right feet together with their left feet and hands by their sides.

He began to explain the simple moves and this went on for the first fifteen minutes of class. Finally, he gave up and had them warm up by running around the perimeter of the room. In between, he would instruct them to kick the bag a few times, then punch the bag, and finally work on the beginning of some moves.

She was bored out of her mind but finally got the chance to show him what she could do. Well, at least a little bit. She didn't want to show off and she didn't want him to think that she was messing with him. It was enough that he had three women in the front row drooling over Hank's every move and nagging him every few minutes about showing them again and again how to place their fists and arms just so he would touch them.

It had become quite nauseating.

It was finally her turn toward the last few minutes of class. Hank would show a series of moves, but only a few because the others were beginners and they couldn't memorize the moves as quickly. It took a lot of practice, but Millie had learned a lot in two years.

"Okay, Millie, nice and easy. I want you to watch what I do then repeat it."

She tried to hide her smile as Hank gave just a few moves and she immediately followed them with vigor and perfection. His eyes widened.

"That was great. Want to try another one?" he asked so sweetly, and she didn't want to lead him on making him think she was a natural when really she had expert training. So she did his next moves and then a few more until he decided he had been had and got her back.

"Class, it seems that Millie is a natural. I'd like to spar a little with her and see what she's got. What do you think?"

A series of cheers went through the room and Millie looked to see the four women from the front line with their arms crossed in front of their chest and scowls on their faces. They looked pissed off, but Millie didn't care. Who came to a mixed martial arts class wearing half T-shirts tied in the back and short shorts?

* * * *

Hank tried to hide his smile. It appeared that Millie knew a hell of a lot more about martial arts then she let on. He was impressed as she moved around the mat with such grace and quick speed. He threw a few quick strikes and she was more than ready for them as she blocked and then countered. Round and round they sparred on the mat until Hank bowed before her then shook her hand. Lena, Sage, and the others cheered.

"You and I are talking after class," he told her with a serious expression and then smiled before he addressed the rest of the class.

* * * *

Dalton watched from across the room. He could hear the intakes of breath from the small crowd and then the cheers. It had shocked him to see Millie was sparring a little with his brother, Hank. She had lied about her training and experience. But why?

"Hey, who is that over there?" his brother, Deputy Marco, asked as he wiped the sweat from his brow then took a slug of water from a water bottle.

Dalton felt his heart rate increase. Millie caught the attention of Marco, too? What the heck was this woman after, anyway?

"That's Millie. She's a friend of Stacy's and Anna's. Apparently, she used to live out here years ago then moved to New York."

"Damn, she sure can move across the mat."

Dalton looked at his brother and he knew his facial expression said it all.

"What the hell is wrong with you?" Marco asked.

Dalton shook his head as the other men in their group began to leave, but not before making comments.

"Who is she?" Deputy Taylor McGreever asked and Marco filled him in.

Marco and Dalton made their way over toward the mats.

* * * *

"Damn, Millie, you sure know a lot of moves. Did you train long?" Lena asked, and she and Sage joined her by the back of the room where they grabbed water bottles.

"I trained for two years. Started off with self-defense classes and then the instructor showed me a lot of different techniques from many forms of martial arts. To tell you the truth, I miss it. I love doing it."

"So why did you quit?" Lena asked.

"I didn't want to. My ex-boyfriend wanted me to," Millie stated without thinking and then she looked up to see both Sage and Lena shaking their heads. At first, she thought they were thinking she was an idiot.

"Yeah, sometimes men are such assholes. They think just because they're interested in you they have a right to control you," Lena stated.

Millie chuckled as she recalled the story about Lena's survival on the streets of Detroit.

"Well, at least you can get back into it now, right?" Sage offered, and Millie smiled then nodded her head. With a glance up toward where Lena was looking, Millie noticed the four women from their class gathering around Dalton, Hank, and some other man whom she didn't know. He was very rugged and stern looking. His expression as the women talked to him seemed off. He almost looked annoyed, but how could he be? The four women were very thin, acutely aware of their great bodies, and totally invading the men's space. *My God, those women are really pushy. They sure are interested in Hank, Dalton, and the third guy.*

"Those four women are Stella, Lisa, Paula, and Melody. All four are from Turbank and they come into town for a little action, if you know what I mean," Lena offered, and Millie tried to act as if she really didn't care. She picked up her small bag and tossed the empty bottle of water into a nearby recycling container.

"Well, men sometimes like women like that," Millie offered.

"Not the Lewis brothers," Lena replied and Sage shook her head in disgust.

"They are so trampy. I mean, look at the way Stella is practically wrapping her legs around Hank."

"I think he's showing her how to do the move from class properly," Millie replied.

Lena snorted. "Yeah, right. If he doesn't pull her off of him then she'll have him on the mats in just a few more minutes."

"Well, then let's get the heck out of here. I don't know about you, but I can't take much more of the scene." Millie began to exit the room. It was upsetting for some reason, to watch the men accept women hanging over them in such a way. They could at least try to act professional in the dojo and save the personal stuff for outside.

"By the way, the third guy is Marco Lewis. He's a deputy with my Kenny," Lena whispered and Millie looked back to see if she noticed the resemblances and caught all three men staring at her.

"Millie, could you stick around please?" Hank asked and both Lena and Sage waved good-bye.

The four women however, stared at her, giving her the once-over. She hated women like that. Millie was feeling pretty good about her body right now after such a great workout. Kickboxing and martial arts wasn't for the weak or unserious. She took the workout seriously and knew that in just a week's time she would be in better shape than she was right now. She would feel more energized and healthier.

"If you ladies could excuse us, we need to discuss a few things with Millie," Hank stated with his arms crossed in front of his chest.

Millie watched as Stella and Lisa both touched his arm and ran their hands down his forearms as they winked and swayed away.

"Talk to you later, Hank. Maybe we'll see you over at Rocky's," Stella stated, and Millie noticed how Paula and Melody licked their lips and tried to gain Marco's and Dalton's attention, but the other two men looked aggravated.

The four women walked by Millie. She, in return, smiled and wished them a good day, which surprised them and apparently ticked them off.

When she looked back toward the three men, only Hank looked amused.

"So, care to explain why you didn't come clean yesterday about your experience with your sensei?" Hank asked, and oh, God, the way he said *sensei* made her belly quiver. *My sensei? Oh Lord, does he sound incredible.*

Millie shrugged her shoulders and thought she'd get away with a nice conversation about quitting but not getting into the details when Sensei Dalton yelled out, "Attention!"

Immediately, Millie found herself standing up straight at attention and Dalton walked around her.

"We don't know one another. Understandable. However, I don't appreciate being lied to, nor does my brother, Hank. Why did you lie about your experience?"

"I didn't lie, Sensei."

"No?" Hank chimed in.

She kept her eyes straight ahead and it was difficult, considering that she was standing in a dojo with three very large, capable men. Although she knew nothing about Marco, the man had a major body on him and she noticed his sparring session during her boring class. He now stood in martial arts pants and a tight black T-shirt that stretched across large pectoral muscles. His tattoos were peeking from the sleeves on both arms. The man was definitely attractive, but his facial expression was so very serious.

"Explain," Hank said, interrupting her ogling over the hunk of man in front of her.

"You asked me my experience and I told you. I started off with self-defense classes and my instructor, my sensei, saw my interest and desire to learn more so he began to introduce different types of martial arts and fighting techniques to me. You never asked me to what intensity."

"Did you move up in belts?" Dalton asked and she could feel him a few feet behind her in a stance that she knew would be attack mode. He was going to test her abilities, not Hank.

"I had to leave before my final test as a black belt."

Dalton didn't just make a move. She knew he wasn't out to hurt her. She had been around martial artists, MMA fighters, and kickboxers for the past two years. They were always challenging on a moment's notice, hoping that a student had truly absorbed their trainer's teachings. Dalton and Hank would be no different, but she wondered how far they would push and whether she could handle it. It had been a few months, after all, and she was a bit rusty.

"Begin!" Hank stated. That was her only warning before Dalton gave a stomp and growl before his first strike. Millie turned, ducked, and counterstruck with a right punch. Her knuckles grazed Dalton's gi on his wrist. His expression was surprise, but she knew he hadn't meant to start off hard with her. Now she had the feeling that he would turn up the heat.

They sparred around the matted room. He gave a high kick and she would strike and step toward him in challenge. They did this for some time and the adrenaline began to take over. She loved sparring and felt alive and confident as she did it. Dalton got a little tougher, but he still held back. She wasn't a fool. This was a test in her training and experience.

"Follow what I do if you can," he told her and she gave a small, quick nod of her head. He came toward her in one of those wild *Crouching Tiger, Hidden Dragon* moves and then jumped into a roll across the mats, pushing up to his feet before standing upright, feet a few inches apart, fists ready to strike. She did the same move with little effort and she thought she saw a small smile on his face. But then he nodded and someone moved in behind her.

Quickly, she jumped to the left and Hank was there. The two of them began to move around her, taking different strikes while she countered two opponents. She had done that in her dojo, too, and wasn't rusty as expected. In fact, her sensei knew her story and about how Frank attacked her. He prepared her as best he could to fight her fears and so many times she was challenged by four opponents at once. At that exact moment she sensed the third body shift to her right. *Oh crap, their brother, Marco, is going to join in, too?*

She lowered, and then twisted, striking forward in a punch to Marco's stomach and he grunted then raised his voice.

"I'm not fighting, I was just moving out of the way."

She dropped her hands and grabbed on to him.

"Oh my God, I'm so sorry. I totally didn't mean to hit you. I sensed you move behind me and just assumed."

Before she finished her sentence, someone swept her feet out from underneath her and she fell right on her ass in front of all three men.

Marco and Hank chuckled, making her realize she had just been tricked, and Dalton stared at her with a serious expression. He looked a bit winded and that made her feel pretty good.

He reached his hand out to her. "Nice job, Millie," he whispered and when she reached up to accept his hand their skin touched and she nearly gasped at the intense sting of electricity.

* * * *

Dalton was trying his hardest to not show the attraction he felt to Millie. She was a dream come true if she were for real. However, she had already lied to them about her experience in martial arts and he wondered why.

He pulled her up a little harder than he meant and she stumbled into him. Immediately, Hank had his hands on her waist behind her and the thought of him and his brothers sharing this woman entered his mind. It was unreal and it scared the crap out of him. He steadied her then released her. Her abrupt move away from Hank and him caused some unnerving feelings to collide with his previous sexual thoughts. She appeared scared. Marco must have sensed the situation because he took over the conversation.

"I'm Marco, their brother, by the way." Marco reached between Hank and Dalton to shake Millie's hand. She looked a little unsure and Dalton wondered if she felt the same reaction to his touch that he felt from hers.

"Nice to meet you, Marco." She smiled when their hands met. She locked gazes with Marco and her cheeks grew pinker. Marco smiled then released her hand.

"You looked fantastic out there, Millie. I'm really impressed," Marco told her.

"Can I go now?" she replied and Dalton hadn't expected that immediate response.

"What's the hurry?" Hank asked her and Dalton waited to hear her response.

"I have work to do back on the Triple C and Lena's giving me a ride over because my aunt's truck was giving me some problems. I had to drop it at the mechanic's shop on my way here."

Marco and Dalton looked toward the front of the dojo. No one was around.

"They left, sweetheart," Hank stated.

Millie looked like she was surprised and then a flash of something else caused a change in her facial expression.

"I must have forgotten to ask her. No big deal. I'll just walk. Am I free to go now, Sensei?" she asked then smirked. Her attempt at trying to change the subject failed.

"Yes, you are released and Sensei Dalton and I will discuss which class would better suit your abilities. But you are not walking five miles back to the Triple C," Hank stated.

"I'll drive you, honey. I have to head home to shower and then be at work for a four-to-twelve shift," Marco stated.

Millie stepped back and began to head toward the front of the dojo.

She was shaking her head.

"No, thank you. I'm fine, really. As a matter of fact, I could use the exercise."

Dalton looked at her strangely. Did she think she was fat or something? Because from where he stood, she was definitely all woman. The gi couldn't hide her large breasts and the way her waist dipped in then her hips curved out and then dipped back in at her legs. He wanted to see her without the gi on, that was for sure.

"There's no way I'm letting you travel that far on foot," Marco scolded as he headed toward the front and grabbed his bag that lay in one of the cubbies by the front door.

Millie placed her hands on her hips and stared at him.

"Excuse me, Deputy Lewis, but I don't know you or your brothers, so if you don't mind, I feel more comfortable taking care of myself and jogging back to the Triple C. I appreciate your kind and hospitable offer, but no, thank you."

Millie grabbed her things, bowed her head before exiting the dojo, and left.

"Hot damn, that woman's got a fire in her." Marco watched her head down the street, adjust her bag so it was a backpack, and begin to walk out of town.

Dalton was beside himself. They each had women like Stella, Paula, Lisa, and Melody throwing themselves at them, which drove them mad with annoyance. Now here was Millie, a sweet, very interesting young woman and she avoided him and his brothers like a plague.

"She is something else, isn't she?" Hank whispered.

"Sure is," Marco replied.

"Did you feel it when you touched her?" Marco asked Dalton, but Dalton didn't want to go there. Women were trouble and he was farthest from good enough for a woman as beautiful as Millie.

"Naw. Not a thing," Dalton said then attempted to walk away.

"Bullshit, 'not a thing.' When you touched her hand to help her up the two of you were locked in a deep gaze and even I felt the electrical current around us," Marco stated.

"Me, too. When we were both touching her at once, I had flashes of images moving in my head." Hank sounded shocked himself.

Dalton knew he had the same thoughts.

"Well, don't go acting on those thoughts. She seems really sweet but also like she's hiding something. Why is she here and how long is she planning on staying in Pearl?" Dalton asked aloud and his brothers mumbled.

"As the local deputy in town, I may be able to find out that information, brother," Marco said then grabbed his bag and headed out of the dojo with a smirk on his face. Dalton and Hank shook their heads then went about getting ready for the next class.

Chapter 9

Millie was leaning against the doorframe, cringing at the thought that tomorrow she would be climbing up ladders and painting the rec center along with Anna, Stacy, Lena, and Sage. After her excursion this morning of working out at the dojo, sparring with the Lewis brothers, and then running the five miles back to the Triple C, her body was in pain. *What the hell was I thinking?*

She watched Stacy labeling which areas in the rec center would be painted specific colors. She had to admit that Stacy was definitely a control freak and enjoyed being in charge. At the moment, that suited Millie just fine. She adjusted her stance and swallowed hard at the achiness. She figured a few months out of her routine of working out would leave her achy on her returning days, but this was crazy. It had to do with the run back to the ranch. She hadn't run like that in ages. But it was better than accepting a ride from a man she didn't know, despite her body's cry to accept the ride and spend some more time in the hottie's presence. She shook her head at the thought. She couldn't trust her judgment of men anymore. She sure as hell wasn't going to allow her physical attraction to any man to make decisions for her.

"Hello, Millie. Did you hear me?" Stacy asked and both Lena and Anna smiled at Millie.

"Sorry. I'm just a bit tired, I guess. Being out of practice from the dojo for a few months had really set me back. I'm not as good as I used to be."

"I tend to argue with you there, Millie. Sage and I saw you sparring with Marco, Hank, and Dalton. You looked amazing."

Millie felt her cheeks warm at the compliment.

"Thanks."

"She was sparring with Marco, Dalton, and Hank?" Stacy asked as she walked closer to Millie and crossed her arms in front of her chest.

"Spill the beans, sister, or else," Stacy demanded.

"What?"

"What went down?" Anna asked.

"Nothing went down. I sparred a little with them. They were testing my abilities to see what class I would fit into better."

"Oh, there was some testing going on, all right," Sage chimed in and both Stacy and Anna smiled.

"Did you get really touchy feely with the Lewis brothers? You know we saw how Anthony and Jeremy were talking to you before. Both were standing real close and looked a bit annoyed when their workers were checking you out," Stacy teased.

"Oh, cut it out. They were not flirting and no one was getting touchy feely," Millie replied.

"You should have seen how annoyed Paula and the girls at the dojo were that the men were paying them no attention and giving Millie full attention," Lena added.

"Stop that. Nothing happened. It wasn't a big deal."

"They like her," Sage whispered then glanced around just as Deputy Marco Lewis pulled up in the patrol car outside.

"Look who's coming to visit our Millie," Anna teased.

"Let's go see if the guys delivered the supplies for tomorrow," Stacy suggested.

"Don't you dare leave me here alone with—"

"Why hello, Deputy Lewis, how are you doing?" Anna interrupted.

"Doing well, Anna. I came by to check out the construction. Spoke with Jeremy and Anthony a little while ago. Said things are moving along smoothly," Marco stated.

"They sure are. We're actually headed out to check on supplies for painting tomorrow. Millie can show you around." Stacy ushered the others out of the building. Millie shook her head. She was going to have to tell the women to stop playing matchmaker. She wasn't interested.

Although, Marco looked exceptionally good in a uniform.

"So you made it back in one piece after all?" he teased as he took off his hat and held it with his hands. His fingers played with the rim of it and she imagined those fingers on her skin, brushing against her cheek. She shook the thoughts. Hadn't she just said "no way" to men?

"Yeah, well, I may look like I'm in one piece, but I'm definitely feeling a bit exhausted. I haven't worked out like that or ran that far in a while. My poor body is paying the price."

"Well, you looked really good on the mat. My brothers and I were impressed. Also I'm curious about what else you know how to do."

She locked gazes with him a moment, wondering what he meant. Why did it feel like this conversation was going to supply hidden innuendoes and flirtatious retorts?

"I told you guys back in the dojo about my experience in the martial arts."

"I think you held back a bit. Should be fun to see how Dalton and Hank pull out some more of your hidden secrets," he teased and she felt her cheeks warm and her throat close up.

How would they feel when they knew she had been involved with an abusive man, was nearly killed, and was now being hunted by him? Or the fact that she hadn't learned her lesson the first time around and got involved with an egocentric, verbal abuser like Stewart? *Shit!*

She felt her confidence deflate and the battle within herself turn to defeat and disgust. Why had she been so stupid?

"Hey, what's wrong? You look upset," he said, and she snapped her head back up to look at him.

She pulled away from the wall and stepped toward the doorway.

"Listen, there's nothing interesting about me. I'm just trying to live my life and make some big decisions about my future plans either here in Pearl or elsewhere. I like martial arts and I definitely could use the exercise. There're no hidden secrets, so please just let me be."

She began to walk away when Marco stepped in her path. He didn't touch her and she was grateful. He seemed to sense her need for space.

"Sweetheart, I'd have to disagree with you on a few points. First of all, you are a fine-looking woman." He looked her body over from head to toe. His expression and tone made her belly quiver and her pussy come alive like no words had ever done before. It was wild.

"You are most definitely interesting enough to get to know. I'm not trying to be pushy, I'm just interested. So why don't you show me around the center here and let me know what the plans are. I'd love to help out if I could."

Millie was surprised by his words and actions but grabbed the opportunity to speak on a lighter subject. She nodded her head then began to show Marco around the rec center and what they planned on doing there.

* * * *

The following day, Millie was sitting on the porch, trying to get her cell phone to turn on. The battery had died on her trip to Texas and she had forgotten to check it. A few days had passed and she had been so busy she forgot all about charging it. Last night she had charged it up and she couldn't help but feel some anxiety about who may have called or left messages for her.

Surprisingly, there were messages from Clare and a few people she worked with during the women's shelter project. As she listened to the voice messages she felt good that they complimented her and bad-mouthed her boss and Stewart. Apparently, they knew Stewart caused her to lose her job. Hopefully, his reputation suffered a bit.

She smirked just thinking about it. She guessed the old saying, "what goes around, comes around," really was true.

She listened to a call from Clare stating that she had her award and wanted to drop it off at the apartment. Then she went on to say that their boss was a jerk and Stewart was a huge asshole. She chuckled and went to her text messages.

There were numerous texts from Clare.

She scanned through them until she got to the one about her award and Clare standing outside of her apartment. Millie heard some vehicles approaching and looked up to see the sheriff's truck and a car driving rather quickly toward the ranch and her cottage.

She was eager to read Clare's text message. Glancing back down at the cell phone and ignoring the fast-approaching vehicles, she read the text.

"Hi, Mill. I'm at you apartment w/ award. U R not here. Where R U?"

Millie read the next text.

"Your X is HOT*! If U don't arrive soon he's MINE!* ☺*"*

Millie didn't get the message. Did Clare mean Stewart? What the hell?

She sent a text back.

"Hey, Clare. Sorry I wasn't home. What x bf? A few seconds passed. *Clare must have her phone in hand.*

"The tall, muscular, sexy one. Ur favorite."

"Who? Where r u?"

Millie had a funny feeling in her gut. What the hell was this about? But now Wyatt and his deputies took precedence over the texts. *Why are they here and looking...upset?*

She stood up and looked at Wyatt as he got out of his truck. He appeared determined as he approached in quick strides toward her and then she saw Marco and Deputy Kenny Jones get out of the cruiser.

"Who's on the phone?" Wyatt asked and his tone frightened her.

"What's wrong?" she replied.

"You're not talking to anyone on there, are you?" Marco asked with just as intense of a tone as Wyatt. All three men looked angry.

"No. I was just checking voice mail and text messages. I was texting my friend Clare back. She just texted me."

"Millie, give me the phone," Wyatt commanded as he reached out for it and climbed the porch steps. Marco and Kenny were following close behind him. Millie stepped back and held the phone away from them.

"No. What the hell is going on?" she demanded to know as she looked up at all three men. They were each very big and filled with muscles. She knew she shouldn't challenge their authority, but she wanted an explanation for their abrupt behavior.

"Give it to him now," Marco demanded She jumped and then immediately handed her phone over to Wyatt without a word, shocking herself. Wyatt glanced down at the phone and scrolled over the messages.

"Shit! She didn't say where she was so it should be okay," Wyatt told the other deputies, but he still hadn't made Millie aware of the situation. Millie felt her gut clench with fear. Something was wrong.

"Please, tell me what's going on?" Millie asked.

"Millie, honey, I heard from Detective Flynn."

She glanced at Marco and Kenny.

"Wyatt, maybe we can discuss this in private."

She didn't want them to know what was going on.

Wyatt continued. "They know what's going on. Marco and Kenny, as well as the other deputies, know what the situation is. I told you that we protect the people we care about."

She felt the tears reach her eyes.

"You're scaring me," she whispered then felt someone touch her hand. She flinched a moment then looked to the side to see that it was Marco. He squeezed her hand and she looked up until she locked gazes with his eyes. They were dark blue and appeared beyond concerned. Marco was stocky and a bit over six feet tall. She felt his presence entirely. She looked back toward Wyatt as he spoke and simultaneously her cell phone chimed, indicating another text message.

"Honey, Detective Flynn called from New York. Your friend, Clare, has gone missing."

"No, that can't be. I was just texting…"

Millie realized as the words left her lips what exactly was happening here. *Clare texted me last night. She was at my apartment with the award. Detective Flynn called Wyatt. Clare is missing.*

She covered her mouth with her free hand and gasped. She was shocked and then she reached for the phone.

Wyatt pulled it away.

"That could be her. I was just talking with her through texting."

He shook his head.

"She was reported missing yesterday."

"So it's probably a mistake. She went to my apartment to drop off the award."

"Honey…Millie…her body was found in your apartment. She's dead," Wyatt told her, and Millie felt as if she were going to faint. Immediately, Marco guided her toward the porch bench and knelt down beside her.

She shook her head. "No, it can't be. Who would do that?" She looked up toward Wyatt, who was reading the text on her phone.

"Frank?" she whispered as the tears hit her eyes and her stomach clenched.

He nodded his head.

"What does the text say?" Kenny asked as he stood next to Wyatt.

"A response to Millie's last text."

"Your friend was really nice but couldn't give me the answers I wanted. Come back to me, Millie. Don't make me come for you."

"Oh God, no!" Millie stood up and Marco joined her. He held her by her waist.

"Calm down, sugar. It's going to be okay. We'll protect you," Marco whispered down to her. She shook her head and covered her mouth. Their words were sinking in. *Frank killed Clare. Oh God, poor Clare.*

She tried to push past Marco.

"Honey, slow down. Where are you going?" he asked.

"I'm going to be sick," she blurted out with her hand over her mouth as she rushed inside to the bathroom.

* * * *

"Son of a bitch, Wyatt. What the hell is this all about? Who is this guy and what does he want with Millie?" Marco asked.

Wyatt took a deep breath then slowly released it. He glanced toward the doorway that Millie had just disappeared through.

"Over two years ago when Stacy, Millie, and Anna lived in New York, Millie started dating this guy, Frank. They were together for a while and he was abusive," Wyatt began to tell Marco and Kenny. Marco had to hide his anger. The thought of some asshole hitting a woman pissed him off. But it especially made him angry that it had been Millie.

"He was dealing in steroids and guns, supposedly, but lost it one night and nearly killed Millie. He beat the hell out of her and was about to kill her when Stacy arrived and saved her life. It was intense, and Stacy suffered some injuries, but nothing compared to Millie. She was hospitalized for weeks and nearly didn't survive. Her total recovery took months. Apparently, this Frank character still wants her."

"How the hell did the bastard get out of jail so darn quick?" Kenny asked as they made their way into Millie's cottage.

"Apparently, he got out early on good behavior and from the recommendation of his therapist. It's a fucked-up situation. He called Millie, she called the detective that worked her case in New York, and he recommended she leave town for a bit. He hasn't been able to locate Frank and Frank hasn't been to see his parole officer."

"Well, big fucking surprise there," Kenny added.

Marco turned toward the hallway just as Millie emerged from the bathroom.

She looked scared and he was compelled to go to her, to protect her from this monster. He couldn't imagine why this was happening to her.

"Come sit down, Millie." Marco reached for her to guide her to the couch, but she shook her head.

"What do we need to do, Wyatt?" she asked, then took a deep breath and straightened her shoulders. She was trying to be tough, but he could tell that she was shaking.

"They're on the hunt for him in New York, Millie. Detective Flynn said to keep you here and safe and that's what my men and I plan on doing." Wyatt stood there with his hand leaning on the butt of his gun.

"It's my fault that Clare is dead," she whispered and Wyatt moved in front of her.

"You listen to me, Millie. I know a bit about individuals like this and believe me when I tell you that this is not your fault. The damn system failed you and it failed Clare. Now it's our job and Flynn's job to ensure that Frank is captured and that you remain safe. I'd say you have a lot of people around here to care for you, so you're not alone in this."

"I can't stay here. What if Frank found out I came to Pearl? What if he goes after Stacy or Anna or the other women in the shelter? Then what? He'll board a plane or take buses or whatever he has to in order to get to me. You don't know him, Wyatt. None of you know this type of man," she blurted out as tears rolled down her cheeks.

Marco wrapped an arm around her waist and pulled her against his chest. She cried as he consoled her.

"I know you're scared, Millie, but trust that Wyatt and the rest of us know what we're doing here. He won't step near this town without us knowing first." Marco continued to caress her back and hold her tight. She clung to him despite not knowing him well.

Just as he thought that, she began to pull away and wiped the tears from her eyes.

"I'm sorry. I didn't mean to slobber all over your uniform." She caressed her hand against his chest as if to wipe her tears away, but all it did was make his body warm and want things he shouldn't want from a woman he hardly even knew.

"Don't jump the gun, Millie. Marco is going to stay here with you while Kenny and I inform the others about the situation so they're all on board. I'm taking your phone with me and calling Flynn so he can look into these texts. If in fact that was Frank texting, then he just incriminated himself. It can also help to establish a timeline. I know that Flynn is contacting Frank's therapist and the parole board. He'll be back behind bars in no time," Wyatt explained.

"He doesn't care. You read the texts, Wyatt. He was toying with me and he killed Clare so easily just because she hadn't told him what he wanted to know."

"Clare didn't know about Pearl or Stacy and Anna?" Marco asked and she looked up into his eyes and shook her head.

"We worked together but never really hung out until the gala. She had a great personality and we hit it off, but she didn't know about my personal life. If she did…"

Marco placed his hand on her shoulder.

"It's not your fault. It's this asshole's fault and he will be captured."

"Let's hope so," Millie replied.

Chapter 10

Detective Flynn and his partner, Detective Mario Bower, stood in the examination room at the coroner's office. The medical examiner, Dr. Lawrence Martin, looked over the various wounds he found on twenty-two-year-old Clare Brown. He announced his findings into a recorder as Flynn and Bower looked on in disgust and sadness. Detective Flynn still couldn't believe that Frank Bennett had done this and for no apparent reason except to find out where Millie Donovan was hiding. He really shouldn't be surprised by the brutality of such a man as Frank. However, his behavior didn't coincide with his therapist Dr. Sheila Perkin's notes and findings. She stood before the parole board and placed her medical reputation on the line for Bennett and showed medical proof in counseling sessions. Could Frank Bennett have manipulated the therapist? They wouldn't know the answer to that until they located the doctor. Currently, she was unaccounted for.

"You see these marks right here along the thigh that can also be seen along other parts of the victim's body?" Dr. Martin asked them.

"Yeah," Flynn and Bower both replied.

"Well, it appears to be from a knife. However, up here along the breast line and abdomen are more scratch-like gashes."

"So what are you thinking, doctor?" Flynn asked.

"This woman was tortured for hours. The killer used at least four types of weapons to assault, abuse, and ultimately kill her."

Flynn gave a disgusted sigh.

"He left a lot of prints at the scene. I'm confident we can gather enough evidence to charge this guy. He won't be able to run for long. We'll catch him," Flynn added.

"That's good to know, because a person who could commit such a brutal sexual assault like this does not deserve to be alive or living free. May God help you find him quickly."

* * * *

Millie heard what sounded like trucks pulling up in front of the cottage. It was only seven in the morning and she felt a splitting headache. She glanced toward the nightstand and then covered her head with a pillow. Thoughts of last night's tragic news resurfaced in her brain. *Clare was murdered. Frank killed Clare.*

She suddenly smelled coffee and wondered who would be making coffee in her house. It was more than likely Anna or Stacy. They stayed with her until midnight along with Ben, Charlie, Marco, and Wyatt.

Marco was insisting that he could stay the night on the couch and finally she was so exhausted and sick to her stomach she walked out of the room and went to bed. She didn't want to argue with him, but he was stubborn as damn hell.

Her eyes popped open under the pillow.

Is he still here? Did he spend the night?

A panicky feeling filled her at the thought. She slowly got out of bed and peeked through a small opening on her bedroom door. Sure as shit, Marco was standing there in casual clothes, sipping a cup of coffee and meeting someone at the front door. His dark jeans stretched across a perfect ass and the material looked plastered against his muscular thighs. She licked her lips and felt her nipples pebble. *Damn, he is a fine-looking man.*

She felt the tears reach her eyes as she leaned her aching head against the door.

She had the worst luck with men and even if Marco seemed sincere and thoroughly delicious, she couldn't entertain her attraction to him or any other man. How could she even be thinking such thoughts when Clare was murdered because of her? Clare was dead and Frank was out there somewhere.

She walked back over toward her bedroom mirror.

She wasn't surprised to see the red-rimmed eyes, blotches over her breasts, and hair rumpled. She'd had a sleepless night. She ran her fingers through her hair, annoyed that the hairbrush was in the bathroom down the hallway. She'd sneak in there first and make herself look decent before venturing into the living room.

She adjusted her T-shirt then grabbed her robe.

Her plan was to go take a shower then tell Marco he could leave and that she would be just fine, but as she slowly opened the door she caught sight of both Anthony and Jeremy Lewis doing something to her front door.

"Excuse me, but what the hell is going on?"

* * * *

Anthony was measuring the door to see where to place the dead bolt and provide extra security in case someone attempted to break into Millie's cottage.

Marco had spent the night and that gave them all a little peace of mind about Millie. None of them could believe what had happened to her. Anthony and his brother Jeremy had immediately suggested coming over to the cottage in the morning to secure it better. Marco had said that Millie hadn't been too keen on him staying over last night.

Just then, Millie entered the living room and she didn't seem too happy about them being there, either.

Marco turned toward Millie and just stared at her. She looked tired and her eyes were red and swollen as if she had been crying, and she seemed angry.

"Anthony and Jeremy came over to do some security upgrades. They won't get in your way and should be done in a little while."

"Security upgrades? What the hell are you talking about?" She held her head between her hands.

"You okay, Millie? You have a headache?" Jeremy asked, and she nodded her head then walked toward the kitchen.

Jeremy stopped what he was doing and headed after her. Marco felt a tinge of jealousy that stemmed from his need to protect Millie. His feelings grew stronger for her overnight as he checked on her while she slept. He wanted to hold her as she moaned in her sleep and tossed and turned. She even cried a few times but was so exhausted she slept right through it. He gathered more information on Frank while she slept and he even spoke with Wyatt first thing this morning.

Things seemed to be getting worse.

* * * *

Jeremy met her by the small island in the kitchen.

"Where do you keep the aspirin?" he asked her.

"I don't know. I just moved in here a few days ago," she whispered as if it would provide less noise for her headache.

He began to gently open cabinets until he found the one filled with a few different over-the-counter cold remedies and ibuprofen.

"Here, I found some. Let me get you a glass of water."

He walked toward the refrigerator, poured some water into a cup, and brought the meds and drink to her.

"Take two of these, honey, and it will help in no time."

She looked up into his eyes and he could see the sadness and weakness there. Her long thick lashes nearly hid her dark blue eyes.

"Thank you." She took the pills.

Her head must have really been hurting her because she crossed her arms onto the table and laid her head down.

She was an attractive woman. Jeremy thought so the moment he met her the first day she arrived in Pearl and on the Triple C Ranch. As he saw her the days to follow and they shared a few friendly words, he began to think about her more and had realized that he was attracted to her. Apparently, his brothers were, too. That was okay by him. However, he had a feeling that Millie wasn't going to entertain the idea.

"Can I get you anything else?" he whispered next to her.

"I just need a few more minutes for these to kick in. God, I feel like crap."

He took a deep breath then released it. "It's understandable. You probably didn't sleep very well, either," Jeremy replied then caressed her back. He felt her body tense under his touch and then she relaxed.

"She didn't have much sleep last night. She was tossing and turning," Marco added to the conversation.

Before she could respond to Marco's comment, they heard Anthony bang something against the door.

"What the heck is he doing?" Millie asked then slowly raised her head up.

Jeremy was certain that the painkillers hadn't kicked in yet, but she seemed determined to not show defeat.

"We told you, sweets, he's updating your security," Marco told her.

"That really isn't necessary."

"Don't you worry about a thing, Millie. We know what we're doing," Anthony stated firmly from across the room.

* * * *

Millie didn't know what was happening. These men were awfully bossy yet sweet at the same time. She didn't know any of them well enough, yet she felt comfortable to some extent. She needed to get a grip. But she understood how relationships worked around Pearl. When multiple men in one family started paying attention to a woman, protecting her, caring for her, then they were interested in more than just friendship. That was something she sure couldn't entertain right now or perhaps ever. A sexual relationship between her and one man did not mix well. She sure as hell didn't need to involve herself with multiple men. She cringed as the deep thoughts added pain to her already aching head.

God, I wish I could just go somewhere and hide. All alone in a nice guarded room tucked under blankets where nothing could touch me or make me feel, and I wouldn't have to deal with everything.

She watched as Anthony knelt down in front of the open door and began to measure and then lift the drill to it. She clutched her ears, expecting the drill to sound harsh against her bad headache, but instead it hummed. She absorbed the sight of Anthony kneeling in jeans and scuffed-up cowboy boots with the utility belt hanging somewhat loose against his waist. His forearms flexed as he pressed the drill bit into the wood, making a hole. She watched in fascination how quickly he did the job and then he stood up. The man was at minimum six feet tall. The sight of his side profile, dark brown crew-cut hair with the small pencil hugged against the back of his ear, was sexy for some really strange reason. His dark-blue T-shirt with the Lewis company logo stretched across his wide chest. He looked a lot like Marco and she wondered if his eyes were blue like Marco's, too.

"There. Now check this out," Anthony stated as he closed the door and showed off his handy work.

Millie watched Jeremy swagger across the room in his tight, dark jeans and joined Anthony by the door and checked the two new dead bolts that Anthony installed. He pulled on the door and Millie watched him. Jeremy was younger than Anthony and definitely Marco, if she had to guess. He seemed closer to her twenty-three years than the others. That thought made her feel funny. Why, when she thought about one Lewis, did she think about the others and compare? She didn't like the direction her mind was heading in. She needed to nip this in the bud before it got out of control.

"You should go lie down again, Millie. I'll stick around until twelve or so and then Hank or Dalton will be by. Jeremy and Anthony are headed to the Triple C for work." Marco sounded bossy and controlling. She didn't want bossy and controlling. The attraction to a man in control and with authority sent her in the wrong direction. Why was she even thinking that these men would be interested in her, anyway? She wasn't thin, glamorous, and sexy. She was average and some psycho killer was after her.

She stood up a little too quickly and grabbed on to the counter before she fell. Marco went to reach for her, but she swatted his hand away. He scrunched his eyebrows up in an expression of surprise at her reaction. She couldn't falter.

"I don't need you to stick around, Marco, or your brothers to stop by and babysit. I'll be fine alone and I don't need you telling me what to do. Now make good use of the door and show yourselves out. I'm taking a shower and then I'll be headed over to the Triple C to paint."

She glanced over her shoulder. They watched her walk away and she saw their surprised expressions. She ignored the tug in her belly of guilt and regret. She was losing her mind, filled with mixed emotions and feelings she just didn't want to be filled with at a time like this. She had some serious thinking and planning to do.

* * * *

"What the hell was that all about?" Jeremy asked.

"She's being stubborn and she's afraid," Anthony offered as he began to gather his things.

"I don't want to leave her here alone." Jeremy walked over to the sink, washed his mug from the coffee he had.

"She's under a lot of stress right now Jeremy. I looked into this Frank guy last night and I plan on talking with Stacy today, too. I want to know the whole story. Plus I think the five of us need to sit down and talk tonight."

"Talk? About what?" Jeremy asked.

"About our attraction to Millie and how we plan on getting to know her and whether or not Hank and Dalton are on board," Anthony said then nodded his head toward the door. Jeremy walked out first and then Anthony and Marco followed, except Marco sat on the front porch waiting for Millie to get ready to go. She more than likely forgot that the truck was in the shop and she would need a ride to the ranch.

* * * *

Millie walked out of the cottage and was surprised to see that Marco was still there. His blue eyes bore into her as he leaned against a rather large truck with tinted windows that nearly shared the color of his eyes. She turned from him, giving an annoyed expression, but truly she was relieved that he was there. While alone in the shower and her bedroom, she thought about the events of the last week and couldn't shake the feeling of guilt over Clare's murder. It didn't matter what Wyatt and the deputies told her. She was to blame.

She locked the door and turned toward Marco.

"I told you that I was fine. I don't need babysitting."

He looked her over and it made her body hum in an awareness she was finding difficult to fight off. Her conversation with herself about staying away from Lewis men appeared to have been forgotten every time one of them looked at her like that.

"Your aunt's truck is in the shop, remember? I figured you might not feel up to walking in the heat all the way to the Triple C."

She had completely forgotten and she shook her head then looked out across the yard toward the horse stables. The sound of pebbles and dirt crunching under Marco's boots warned her of his quick approach.

She stood at the top of the three steps to the porch and he stood level with the walkway. He was still taller despite her position.

She locked gazes with him, and damn, did he look commanding.

"If you think I'm going to let you get a ride with some other cowboy besides me or one of my brothers, you've got another thing coming, woman. Now let's get a move on it, I've got a couple of hours before work."

He reached his hand out for her to take it, but she was trying to get over the emotions his words brought out in her. In an attempt to hide their effect, she skimmed past him, brushing against his body without his assistance toward the truck.

Before she could reach for the handle of the door, Marco was there. Their fingers brushed against one another's and she pulled back only to bump into his chest.

His hand landed on her waist to support her, and she froze in place.

Near inches from her head and neck she heard his intake of breath as his body gently swayed against hers. She felt the thick, long, ridge of his cock against her backside and unintentionally gasped. The heat hit her cheeks. She felt flush with instant desire and was grateful that her back was toward him. Marco then pulled away before she could enjoy the close proximity.

"You smell real good, Millie."

She swallowed hard, trying to destroy the lustful feelings circulating through her veins as he opened the door and guided her toward the seat with a hand still at her waist. It was high up, so she grabbed the roll bar on the door and was about to hoist herself up, but Marco lifted her as if she weighed nothing at all and placed her in the seat.

She squealed slightly and more out of shock and surprise at his move, but then he went further by leaning across her to push some papers toward the middle compartment. His muscular arm brushed against her breasts, and damn it, did her body renege on the agreement of ignoring her attraction to this man.

His face was inches from hers as he turned toward her.

"Not all men are assholes, sweetness."

What?

"Safety first, honey. Let's get this seat belt on and head to the Triple C."

She sat in utter shock as he guided the strap across her body, buckled her in, and then stepped down from the truck. He closed the door and she ordered herself to breathe and not look into what his comment meant.

Was he trying to justify his actions? Was he trying to tell her that he was interested in her? Maybe he just wanted her to know that not all men were assholes so she didn't feel like crap for ever getting involved with Frank?

She hadn't a clue and she knew she was in trouble. She couldn't even have a regular conversation with a man without analyzing his intentions, or, at minimum, confusing herself about them.

She stared straight ahead as Marco started the truck and chuckled as he headed out of the driveway.

* * * *

Millie was lost in thought as she painted the walls of the rec center. She had spent time talking with Anna and Stacy when she first arrived at the ranch. Stacy had gone outside to talk with Marco while Lena and Anna discussed the events from last night and how Millie was handling things. She knew that Anna, Stacy, and Lena understood what she felt like. But no matter what they told her, she felt guilty about Clare.

As she walked toward the other room and began painting, she was soon lost in her own thoughts. Millie figured that she had a few decisions to make. After going over every scenario in her head, she realized that she had to give Detective Flynn time to locate Frank and handle things. She also decided that Anna and Stacy were right about her being protected in Pearl. There were plenty of men around the area and, due to the new facility, security had to be good. She had learned that Hank and Dalton had trained all of the deputies in town. Apparently, there were a lot of ex-military and active military living on the outskirts of town as well as inside Pearl. Her concern over baby Hope as well as Stacy and Anna would be resolved by Millie staying toward the edge of town at her aunt's ranch. She might be alone most of the time, but that's where her other decision had been made.

She was going to have to take care of herself and her own safety, beginning with getting Hank to train her as if she were law enforcement or military. If Frank came looking for her in Pearl, she wanted to be physically ready to fight for her life since mentally she was scared of him. She needed to learn how to turn off that fear and rely on her abilities and training. If she were going to die by Frank's hands, then she would die fighting.

"It looks great in here."

Millie jumped at the sound of the male voice. When she turned to look and see who was there, she was surprised to see Hank.

"Thanks," she whispered then mentally tried to prepare herself to ask him for assistance with the training.

"How are you doing?" he asked as she stepped down from the ladder, placed the brush on the top, and looked around the room.

"Okay."

"Do you need some help?" he asked, and she realized that he was there because Marco probably asked him to come and babysit her. Damn, why was Marco so controlling and bossy?

"Listen, I don't need a damn babysitter," she stated with a bit more attitude than she intended.

Just then, Dalton walked in. He glared at her as if he had heard her tone and for some odd reason she felt intimidated. He always looked so damn angry. Did the man know how to smile? And that scar of his made him look hard and intense. He wore it well, though, like a pirate with a black patch over his eye.

"Hey, we're not here to babysit you, as you called it. We stopped in to see Lena, Anna, Stacy, and you to discuss the schedule for offering self-defense classes here at the rec center," Hank replied.

She took a deep breath and felt guilty for accusing him of something he hadn't done. She was on edge, and now would be as good a time as any to ask for the help.

"I'm sorry." She looked down toward the ground then back up into Hank's eyes. Now Dalton stood next to his brother, and Dalton just stared at her.

"I'm a bit on edge. I know everyone is concerned and I have a lot going on in my head. I'm sorry."

"That's understandable." Hank gave her a small smile. She noticed how bright his blue eyes were and also the slight dimple in his left cheek.

"I'm actually glad that you're here, Hank," she began after staring at him for an awkward few moments.

And Dalton raised his eyebrows at her as if he were offended that he wasn't included in that "glad you're here" sentence. Deep inside, she was happy to see them both. What woman wouldn't like a visit from two big, strong, sexy cowboys? But she had a plan here that needed to be set in motion.

"I was hoping to talk with you about me taking a different class at your dojo."

"Well, that's a definite, or you'd be bored in the class you're in now," Hank stated with a small smile. "Well, actually, I had an idea and was hoping that you could maybe train me like you train the law enforcement and military around town."

"What? Why?" Dalton asked, interrupting her conversation with Hank. His voice was deep and firm and she actually shuddered from it.

She felt her cheeks warm and she placed her hand on the ladder for a bit of support.

"What exactly is going on in that head of yours, Millie?" Hank asked.

"I'm interested in that type of training."

"No, you're thinking that those detectives aren't going to locate this guy Frank in New York and that he's going to come here to Pearl," Dalton stated and Hank looked at his brother and then back at Millie.

"Will you help me or not?" she asked.

"You're a beautiful young woman, why would you want to learn such things?" Dalton asked.

"Listen, I don't need to explain myself to you." She attempted to walk away, but Dalton blocked her path and grabbed her wrist. She froze in place as she looked up into his mean, green eyes.

"That's where you're wrong. You need a damn good reason to get that type of training and 'for self-defense' isn't good enough."

She clenched her fists despite his hold on her one wrist.

She glared up at him. "How about for survival? Would that be good enough reason, Dalton? Maybe because I've been abused and nearly killed by the man before and I'm scared of him and I'm tired of being a victim!" She shook with emotion. The man surely got under her skin.

He released her wrist and crossed his arms in front of his chest.

"I don't think you know what this type of training entails, Millie. This isn't like in the movies, where you learn things in one try. We don't take it easy on our students male or female. We teach survival and the principle of 'kill or be killed' as the final and last resort."

"You're not military and you're not law enforcement," Hank added.

"I just want to be better trained and somewhat prepared if they don't catch Frank in New York. I know you offer the training, but if you're not willing to help me, then I suppose I'll be forced to look elsewhere. I've already looked up a few places in Turbank and farther south."

They were both silent a moment and then Hank spoke. "Come to the dojo tomorrow at seven."

"Okay," she whispered as Hank and Dalton exited the building.

Millie released a long sigh and shook with fear she had been desperately trying to hide. That hadn't gone as badly as she feared it might have. They could have downright refused her.

They were seriously intense men and she hoped that she could follow through with her decision. She was truly tired of living in fear and being scared of Frank. Perhaps Dalton and Hank could help her gain some confidence back so she wouldn't be such a scaredy-cat anymore.

Chapter 11

"Why are you doing this, Frank? Please talk to me. We can discuss the feelings that you're having," Sheila pleaded as Frank pulled the restraints tighter. She had opened up a savings account for him after he cried about not being able to get a job as an ex-con. His acting and sob story worked and he was fifty thousand richer. He had withdrawn the money and decided to keep her around for a little longer. He had gotten a little information from Clare about Millie's ex-lover, Stewart. The little fuck used Millie for her body and now he would suffer. Millie never should have been with another man. She belonged to him and no one else. Hadn't he made himself clear the last time they were together? He walked over to the piece of shit and tugged on the ropes.

"I know you're awake. You can't be that much of a wuss," he yelled at Stewart, who was tied to chair, bloody and nearly unconscious.

"Please, I don't know what you want," Stewart moaned.

Frank looked over at Sheila, who was as white as a ghost and perspiring with fear. The good doctor would see firsthand what he was capable of. No therapy of any kind could truly help a man like him. He wasn't sick. He was in love and would do anything for that love. No one was going to stand in his way.

"Where is she?" Frank asked Stewart.

"I don't know," Stewart cried like a blubbering sissy.

Frank struck him with a backhand across the cheek. Stewart moaned.

"Don't, Frank. Leave him alone," Sheila cried out.

He pointed at her from a few feet away.

"Shut up, bitch! You're next."

He grabbed Stewart by his shirt and shook him.

"Think, Stewart! Think, damn it. Where the hell is Millie? I want my woman back, asshole."

"I don't know. I can't think."

Frank punched Stewart in the stomach.

"You worthless piece of shit. You hurt her. You destroyed her with your evil words. I'm going to kill you, Stewart."

Sheila screamed and Stewart cried out.

"She has friends. Her friends from Texas. She talks to them all the time. Maybe she's there."

Frank stopped and stared at Stewart.

Millie used to live somewhere in Texas. Did Stacy and Anna move out there? Is that where my baby is? Stacy probably talked Millie into leaving. That bitch will die for interfering again. I should have killed Stacy then the bitch wouldn't be such a problem right now.

"Please don't kill me. Please," Stewart begged, and Frank smiled as he walked away from Stewart and toward the duffle bag.

He watched Sheila, her eyes red with fear and her body shaking.

"You think you could make me forget about my woman, Sheila? You think you know me and know what it's like to feel true pain?"

Sheila shook her head.

"Please, Frank. Don't kill him. Let us go and get the help you need."

Frank smiled.

"I don't need any help. I know exactly who I am and what I want. It's people like you and Stewart here that hide behind your money and education, thinking that you own this world and can manipulate anyone you choose to. He took my woman. He hurt her and now he's going to die."

"I can help you, Frank. Listen to me. You don't want to do this. You don't really want to take another life. Let's talk this through. I care about you. I stood behind you when no one else believed that you were cured. Come on, Frank. Put down the knife." Sheila spoke in that condescending, therapeutic tone that irked him.

"I think you've read too many text books, doc. You can't cure men like me. I like to kill and to cause pain when I don't get what I want and what I deserve. I deserve Millie. I want Millie. If I have to kill to get her, then so be it. Besides, it makes me feel good inside."

"No, I don't believe you. You love me. You told me so and promised that we would start a new life together," Sheila replied.

"Ha. I lied. I would do anything to get what I want. I have determination, desire, and hunger. People like you and this sniveling idiot frown upon people like me. I'm the underdog. I don't need to be rich or have some mansion or fancy car. No, all I need is the love of my woman. I'm going to find Millie. First, I'm going to kill this piece of crap nice and slowly while you watch and then you and I are going to have some fun. You're going to learn firsthand what it's like to be a victim, doc. All those people you helped get out of jail only for them to kill again was because of you. I'm going to help you see reality before you die."

* * * *

Wyatt had given Millie a ride into town on his way into work so she could start her training with Dalton and Hank. Her truck would be ready by nine and she would wait around for it after the workout.

Wyatt informed her that Frank's therapist was still missing and so was her car.

Detective Flynn discovered evidence indicating that Frank's therapist was in fact aiding him on a personal level. She had notes indicating that she was falling in love with Frank and he was falling in love with her. She apparently set up a savings account with fifty thousand dollars in it for him, and he drained the account. Millie felt sick to her stomach. But the fact that a therapist was so unethical and that she chose to fall for Frank was more bad luck for Millie. It seemed that odds were against Millie to ever be free from Frank's threats and abuse. The news made her feel worse, but Wyatt reminded her of how cunning and manipulative Frank had become. Wyatt said that Flynn believed Frank manipulated his therapist and lied to her to get out of prison so he could find Millie. Some notes from his doctor explained counseling sessions where Frank admitted feeling incomplete for not killing Millie or possessing her fully for eternity. Millie couldn't handle some of the other information Flynn told Wyatt. The bottom line was that Frank could be anywhere at this time.

Millie knocked on the door to the dojo because it was locked. At first she wondered if Hank and Dalton had changed their minds, but then she saw Hank.

He wasn't wearing his gi but instead baggy martial arts pants and a tight T-shirt that showed off his perfect physique. "Good morning." He let her in.

"Morning," she replied then he closed the door and relocked it.

"No one else is coming to this session?" she asked, feeling a bit nervous.

"Just you. We don't exactly want to advertise what we're doing here. I don't think that this is the answer for you. You deserve to be taken care of and protected."

She was shocked by his words and couldn't respond as he continued to walk toward the back gym. She wanted to respond but now she had second thoughts. Do this, don't do this, she was totally confused. She gave herself a mental kick. Wasn't this the point of getting the training? Didn't she want a fighting chance if Frank found her? She suddenly felt sick to her stomach and weak again.

She focused on following Hank. The rest of the place was dark and a bit of fear filled her gut. She was going to be alone with a man, a very resourceful man, whom she hardly knew at all.

She was turning into a worrywart. Frank made her weak and made her feel incapable of taking care of herself. She grew stronger after he was behind bars, and the moment she found out that he was free, she felt the need to run for safety within the imaginary shell she created. She felt herself closing into that imaginary world, the one which nearly killed her because she hadn't followed her gut or asked for help. She swallowed hard as she stared at the dark shirt stretched across Hank's wide, muscular back. He was way bigger than Frank.

She reminded herself that people knew where she was. Wyatt knew and he had hinted to the fact that she was safe around the Lewis brothers. Something told her that she didn't know what she was getting into.

Millie entered the room and saw Dalton stretching. He was wearing black karate pants and a tight black T-shirt. She could see tattoos on his upper arms and the same fierce expression he always seemed to have around her. She wasn't expecting him to be there, too. She should have known since she asked both of them for help. Dalton had seemed adamant about her request. Did he have other motives? *Shit.*

The man had major sex appeal, just like the rest of his brothers. Why was she suddenly feeling hot and aroused?

"Put your bag in the corner. We'll do some stretches first," Hank stated firmly and she immediately did as she was told. She dropped her bag in the corner.

"You're going to be hot in that sweatshirt," Hank practically barked at her. He seemed tense.

"I'll take it off when I'm hot," she replied, not wanting to admit that she felt a little self-conscious around such physically fit ex-military men.

Dalton rolled his eyes at her and she felt her cheeks blush. Was he able to read minds?

She sat down and began her stretches until Dalton stood up.

"Attention," he commanded, and she immediately stood at attention with her hands by her sides.

"We're going to start with some general moves to see how you maneuver in hand-to-hand combat. Then we'll take it to the mats," Dalton informed her.

She almost wasn't prepared for the simultaneous moves from both Hank and Dalton. They came at her, first one then the other, and she maneuvered her way between them. One would send a fist toward her as the other tried to take out her legs. This went on for several long minutes until Hank stepped aside and Dalton began a one-on-one assault.

"I'm your attacker. I have a knife in my left hand. What's your first move?" he asked her, and she tried to kick at his wrist and he immediately turned her around and pretended to cut her throat.

"You're dead! Try it again," he yelled and she felt her heart rate increase.

Before she could fully recover from his move and his hard body that was wedged against her, he attempted a pretend stab to her midsection. She did a counter karate chop down on his forearm and he swept her legs out from underneath her, causing her to fall on her ass.

"Think, Millie! It's do or die!" Dalton yelled and she started getting angry at him. He was being so hard on her and all she wanted to do was learn to defend herself and fight off Frank if he found her.

She stood up and took a deep breath, feeling both angry and discouraged. Could she do this? That imaginary shell was beginning to enter her mind. She was safe there. She didn't feel pain there. She wasn't inferior there.

They circled one another around the mat and Dalton tried to strike again, but this time she sidestepped and hit him. He was surprised, but he came back again and again, and each time he was rougher and harder, but she evaded his strikes until he tackled her to the mat.

He was huge and immediately he had her pinned to the mat with his body.

She had cried out. The instant fear brought images to her mind she hadn't thought about in quite some time. Her heart pounded against her chest as she absorbed everything with full force.

He felt so heavy and hard as steel against her more feminine frame. Her breasts were pressed against his chest. She could smell his cologne or deodorant, but she was filled with fear, caught up in the moment and scenario. It reminded her of being attacked and she felt herself losing focus and giving in. The walls were beginning to close up. That shell began to appear thicker and surrounded her in her mind. It was her imaginary escape every time Frank hit her or hurt her. It was her only source of survival and it had nearly killed her that one fateful night.

"Fight him, Millie. Try to get free," Hank commanded, snapping her out of her thoughts and back to the present reality. He was kneeling to the side of her. He brought her back to the present and let her know that this was training. She tried shoving and moving her legs free, but in all honesty, she was barely trying. She was giving up. She wanted to quit and just get the beating over with. She felt the urge to give up and cry in defeat, but she didn't want to be weak anymore. She was fighting against herself now, not just against Dalton.

As if Hank saw the emotional struggle in her eyes and her body language, he gave her instructions. "Get your legs free, Millie, and wrap them around his waist against his ribs, high so you can impede his breathing. That's it, baby, just like that." She wiggled her hips while gasping for every breath. Dalton was so big and heavy, all muscle and unbeatable.

"Do it, Millie, don't give up!" Hank yelled, and she maneuvered her legs until she somehow got free and wrapped them around Dalton's waist.

"Squeeze, Millie!" he yelled and she squeezed, but it didn't matter. The fear of being restrained by Dalton was overwhelming and she gave up.

"Damn it! I told you this wasn't for you!" Dalton yelled as he banged his fist down on the mat before he stood up, making her jump and close her eyes at his intensity and anger.

She caught her breath and was struck by his tone and belief that she couldn't do this.

"I've never done anything like this before!" she yelled at him. Her voice cracked and he stared at her with annoyance. He was disappointed in her and she felt guilty, deep inside her heart. God, she should just tell them what had happened and about her own inner struggles right now. She stared at Dalton. He would find her weak and she didn't want that. She wanted him to respect her and to support her. *I'm making myself crazy.*

"I don't know what to do or how to fight against myself. I've never done anything like this before," she repeated in desperation.

"Because you shouldn't have to!" Dalton yelled back then paced a few steps, running his hand through his crew-cut hair.

Hank looked at her and touched her knee.

"You have to be able to think quickly, Millie. You can't fight against the thoughts in your mind or the weaknesses from other things in the past. You have to be in the now, Millie. You almost have to have a sense as to what move your attacker will make. When you see Dalton come down low at you, you need to prepare to get out of the way or get into the immediate position to counteract. As he goes to grab you, I want you to immediately wrap your arms around his neck and latch your legs around his waist, closer to his ribs, and squeeze against him. Make him use his strength and energy trying to get you off."

"That's going to hurt when I hit the floor. He's huge," Millie replied.

"If you're attacked, it could be by anyone of any size."

She nodded in understanding.

"She's not focused," Dalton chimed in.

She glared at him as she stood up and unzipped her sweatshirt.

"I am focused," she replied with attitude then pulled off her sweatshirt and tossed it to the corner. She wore a tight-fitting black tank top tucked into her loose, thin yoga pants. Both men seemed to look her over before she got into a ready stance.

* * * *

Dalton was trying his hardest to act professional and understand what the hell Millie was thinking, but it was difficult. She smelled incredible and was very tough, but he didn't want her to feel like she needed to fight. He was compelled to protect her, but she seemed distant and independent to the point of frustrating him and his brothers. They had all met last night and talked about her. His brothers were interested, but they knew they needed to tread carefully. His patience and control were being tested especially when rolling around on the mats with her breasts pressed against his body. His dick was so fucking hard he was having trouble concentrating, and now she took off her sweatshirt. Sweet mother of God, she was gorgeous, and for crying out loud she seemed oblivious to it. Most women would have come in here wearing far less and strutting their bodies for attention from him and his brothers, but not Millie. She hid behind loose-fitting clothing and sweatshirts.

"Okay, start again." Hank interrupted Dalton's thoughts.

He maneuvered around the room, striking when he thought he could catch Millie off guard, but she surprised him by countering his strikes with hits. She was very angry and her determination to succeed was commendable, but she was far from ready.

He pretended to have the knife again and he struck. She turned and jabbed him in the side. He hid his response and stabbed at her again. This time she nearly tripped but recovered and dodged his move again. He went for the kill and got down low to tackle her.

This time Millie was ready as she wrapped her arms around his neck and her legs around his hips as he took her to the mat. He used his knee to break the fall slightly because she was so much smaller than him.

"Tighten those legs, Millie, and hug him to you so he has to exert the energy to get you off of him," Hank told her, and she did. She was very strong and nearly choking him as he worked her body with his hands. He could feel her heart racing and he knew his was, too, not from overexertion, but from lust.

She felt good in his arms, all feminine and curvy. He was a big man and would love the feel of a solid, voluptuous woman like Millie in his arms whenever he wanted.

She seemed to be lessening her hold on him and slowly pulled her head back from his shoulder.

They locked gazes as they both breathed heavily, his body covering hers as she lay flat on the mat.

He had no control over his next move and lowered his head, touching his lips to her soft full ones.

* * * *

Millie didn't know what had come over her or them, for that matter. One minute she was annoyed and angry at Dalton's words and actions and the next she was absorbed with his scent and his muscles surrounding her. He obviously felt the same attraction and now he was kissing her. He was thorough with his tongue, exploring her mouth as his hands explored her body. She relaxed her legs and he pressed his groin firmly against her mound. Millie moaned as she realized just how big Dalton was and how hard and long his cock felt against her.

She ran her fingers through his hair, kissing him back with as much vigor as he was kissing her. It was intense and then she realized how irrational their behavior was and she tensed up.

Slowly, he released her lips and she just stared at him.

"I…" she began and Dalton remained above her with his hands on either side of her as he raised his chest up, causing her legs to fall awkwardly open and away from his hips. His thick body remained wedged between them.

She tried to scoot back so she could sit up, but he grabbed her thighs, keeping them open and against his rock-solid ones.

He seemed to be breathing just as heavy as she was.

"You're a beautiful woman who should be pampered and protected. You shouldn't have to be trained to fight for your life, Millie. It's wrong." She felt his indignation against her choice to seek such training. She was past her shock of kissing him and now her determination to fight her fear led her to her response.

"In a perfect world I wouldn't have to do this, but you don't know him, Dalton. He beat me and tried to kill me. I'm ashamed of what I allowed him to do for so long. I should have died then." Tears filled her eyes. For some strange reason, she felt emotional about telling him and Hank.

Oh God, Hank.

She turned toward the side and Hank stared at her. He looked…hungry.

Dalton placed his hand against her cheek. She closed her eyes and absorbed the masculine show of affection.

"Come on. Enough for today," Dalton said then scooted back, took her hand, and pulled her up. The significant difference between her height and theirs struck her momentarily until Hank took her hand and pulled her to him. Before she knew what he was going to do, she felt his hand against her neck and head and his arm around her waist.

"We can protect you, Millie. My brothers and I want to take care of you." Hank lowered his mouth to hers and kissed her.

She had just kissed Dalton and now his brother Hank was kissing her, and instead of feeling cheap or guilty, she felt aroused. Did she want this? Was she ready to jump into something so crazy when her track record showed nothing but grief and failure with her choice of men?

She began to pull away from Hank's kiss and he pulled her tightly against him, kissing her more fully until he was ready to release her. By the time their lips mutually drifted apart, her eyes were closed and she was lost in the moment.

"You taste incredible, baby. Better than I imagined." Hank caressed her cheek with his thumb.

The sound of someone knocking on the front door to the dojo interrupted them and Millie pulled away.

* * * *

Hank walked out of the room to go answer the door and Millie gathered up her belongings. A quick glance at the clock and she saw it was nearly nine o'clock. Had they really been rolling around on the mat for two hours? She swallowed hard then lifted the water bottle to her lips, hoping it would ease some of the heat she felt throughout her entire body.

"You feel okay? I didn't hurt you, did I?" Dalton asked, and she was startled by his deep voice. He stood inches behind her. She could sense his bulk and it just made her heat up all over again.

"I'm good, Dalton."

He touched her arm and turned her toward him. She looked up, her head tilting back, and locked gazes with his firm expression. He gave her a look that challenged her initial response to his question. He was quite intimidating and she was achy from their workout, especially from him initially landing on top of her. Truth was, she didn't care at all. The way he had claimed her mouth and controlled her body in such a way wiped all pain from her thoughts. If she could wrap him or his brothers around her like a blanket, she was certain she would feel safer and more content than ever in her lifetime. That was frightening.

"You wouldn't lie to me, would you?" he asked, and she couldn't help but feel guilty and also a bit worried. He looked so darn dangerous with his cocky expression, perfect body, and that scar from neck to shoulder. She had to remind herself that he had shown compassion and gentleness, too.

"I'm a big girl, Dalton. The extra padding helps, so don't worry." She tried to joke around by making fun of herself, but Dalton's expression changed.

He stepped closer and placed the palm of his hand against her cheek and his other against her waist.

"You really don't know how perfect you are, do you?"

"What?" she asked in a whisper, not expecting that particular reply from him. Stewart had always initiated the insults about her chunky body and overlarge breasts. She was used to making fun of herself first or accepting Stewart's insults. Frank complimented her body but also abused it. Dalton confused her and she attempted to step away as she lowered her head, but Dalton stepped with her.

Somehow she was cornered against the wall. One of his hands was pressed against the padding above her shoulder and the other held her waist.

"Look at me, Millie. You are beautiful and you are perfect. Any man that said otherwise was a fucking idiot."

She gulped as the tears reached her eyes then jerked slightly when the hand that was pressed against her waist moved slowly up to her ribs.

"Your legs are perfect, your hips curved and muscular the way they should be. I love the way your waist dips in and your ass slightly sticks out, round and solid. You are perfect, baby." He softly caressed her, moving his hand farther up her body as he inched closer. His breath was warm against her neck as she tilted back against the wall. His lips gently touched her skin, causing tingling goose bumps to scatter about and run amok throughout her body.

Oh God!

She felt her pussy moisten from his words then tighten up with need and hunger.

When his hand began to glide up the side of her right breast, she gasped.

He glided a thumb over her nipple, back and forth, and she wished she weren't wearing any clothing. If they were skin to skin, she would go up in flames.

"You have big, full, beautiful breasts, too. I have big hands, Millie, and they're still not enough to cover your breasts completely. That's fucking hot. Do you feel how hard your little nipples are, Millie? See what my touch does to you? Touch me, Millie. Reach your hand down and feel how hard you make me. This is just from looking at you, caressing your sexy body."

Millie couldn't move and she didn't have to.

"Ah, hell." He leaned forward and covered her mouth with his own and began a sensual exploration of her mouth.

She kissed him back, wanting more of him and giving in to her attraction. His thick thigh pushed between her legs and she moaned against him. Every sensation grew stronger with every touch and roll of his tongue. The feel of stone beneath her fingertips and the dips and ridges of muscle were making her so damn needy for more of him. His large hands pressed against her breasts, pulling and tweaking her nipples then massaging her breasts until he continued a path up her shoulder to her neck.

His long, rough fingers caressed her throat and then both hands held her face.

His kisses slowed down and she was grateful as the sound of approaching voices could be heard.

He slowly released her lips. They both were breathing hard.

"You make me want to do things, wild, wicked things to your amazing body."

She was startled and utterly turned on by his words, never mind his actions. She was holding on to him still and the voices came closer.

He must have read her fearful expression and he stepped back, adjusting his pants and walking back a few steps.

Millie lowered to the floor and picked up the water bottle and bag she had dropped.

"Good morning, Dalton! Are we too early?" Stella asked with Lisa, Paula, and Melody following close behind. The four women were dressed kind of odd for a martial arts class. They had short shorts and half tank tops on with their breasts pouring from the tops. If Stella, Paula, or even Melody bent over, their boobs would vacate their tops. The one woman Lisa's breasts were so small, she had the opposite problem.

Dalton glanced at the clock.

"You're fifteen minutes early. No one else has arrived yet."

"Well, we can maybe warm up a little. I was having some trouble with the moves you taught us on Monday," Stella whined as she ran her hand up and down Dalton's arm. Millie wanted to grab that hand and smack Stella with it, but she had no right to act jealous and possessive. Then Dalton did something unexpected.

He pressed Stella's hand away from him and scowled at her. She turned red but looked determined.

Then Millie sensed movement toward the doorway and saw Lena and Sage had arrived. They waved at her and Millie looked to pass Stella and the others to leave, but Stella made no effort to get out of Millie's way. Stella had her arms crossed in front of her chest.

"You running some sort of toning class or something for her?"

Millie was not surprised by the thin bitch's comment, and she saw that Lena and Sage were about to say something when Dalton spoke.

He blatantly looked Millie over from head to toe extremely slowly. So much so that Millie felt body parts tremble and her nipples harden to pebbles.

"Naw, Millie is fucking perfect."

She heard gasps but she was too absorbed in staring at Dalton to notice. He reached out his hand and she immediately accepted it as he practically walked over Stella and her friends and escorted her to the front.

"You better go sniffing somewhere else, girls, looks like the Lewis brothers are staking a claim," she heard Lena say and Dalton hugged her closer to his side, laying a hand over her waist, and nearly her ass, possessively.

Chapter 12

"Let me get this straight. You actually had her meet you and Dalton at the dojo so you could teach her how to fight to the death? Are you out of your fucking minds? She's a beautiful young woman, living in fear right now because of some asshole," Anthony said, raising his voice. They were all sitting around the back porch talking about Millie.

"That's exactly why we met her, Ant. She's used to handling things on her own, but she's scared out of mind over this jerk. She said she should have died the last time the asshole got ahold of her. She seems to be at war with herself right now and the decisions she made over the years," Hank replied.

"She wasn't just fighting me on that mat. She was fighting herself," Dalton whispered before he took a slug of beer from the bottle he held.

Hank nodded his head then continued.

"She would have gone and tried to find someone else to help her. It was our opportunity to gain her trust and get to know her. Dalton and I talked about it. We figured we could get her to see that she wasn't alone in this."

"Well, did you change her mind about it? You could have hurt her, Dalton. You're huge compared to her and used to pushing the limit in your classes," Marco added as he eyed his brother. Anthony didn't want this to turn into a pissing contest over Millie and who cared for her more.

"I didn't hurt her. I wouldn't hurt her ever," Dalton shot back at Marco.

"He didn't hurt her. It worked out in the end. He pushed her, telling her she wasn't ready. She pushed back and handled his counterattacks and eventually he wound up on top of her on the mat, between her legs. It was fucking incredible to watch and then he kissed her. They completely forgot that I was there." Hank chuckled before taking a slug of beer from the bottle he held.

"So after you kissed her, did you tell her that she doesn't need that type of training? That we're all here to protect her?" Jeremy asked.

"I was about to, but then Stella and the crew showed up and interrupted," Dalton stated, looking annoyed to Anthony.

"What happened?" Anthony asked and Dalton explained.

"She's hard on herself and thinks she's not attractive," Dalton added.

"What?" They each responded with similar comments of surprise.

"She is such a stunning woman with her dark blue eyes and long, wavy brown hair," Jeremy stated.

"She has a hell of a body, too." Dalton sat back and stared out across the yard.

"Damn straight, she does. She's perfect," Jeremy stated.

"Well, we'll just have to show her how beautiful and perfect we think she is. It's good that you kissed her, Dalton. She needs to start accepting her attraction to each of us. Jeremy and I need to make our position known with her, too. We'll start tomorrow at the Triple C," Anthony told them.

"I kissed her, too. Right after Dalton did. She looked so beautiful, her lips all swollen and wet from Dalton's kisses. She came to me willingly and didn't resist my touch or my kisses. It was a positive sign," Hank told them.

"Sure is. I can't wait to kiss her and hold her, too," Jeremy added and they were quiet a moment before Marco, the oldest, spoke up.

"I think you all need to know what I found out from Stacy, Anna, and of course, the detective from New York."

"Sure, Marco, anything you can tell us will help us to protect her and understand where her thinking may be at," Anthony replied.

* * * *

Marco began to explain Millie's relationship with Frank, Stacy's saving her from being killed, and Millie's recovery time in the hospital. His brothers were all shocked and equally upset with the details. He had been, too, as he spoke with the women and then the detectives.

"This guy, Frank, is apparently obsessed with Millie. The detectives had notes from the therapist in their possession that state Frank admitted that he regretted failing to kill Millie. He supposedly felt incomplete."

"Lousy, sick bastard," Jeremy stated.

"They think this therapist is aiding Frank right now?" Anthony asked.

"It appears that she was helping him all along and fell in love. He led her to believe that he loved her, too. So she used her professional pull to get him out of jail on good behavior. She even set up a bank account for him with fifty grand in it. Of course, he emptied the entire account within twenty-four hours of her opening it. Then she disappears."

"Do the detectives think that he killed the therapist?" Anthony asked.

"They don't know. He's capable, that's for sure, and he did kill Clare from Millie's job. She was really upset about that. She blames herself," Marco told them.

"She's not at fault. This guy is out of control and it scares me to think how obsessed he is. What if he does get here to Pearl? We need to keep Millie close by," Hank stated.

"She'll fight us tooth and nail," Dalton added.

"Well, we want to get to know her and convince her to get involved with all five of us and that's going to take some time," Jeremy told them.

"It sure is. The only way to get to know her is by spending time with her," Marco stated.

"As far as I'm concerned, she's already my woman. She'll come around and accept it," Dalton stated firmly and Marco nodded his head in agreement.

Chapter 13

"Okay, spill the beans. What the hell happened between you, Hank, and Dalton at the Dojo this morning?" Stacy asked as Millie, Lena, and Anna painted the rec center together.

"Nothing happened," Millie replied, but she smiled.

"Bullshit. They kissed you and you liked it, didn't you?" Anna asked.

"Were you rolling around on the mat with them? How was it? Are they good kissers?" Stacy asked.

"Oh my God! Cut it out, will you?" Millie replied, sounding shocked. But she couldn't help but giggle. It was just like old times. It was just like the dream she had about when they were young. She became quiet as she thought about the past and her friendship with Anna and Stacy.

"Oh, don't even think that you're getting off with giving us the silent treatment," Anna added, and Lena laughed.

"You three are so funny. You act like sisters," Lena stated.

"We might as well be sisters. We always did everything together," Stacy added.

"We never have any secrets between one another," Anna stated.

"And these two sure can nag like nosey sisters trying to get info from their sibling," Millie said, and Lena laughed, but Anna and Stacy gasped. Then Stacy picked up the bag of popcorn they had been munching on, reached in, took out a handful, and threw it at Millie.

"Hey!" Millie raised her voice then giggled before she reached into the bag of pretzels she had and started tossing them at Stacy and Anna and then Lena.

"Why are you hitting me? I wasn't the one trying to force info from you. I'm just an innocent bystander." Lena laughed and covered her head so flying snacks wouldn't hit her.

"Oh, don't you get all 'I'm innocent' with me. You were at the dojo. You told these two crazy women about what you think you saw."

"I know what I saw and it was you looking incredibly beautiful and happy," Lena stated, and Millie, Stacy, and Anna stopped what they were doing.

Millie lowered her eyes and then looked back up to Lena, who was now standing in front of her.

"It's crazy, isn't it? To come to this spectacular town and run from your troubles, the fear, the worry, and start over? To think that you're alone in that fear, to find the fight within you and then get unexpectedly hit out of thin air by love, attraction, lust, if you want to call it that? To think that you could never have a relationship, never mind one with multiple men, and suddenly you're considering it?" Lena asked in a whisper but loud enough for the others to hear. Then she placed her hand on Millie's shoulder.

"It's going to be okay. The way the Lewis brothers look at you, absorbing your every emotion, caring about what you say, and your response to them is amazing to watch. It makes me feel so good and alive inside to think that my men look at me in that same way. Forget about your past, the men who hurt you, and embrace what is right in front of you. You're special, Millie, and stronger than you give yourself credit for. I watched you in the dojo. I saw the passion and excitement in your eyes as you sparred with Hank. I also felt the intensity in the air when I walked into the dojo with Sage to find you and Dalton alone. I knew something was up and he made his declaration clear to those bimbos. I believe his words were 'Millie is fucking perfect.'"

Millie was touched by Lena's words and she didn't know what else to do but pull her into a bear hug. Then she felt Anna and Stacy join in the hugging and they all giggled.

"Hey, what's going on in here? I want to be part of a group hug," they heard Sage state and then a moment later Sage was trying to wrap her arms around them, too.

Millie felt Lena's words to her heart. Everything was going to be okay. This was her new start and she needed to move on from her past. It wasn't like Frank would be out of her mind. She would always remain on guard as long as he was out there as a free man. But she had a life, and he wouldn't take that from her without a fight.

* * * *

Millie walked out toward the back of the building to find a broom so she could sweep up the mess she and the ladies had made inside. She was smiling and looking down to the ground thinking about Lena's words. Did all five of the Lewis brothers find Millie attractive? Were they all interested? The thought made her belly quiver and a giddy feeling fill her. As she rounded the corner rather quickly, she walked right into a brick wall.

"Oh God!" she squealed then grabbed on to the man she nearly plowed over.

Anthony chuckled as he turned around and held Millie.

Millie looked up and up until she locked gazes with Anthony and his sparkling brown eyes.

His chiseled features and hard lines by his eyes, combined with the tan complexion, made him appear mature and in charge. She knew he was the manager of the company. Anna had informed her.

"I'm so sorry. I was looking down instead of up." She took a step back. His eyes never left hers.

"Darlin', you can bump into me any time you like," he teased then winked, and damn it, did her belly just do a series of somersaults.

She lowered her eyes and then looked around for the broom.

"Can I help you find something?" He slowly took a step toward her. He looked her over with hungry eyes, then damn it his tongue peeked out to lick his lower lip and she almost moaned. There was a magnetic feeling surrounding her body, and as she hit the wall of the building behind her, Anthony made his move.

In a flash, she felt Anthony's hand on her waist and the other over her shoulder, palm against the wall. She smelled his cologne, felt his masculine presence, and she was everything but scared. Utterly turned on was more like it. She was in tune with his body just like she had been with Dalton's and Hank's. His tool belt slightly pressed against her waist and his eyes held hers while his thumb rubbed gently back and forth across her hip bone.

"Don't be scared of me," he whispered, and it sounded more like a plea than a demand. Was he worried that he might scare her?

"I'm not afraid of you," she replied with more oomph than she intended, and Anthony raised one eyebrow then smirked.

"I'm going to kiss you, sweet Millie. Your lips have been calling to me for days," he whispered then swallowed hard. He appeared as nervous as she felt.

"Are you sure that's a good idea? I kissed Dalton and Hank, too. They might get upset."

She didn't know why she rambled on or even said the words. She figured somewhere deep inside she needed Anthony to condone this fact and state that it was fine.

"Honey, that fucking turns me on like you wouldn't believe."

She felt the hand that was against the wall move to her neck as he stepped closer, nearly pinning her against the wall. Not that she wanted to move. She watched his lips with anticipation of how they would feel against her lips.

"My brothers and I have a good relationship. We like to share." He moved closer and then his lips touched hers, devouring any words of response.

He kissed her tenderly and so slowly, as if he was savoring her like she was a delicacy. She found herself leaning into him and then he pressed her back against the wall and suddenly that kiss deepened. He had waited for her response, and because she showed her need for him to take her lips more deeply, he complied.

God, these Lewis men could kiss well. She was lost in his possession of her mouth. The feel of his strong fingers, holding her head in place as his tongue explored her mouth, took her breath away and filled her heart with such desire she moaned into his mouth.

A moment later, his other arm wrapped around her waist and hoisted her up against his body. God, she was on fire with such need. She rubbed her pelvis against him and he moaned into her mouth.

She felt Anthony's body tense a moment and then he was turning her away from the wall but remained making love to her mouth. Suddenly, she felt another set of hands on her from behind. She froze as those hands rubbed slowly up her back to her shoulders and then the utility belt rubbed against her spine.

"So sweet and beautiful, Millie. I want to feel those lips of yours, too. I can't let my brother have all the fun."

Jeremy!

Millie's body seemed to react in a totally surprising way as both men caressed and pet her. As Anthony slowly released her lips, trailing kisses along her neck, she turned to the side only to have Jeremy cup her cheeks between his hands and smile at her.

"You are gorgeous, woman. I need to feel your lips against mine, darling. I've waited too long."

He winked at her and she felt as if his aura hugged her. He was a flirt, a jokester, and his brown eyes sparkled with mischief right before he lowered his mouth to hers. On cue, Anthony relinquished his hold on her to his brother and now Jeremy was kissing her, exploring her mouth as his hands firmly traveled along the curves of her body. She kissed him back, absorbing the differences between Jeremy and Anthony. They were similar in height and in body type, but as her hands pressed against his back she felt her fingers reach his hair. She envisioned how he always kept it tied back neatly and it looked shiny and soft.

Slowly, Jeremy released her lips and pressed soft kisses against her mouth and cheeks before he locked gazes with her.

"Way better than I fantasized about," he admitted, and she felt her cheeks blush. Then Anthony gently rubbed his knuckles along her other cheek and she looked toward him and he smiled.

"Beautiful," he whispered, and she shyly lowered her eyes then stepped from Jeremy's embrace.

"Hey, did you get lost? Ohhh." Anna smiled wide. "I'm sorry to interrupt. I'll just leave you three to what you were doing." She back stepped toward the other side of the building.

"I'm coming." Millie reached for the broom and began to follow Anna. Then she felt a strong, large hand against her upper arm stop her from exiting.

"Wait," Jeremy stated.

She looked at both Jeremy and Anthony. They appeared uncertain and almost desperate for her to remain there.

"Don't go. We'd like to talk to you, get to know you better, and make some plans. Would you like to come over for dinner tonight?" Jeremy asked her. She nibbled her bottom lip. Dinner at the Lewis brothers' place with possibly all five of them? *Oh shit!*

As if sensing her anxiety, Anthony stepped forward, locking gazes with her as he took her other hand. Now both men were touching her again, and damn it, did her body betray her mind's warning to take things slow.

"Just dinner, Millie. We really do want to get to know you better. And maybe fool around a little more. Your kisses are going to be addicting, I can tell already," Jeremy teased, and she chuckled.

What the hell did she have to lose? It was just dinner and getting to know five sexy, intimidating cowboys.

"Okay."

Both men smiled wide.

"I'll pick you up at seven. Is that good?" Anthony asked.

She nodded her head.

"We'll pick you up at seven," Jeremy chimed in then winked, and she laughed before taking the broom she had in a death grip with her and back toward the rec center.

Chapter 14

Millie looked at herself in the mirror. She had chosen a turquoise, A-line sundress that flared slightly above her knees. It accentuated her breasts with scalloped trim along the bustline and straps. She thought she looked really good in it and it was versatile, too. She decided on a pair of white, strappy sandals that had a slight heel.

After showering and blowing her hair straight, it now appeared long and shiny as it silhouetted down her back to nearly her rear.

Looking through her jewelry box, she pulled out a pair of earrings and matching necklace that she had handmade herself. It contained light blue stones and matched her outfit perfectly. She sniffed the air, absorbing the smell of her light perfume before twirling around to get a better look at her appearance. In her mind, she thought about everything all at once, but what really stood out were Stewart's insults. He would frown upon her wearing such a simple dress. He hated the color blue when she loved it.

Stewart filtered through her mind, nearly bursting her bubble of excitement about tonight's dinner with the brothers. She swallowed hard. She couldn't help but think that this was a mistake. She was asking for trouble times five. It could end up disastrous and then what? She liked it here in Pearl. She didn't want to leave. As a matter of fact, subconsciously it seemed she had made the decision to stay. She forced Stewart's words out of her mind. She hated him. She hoped that he was miserable right now and that people told him how much of a jerk he was for getting her fired. She looked into the mirror again and smiled. *No more thoughts of Stewart or men like him.* That was behind her. Tonight was about starting with a clean slate and getting to know the Lewis brothers as individuals and fellow residents of Pearl.

The sound of a truck pulling up outside made her heart race. This was it. She was going to do this.

* * * *

Anthony gave Jeremy an exasperated expression as they climbed the front porch to pick up Millie for dinner.

Jeremy was getting on Anthony's nerves. He had been tapping his hands on his lap and fidgeting the entire way over in the truck and Anthony was fed up.

"Will you calm down?"

"What?" Jeremy asked with confusion.

"You're fidgeting and hopping around like spit in a hot skillet. I can't take it. It's not like you've never been on a date before."

"This is different. Millie is different. I know this."

Just then the front door opened and Millie appeared.

One look at their goddess and Anthony was speechless and felt so damn nervous he should have never reprimanded Jeremy.

"Hi." Millie stared at him and Jeremy as if they were crazy or something. He was tongue-tied and so was Jeremy. Millie looked stunning in a blue dress that accentuated her feminine curves like nothing she had ever worn before. The woman looked sexy in a pair of blue jeans and T-shirt, but damn did she look piping hot in a dress.

"You're gorgeous," Jeremy stated then pulled the door open and smiled wide. He leaned forward to press a kiss to her cheek and she blushed.

"Absolutely gorgeous. Are you ready?" Anthony chimed in then leaned forward to kiss her on the other cheek. She shyly nodded then turned toward the door to lock it, placing the key into her purse she held in one hand.

They both took an arm and led her down the stairs to the truck.

"You sit up front with Anthony. I'll sit in the back seat," Jeremy told her as he helped her step up into the truck. When the material of her dress parted and showed off her tan, muscular thigh, Anthony felt his cock grow hard and tight. This was going to be a hell of a night trying to keep his lust reigned in. She was perfect.

* * * *

The ride over had been pleasant and Jeremy talked a mile a minute, making it easy on Millie as to not force words from her trembling lips. She took the opportunity to absorb the men's attire, which only added to her oversensitive body. She partly listened as Jeremy spoke.

"So it looks like the construction is going well with all the cottages. We heard a few more women showed up yesterday looking for a safe place to stay. I think this was a great idea you all came up with," Jeremy told her from the back seat.

Anthony looked like he had just stepped out of a men's fashion catalog. He wore a crisp, white button-down shirt that he hadn't buttoned fully and exposed some of his tanned, muscular chest. His dark jeans were designer and his boots black and shiny. He looked edible. Millie felt her heart rate increase and then she looked away as Anthony caught her drooling.

"It's got to be difficult, being on your own without anyone to help you, never mind if you have children," Anthony piped in.

"It is difficult. I've seen it many times before in New York. That was one of the main ideas I had for the women's shelter I raised funds for. It was also to provide guidance and support so eventually the women, and if they had children, the family, could get back out on their own. It's not an easy process." Millie looked back toward Jeremy since it seemed Anthony kept glancing at her instead of the road ahead of him.

Jeremy was dressed in a dark blue button-down shirt, black jeans, and he also had on designer boots. His belt buckle showed off the fact that he had ridden a bull and at one point in time won a medal for his bravery or maybe stupidity. She never understood why anyone would find joy in riding on top of a wild, uncontrollable beast weighing anywhere from one thousand to two thousand pounds of angry muscle. But for some strange reason, the thought turned her on. It was sexy and manly even if she thought it was crazy.

When they pulled up to their property Millie was stunned. The gates opened electronically and way up the long, winding road was a stunning, extraordinarily large estate made of modern brick and stonework as well as a traditional wraparound porch.

"Oh my God, your place is huge," Millie whispered, taking in the sight of the horse stables to the left that matched the same woodwork and stone on the house.

"Well, there's five of us living here and we're big men," Jeremy chimed in from the back seat and winked at her.

"It's stunning."

"We built it," Anthony stated, and Millie stared at him in disbelief.

"No way! Really?"

"Yep. We all did and everything inside is custom made. Anthony is amazing with cabinetry and woodwork," Jeremy informed her, and she glanced back at Jeremy and then at Anthony, who appeared embarrassed.

"It's not a big deal." He grunted. He was modest and humble. She liked that. The truck stopped in a spot along the side of the house. Before she could open her door, Hank was making his way down the porch steps and she paused with her hand on the handle of the door as Anthony climbed out of the truck.

Hank looked handsome. He wore blue jeans and a dark sage-colored, collared shirt. He smiled wide as he approached the door. She was suddenly feeling a bit intimidated.

Slowly, she pushed the door open and Hank was there offering her his hand. She smiled. "Hi," he whispered.

"Hi," she replied and when she began to step from the truck, Hank lifted her into his arms and against his chest. She clutched his shoulders, and as he slowly lowered her, he kissed her on the mouth. It was a soft, gentle kiss that ended way too quickly.

"Hey, let me outta here," Jeremy interrupted, and as Hank released her lips he gave Jeremy an annoyed look.

Hank let her down and took her hand, and Jeremy chuckled. It appeared that Jeremy was teasing his brother on purpose.

"You look stunning, sweetness," Hank whispered next to her ear and she felt her belly quiver. He was damn sexy.

"Damn straight, she does." Jeremy winked at her.

His playful side made her feel a little less nervous until she approached the front steps and spotted Dalton.

* * * *

Dalton was trying to calm his breathing. He was so fucking nervous his hands were clammy and he was nearly perspiring. He had served in the damn war, yet this woman made him more nervous with anticipation of what may or may not happen. Or perhaps how many things could go wrong or even right. *Shit.*

As he looked up toward the open doorway, he saw her standing there, dressed in blue, looking like an angel with the sunlight gathered behind her. Hank held her hand, towering over her as Jeremy and Anthony followed suit. She looked stunning and feminine and every nerve ending in his body felt the need to protect her, possess her, and hold her in his arms.

As he stepped toward her, ready to take action and claim what was instinctively his, he stopped short. Perhaps she didn't feel so strongly about him. The thought had him scowling.

Millie must have picked up on it because her smile faltered and Hank cleared his throat.

"Welcome to our home. Let's give you the tour." Hank practically dragged her across the room.

"Wait," Millie whispered and Hank stopped walking. She was a few feet away from Dalton and he watched her intently, wondering what she would say.

She looked him over from head to toe. He wondered if he had dressed too casually or perhaps he should have worn a different color than black but black was his favorite color.

"Hello, Dalton." She reached her hand out for him to—shake it? *What?* He wanted to pull her into his arms and kiss her, not shake her fucking hand as if she were the next-door neighbor. *What the fuck?*

As he slowly reached for her hand, she smiled just as the electrical current he felt between them in the dojo came crashing forward. An instant later she was wrapped up in his arms and he was devouring her mouth.

* * * *

Millie had no idea what the hell was happening, but she was instantly and evenly attracted to the brothers. Initially, she had thought that Dalton may have changed his mind about his attraction to her by the scowl on his face, but then something came over her. She liked him. A lot. She recalled her jealousy toward the other women that found him attractive and flirted with him. She wanted the men to belong to only her. It was a shocking, controlling thought that fed her hunger.

She poured all of that emotion into their kiss, and before long, he was lifting her up, holding her tightly against his chest and loving her mouth.

As if realizing that his behavior and response was compulsive and may have frightened her, he began to pull away. His lips slowly left hers and then he smiled down at her.

"Hot damn, woman, you set my body on fire." She felt the palm of his hand glide across her ass cheek and squeeze. Her nipples hardened and her body rubbed against him.

"I think dessert should come before dinner tonight," Jeremy stated and they all chuckled.

"Millie."

Millie turned from Dalton's heated gaze to Marco, who leaned against the entryway to another room with his arms crossed. From cowboy boots and Wrangler jeans all the way up to his Western-style black shirt and stern expression, she absorbed him completely. Her mouth slightly opened and she nearly moaned from overstimulation and complete appreciation for the five fine-looking cowboys around her.

"Come here," Marco commanded. She widened her eyes in response, but she feared to take the shaky step toward him. She was at a crossroads of sorts at the moment. She had deep feelings for these men. All of them. When she loved, she loved entirely and that had been her downfall twice. First with Frank and then with Stewart. But she did love a man in charge. She wanted one that could take care of her, one she could lean on, and one that could also be commanding in the bedroom but bring her pleasure, not pain. Marco cleared his throat as if she were waiting too long to follow his command. This was a leap of faith. These men had shown her nothing but gentleness and affection. *Third time's a charm, Millie.*

He raised his eyebrows, the cocky, sexy bastard, and she found herself slowly walking the six feet toward him. His eyes sparkled in celebration as she approached.

"Stop right there," he whispered firmly and she forced herself to remain still and not take the last two steps and throw herself into his arms for a hell of a hello.

He uncrossed his arms and looked her over from head to toe. *Oh, please don't say you hate the color blue. Oh, please, don't tell me what you don't like about me.* She wondered why she was being so critical and worrying about them turning out to be like other men. *Give them a chance.* She tensed up entirely until Marco spoke in his deep Texan accent.

"You should dress like this more often. You're a stunning, voluptuous woman, Millie. I'm going to enjoy removing that dress from your body and exploring every inch of you."

Holy Mary, Mother of God!

She closed her eyes and swallowed the moan she felt nearly slip from her lips.

That was the hottest thing any man had ever said to her.

When she felt his arm go around her waist and pull her to him, she opened her eyes and looked up and up until she locked gazes with Marco.

His mouth descended on hers quickly, leaving no room to prepare for his kiss. He was lethal and thorough as he explored her with his mouth as well as his hands.

Lost in the sensations and the constant state of arousal, she hadn't realized that another body was now behind her and two sets of hands began an exploration. As Marco caressed the palm of his right hand up her dress and squeezed her thigh, Anthony moved her hair from her neck on the opposite side of her body and licked and kissed along her skin.

She lost the ability to stand and Anthony held her up.

"Whoa, honey, easy now. You taste really good and whatever perfume you're wearing it is very appealing," Anthony whispered then continued to kiss her neck. Marco slowly released her lips and she couldn't control her heavy breathing no matter how hard she tried.

His hand tapped against her thigh then moved farther up. He held her gaze and his eyes widened probably at the fact that she wore thong bikini underwear. Damn straight she did. If she was going to possibly have sex with five men, she was going to bring in the heavy artillery. She hoped the matching black silk bra was to their satisfaction as well. If they in fact wanted to explore her sexually, she wanted the wrapping to be as good as the present.

Marco's fingers pulled the thin material that started at her hip and disappeared between her ass cheeks. She gasped at his brazen move but was so utterly and completely turned on by both him and Anthony she couldn't move. The pressure from his large hand enticed her body. She felt her pussy clench and she tightened her legs.

"Your choice, Millie. Dessert before dinner or dinner first?" Marco asked. His hand paused on her skin, singeing it and filling her with lust.

"Oh, God, this can't be happening to me."

"It sure is happening to you. We want you," Anthony whispered against her neck as he held her hips.

"Why?" she found herself asking in a raspy, sexy tone.

Marco shook his head as if disappointed at her lack of realization as to why they wanted her. Then he squeezed her to him and held her gaze.

"Because you are sweet, sexy, and all woman. You make me want things I've never wanted before." She gulped then felt Anthony move his hands from her waist up to her breast and squeeze.

"And because you're beautiful and a fantasy come true," Anthony added then squeezed again.

"Oh, God."

"You feel it, Millie, don't you?" Jeremy asked as he moved into her line of sight. Hank and Dalton surrounded them now, too.

She nodded her head.

"Say it. Say you feel what we all feel," Hank demanded, and she felt the intensity of his tone.

She looked at Dalton. "I feel it. I feel it with all of you."

"Dessert first," Jeremy teased.

"Didn't someone say something about a tour?" Millie asked, feeling a bit of stage fright.

She gasped as Marco scooped her up into his arms as if she weighed nothing at all.

"No better place to tour first than the bedroom."

* * * *

Marco slowly lowered Millie's body down his until her feet hit the carpeting. He could sense her uneasiness and was glad his brothers held back joining them. They didn't want to scare her, but they were going to make love to her tonight.

"Are you scared?" he asked as he cupped her cheeks and stared down into her dark blue eyes.

She nodded her head.

"Well, don't be. Anthony and I are going to take things nice and slow, baby. We want you." As he said Anthony's name, his brother took that moment to place his hands on Millie's hips. She tensed a moment until Anthony kissed the top of her head. Anthony massaged her hips then pulled her back as he stepped forward. Her body was wedged between them both.

"Now where were we?" Marco teased while he cupped her cheek, tilted her face up toward him, and kissed her.

She tasted sweeter than honey. He felt Millie relax against Anthony as she reciprocated Marco's kiss. He glided his hand along the hem of her dress and back to her thigh where he stopped earlier. She would tense and then relax with every new move he made. He continued the journey with his hand, grabbing ahold of the thong panties, pressing them to the side then cupping her mound.

Millie moaned into his mouth.

She was hot and wet for him. The evidence made his cock harden and hunger intensify. When she slightly adjusted her stance so he could gain better access to her pussy, he took full advantage and pressed a digit up into her.

"Oh," she moaned after pulling her mouth from Marco's. He continued to kiss her skin, suck along her neck then nibble.

In and out he pressed his finger then added a second digit.

"So hot and wet for us. I want you, Millie. I can't wait to be inside of you."

"Yes, oh God, Marco, please," she begged then thrust her hips against his fingers.

"Baby, you are turning me on. You ever make love to two men at once?" he asked and she shook her head. "Good. We'll be your firsts."

Marco continued to thrust his fingers up into her as Millie rode out the waves of an oncoming orgasm. Marco could feel her vaginal muscles grip his digits and he couldn't help but imagine being inside of her. Anthony began to pull off Millie's dress. He lifted it up and over her head then tossed it onto a nearby chair.

The sight of her body and her large breasts covered in black silk was too much to ignore.

He leaned forward and licked the cleavage.

"Millie, you're a goddess. It's like you were made for us," Anthony stated then licked across her collarbone. Marco smiled from below.

"I have to be inside you."

Marco slowly removed his fingers, causing Millie to moan as Anthony turned her toward him. Anthony began kissing her while Marco pulled off his clothing.

When he was naked, he stared at her body and reached out to caress her ass cheeks.

He pressed up against her, allowing her to feel his cock between her ass cheeks while he rubbed up and down. They were skin to skin and he felt the pull, the attraction so deep he nearly came right there.

"You have a great ass, Millie."

"Oh," she moaned then rolled her head back. Marco made quick use of his hands and unclipped her bra.

The material dropped to the floor and Anthony moaned.

"God almighty, you're perfect," Anthony stated then leaned forward to take a nipple into his mouth.

Marco guided them to the bed.

* * * *

Millie was on fire. She had never felt like this before. Men didn't talk to her this way when she was naked and about to have sex. There was deep meaning behind their words. She was certain of it.

"Please," she begged as Anthony sucked harder on her nipple as he cupped her other breast. His tan hand was a huge contrast to her lighter skin. His fingers were long, thick, and callused. The roughness added to the sensations traveling from beneath where his fingers touched.

Marco was behind her, caressing her ass and talking dirty.

She felt the cream drip from her pussy and she knew she wanted him inside of her.

"Lay her down on the bed," Marco told Anthony. Anthony didn't move right away. He continued to feast on her until he was ready. When he released her breast he stared into her eyes.

"We're going to take good care of you, Millie."

She heard and sensed his sincerity.

"Are you on the pill?" Marco asked from above her shoulder and she nodded.

"Good. We're clean. It's been a long while," he confessed and that thought flooded her with relief. She didn't like thinking about them with other women.

Anthony lifted her up and placed her on the edge of the bed. In an instant he knelt down, caressed her thighs open, and began to play with her pussy lips. He used his fingers to spread her wider then stared at her.

His finger trailed along the scar by her groin and she tightened up. He crunched his eyebrows in concern. "What's this from?"

"The attack," she whispered, and saw the bit of anger cross his expression and then it softened. She was glad he didn't push for more info. Nor did the others. Instead, he leaned forward and kissed along the scar, making her moan and tighten in response. He was so gentle it aroused her need for more of him.

"You're all pretty and pink down here, sweetness." He leaned forward and licked her pussy.

"Oh, God!" she moaned as she gripped the sheets and felt Anthony's mouth latch onto her clit. When he alternated between fingers then tongue she lost all control and came. Her hips thrust up and she shook from the orgasm.

"Now that is fucking hot," Jeremy stated, and Millie opened her eyes. Jeremy joined Marco and Anthony and he was naked.

"Oh, Lord." She absorbed the sight of both Marco and Jeremy completely naked. There were so many muscles and ridges of steel she practically drooled.

"She tastes delicious, too," Anthony said, interrupting her ogling.

"I'm ready for my woman," Marco stated firmly, and her belly quivered.

Three men in the room on a bed with me at the same time. Oh, please let this be amazing and not a mistake.

Anthony kissed both her inner thighs then winked as he stood up. There was Marco taking his place, holding his thick, long cock in his hand.

"Fuck you're beautiful. I need a quick taste." He fell to one knee, leaned forward, and latched onto her clit.

She grabbed ahold of his head and moaned as he ate at her cream.

The bed dipped and there was Jeremy, smiling wide. He cupped her breast and leaned down as if he were about to feast on it, but he kissed her mouth first. When he released her mouth, she opened her eyes, and he winked before he licked across her nipple.

"Perfect."

The warm mouth and breath against her pussy lips disappeared, and there was Marco, standing up and lining his cock up with her entrance.

"Ready for me, baby?" he asked, and she nodded.

Jeremy pulled her nipple between his teeth, causing her to scream as Marco thrust forward into her.

Her inner muscles screamed from lack of use as she accepted the large invasion. Marco was way bigger than any man she had ever been with. Jeremy looked just as thick, and she wondered if the others were as well endowed.

Jeremy released her breast and Marco leaned over her with his cock buried deep inside of her pussy.

"So tight. Damn, woman, you feel like heaven."

She gripped Marco's shoulders and kissed his skin as he thrust slowly into her. Instinctively, she wrapped her legs around his waist and counterthrust.

"Yeah, baby, you feel so damn good. I ain't gonna last, sweetness," he admitted then lifted up and thrust a few more times.

* * * *

Marco didn't recognize the feelings he had inside. He felt possessive and deeply out of control. He increased his speed and thrust into Millie, trying to relieve that sensation and satisfy his hunger. Millie counterthrust against him, dug her nails into his skin, and he couldn't hold back. The scent of her perfume, her cream and response to their touch overrode any comprehensible means to slow down. He wanted to brand her his. He wanted to feel this feeling every day of his life.

"Arrgh!" he yelled as he thrust hard and deep three more times before exploding inside of her. Millie screamed then grabbed ahold of him, pulling him against her tight.

"Oh, God, that was so good. Are you okay?" he asked her and she lifted up to kiss him hard on the mouth. He held her against him and they kissed a few moments longer. When they finally parted lips she smiled at him and his heart lifted with joy.

"Incredible," he whispered then kissed her nose before he lifted up and slowly pulled from her body.

* * * *

The moment Marco moved out of the way, Anthony took his spot and Jeremy began to play with her breasts again.

"You make love so passionately, Millie. I saw the emotion in your eyes. I want that, too," Anthony told her, and she smiled.

"I want you, too," she told him, and he leaned down against her as he entered her slowly.

Her vaginal muscles gripped Anthony's cock tight. It had been over a year since he had made love to a woman. His emotions tore at his heart as he realized how deep his feelings for Millie were already. Now that he was inside of her, making love to her, there would never be another woman. He just knew it. He and Marco were the oldest and fourteen months apart. They chose their lovers wisely and never had he felt such depth so quickly.

"Millie, my sweet angel. God, you feel so good." He kissed her lips. As she kissed him back he thrust in and out of her pussy, feeling his cock grow harder with every stroke.

She ran her fingers through his hair and against his shoulders as she kissed him passionately. When she released his lips he increased his thrusts and she moaned with pleasure, feeding his desire to satisfy her and have her like this for as long as he could. In and out his strokes grew deeper and his emotions overwhelmed him.

"So sexy, so good." He clenched his teeth and thrust two more times before he came inside of her, screaming her name.

* * * *

Millie tried to catch her breath. Sex had never been so good as it was with these men. She felt hungry and desirable. They didn't seem turned off by her chunkiness. In fact, they seemed infatuated with her breasts and the fact that her pussy was shaven bare. She liked to keep it that way and read that men found pleasure with a bare pussy. She giggled to herself as Anthony kissed each breast before he stood up. Then came Jeremy. He winked and caressed her inner thighs.

"Think you can handle me, baby?" he asked sounding all cocky and sure of himself. She wanted to laugh but wasn't sure if he would feel insulted, so she pretended that she wasn't sure. But she knew she was sure. If she was going to have sex with five men then she was doing them all tonight.

"I'm not sure, Jeremy. Go easy," she whispered. His cheeks reddened and he leaned forward to twirl his tongue over her mound then up and into her belly button. She grabbed his hair and lifted her legs so her feet lay flat on the bed.

"Such a pretty pink pussy you have, sweetness. I think I'm gonna love being inside of you."

With those final words, he lined up his cock with her entrance and placed both hands on either knee, pulling her toward the edge of the bed as he thrust into her.

Millie screamed and instantly exploded in pleasure. It appeared that Jeremy was a take-no-prisoners kind of lover. When he caressed his hands lower, pulling her tighter against his cock with every one of his thrusts, she nearly lost her breath from the incredible sensations.

He rocked into her, spreading her ass cheeks then lifting her rear off the bed into the air slightly to penetrate deeper. Her legs were now over his shoulders as he played with her ass and dove deeper into her channel. She barely held on to the comforter as he increased his strokes.

Millie moaned and tried to counterthrust when suddenly she felt his finger at her puckered hole then pressing through the tight rings.

"Oh!" Millie screamed then came again.

"Fuck yeah, you're gonna love having a dick in your ass, baby. That's my girl!" he roared as he thrust three more times then came inside of her.

* * * *

Millie needed a rest after that. She never had anal sex before and after what Jeremy just did to her she was seriously curious and ready to try it.

"Oh, God, Jeremy," she whispered as she placed her arm over her head. He leaned down, placing kisses along her belly after pulling from her body.

"That was really good, baby. I don't think I'll ever get enough of making love to you," he admitted and her heart leaped with joy.

Marco appeared moments later wearing only his jeans with the button undone and holding a washcloth. He cleaned her up and she drooled over his pectoral muscles. Reaching up with her fingernails, she gently glided them over each ridge and he tensed his muscles.

"You're gorgeous," she whispered, and he chuckled.

"You're the gorgeous one. Are you okay? We weren't too rough?" he asked, and she shook her head as emotions she hadn't expected shoved into her heart. These men were really caring and gentle. They actually gave a shit about her. It was so strange and scary. It was also something she could get used to.

Marco helped her sit up and she covered herself with a shirt that was on the side of the bed.

"Hey, no hiding that body from us. You're perfect," Anthony stated.

She lowered her eyes.

"I'm not perfect," she whispered.

"From here you look every bit perfect," she heard Hank state from the doorway. She blushed and he entered the room. Dalton was behind him.

Her stomach tightened.

"You guys want to help me get dinner ready?" Dalton asked and disappointment filled her belly. Dalton didn't plan on making love to her next? What was wrong?

"You bet." Marco leaned down to kiss Millie on the cheek before he headed downstairs. Anthony kissed her next and then Jeremy. Hank remained with Dalton standing in the doorway.

"You are more beautiful than I imagined, Millie," Hank whispered as he took a seat next to her on the bed. He caressed the skin on her arm with the back of his knuckles.

"Are you okay? They weren't too rough?" he asked, and she shook her head then looked back toward Dalton. His expression was dark and intense. He seemed to be struggling with something. As if sensing her tension at watching Dalton, Hank pressed the palm of his hand against her cheek, turning her face toward him.

"I want to make love to you, too, baby. I want to hold you and keep you safe in my arms."

She smiled at him.

"I want you, too, Hank," she whispered, and Hank leaned forward to kiss her.

He made love to her mouth as he removed the shirt from her body and explored with his hands. He was a big man, too, just like his brothers, and his large hands hardly covered her breasts. The feel of his skin and the intensity of the attraction made her wet all over again and soon Millie was reciprocating.

She reached between them and undid the button on Hank's jeans. He stopped kissing her to stand up, and she watched as he removed his jeans and saw that he went commando.

"That is sexy," she told him, and he smiled. She wondered where her brazenness was coming from. She hardly knew these men and was solely going by her gut and her emotions right now. She absorbed his body and the slight blush against his cheeks. Did her words do that to him?

"Glad you think so, sweetness," he whispered then lay down next to her on the bed. He ran his fingers across her torso and she tightened as the goose bumps covered her flesh.

He stared into her eyes and she held his gaze, wishing she could tell him all the things she was feeling at once right now. Millie was overwhelmed with desire and affection for five men. The thought alone overwhelmed her.

"Are you okay? Are we moving too fast?" Hank asked while his fingers gently played against her skin. Her core tightened and her vaginal muscles clamped in response. She knew that she had it bad.

"I'm beyond thinking straight right now, Hank. I feel like there's so much to talk about and confirm, yet the need for you to be inside me is much greater right now. It's wild, isn't it?" she asked him.

He smiled at her. She absorbed his blond hair and watched the sparkle in his bright blue eyes.

"You make us wild, woman. You got under our skin in a flash and there ain't no other woman who ever came close to doing that. I want you so badly it hurts inside, Millie."

His words burned through to her soul.

"Then take me," she whispered and her voice cracked. She thought he would lean over and kiss her or slowly make his way between her legs, but she was wrong. These men were experienced lovers and they were lethal.

"Spread your legs for me, angel," he whispered as he held her gaze, and she practically came from the intensity but immediately did as she was told.

She opened her thighs wide as Hank trailed fingers from breast to mound.

Looking down as his fingers parted her folds and spread her pussy lips turned her on and made her feel hot. Her clit tingled and her nipples hardened. How could she be so aroused and ready to have sex again so quickly?

She lifted her hips, hoping he wouldn't tease her and would press a finger to her pussy.

"Please, Hank," she begged then heard a groan from across the room. There was Dalton with his pants unbuttoned and his cock in his hand.

Hank's words came crashing back into her mind. *"You make us wild, woman."*

Could it be true? Could she really have such a strong effect over five perfect men? The thought gave her confidence and built up her self-esteem in a flash. She looked at Dalton. He appeared aroused, and boy, did he look edible. She wanted to taste him, to touch him and hold him, too.

"Dalton," she moaned just as Hank pressed a finger up into her pussy.

She felt his forearm across her thigh and the muscles hard against the soft swell of her belly. She moaned and lifted her hips. His digit was thick and hard and teased her pussy. She needed him inside of her, but she was so overstimulated if he continued to stroke her she would scream her orgasm any moment.

Hank swooped down to kiss her lips quickly as he thrust his finger in and out. She grabbed hold of his shoulders, tilting her head back while moaning from the effects.

"Sweet Jesus, you're so responsive." Hank pinched her clit as he sat up and moved between her legs. "I can't play around, baby. I'm so hard I'm about to burst. I want to be inside you when I do," he told her.

"Oh, please, Hank. I need you, too."

Hank caressed along her inner thighs until the tips of his thumbs rubbed gently against her pussy. She tilted her hips and he lifted her thighs, getting into a better position to penetrate her.

"So amazing. Get ready, baby. I've got a lot to give you." And he pushed forward.

He was thick and hard, but her pussy was so extra wet from Dalton watching them. She had never thought that knowing someone watched her having sex would turn her on like this. She was wet beyond anything she had ever felt. The sloshing sound filled the air, and she was almost embarrassed.

"Oh fuck, Millie, you're so wet. Our little sweet angel likes being watched, huh? You like knowing that my brother is jerking off as I'm fucking this sweet, wet pussy?"

"Oh!" Millie screamed from Hank's words.

He was covering her now, her hips spread against him wide while he thrust in and out. He kept rocking his hips fast and then he would slow down, nearly torturing her. He placed his hands against her cheeks, holding her head in place. Hank's expression was wild, his breathing rapid, his eyes glazed over in arousal.

"Woman, what you do to me." Hank covered her mouth with his. He kissed her wildly, plunging his tongue into her mouth as he thrust his cock deep into her, making her moan against his mouth. Her vaginal muscles clamped down tighter. It was outrageous and crazy. She kissed him back, giving as good as she was getting. All her lust and sexual desire for this man came pouring out of her. She ran her hands along his skin. She rubbed her fingernails across any bit of flesh she could touch and hold on to as he thrust faster while he lay his face against her neck and shoulder.

She was so aroused and ready to ignite, and then he yelled her name as he came hard inside of her. He thrust his hips twice before falling against her.

She was deaf from the sensations of her orgasm. Her breathing echoed in her ears. It was odd and crazy. As she controlled her breathing she felt Hank kissing her collarbone, her neck, her lips, and then her breasts. He was scattering kisses everywhere.

"So beautiful. So soft and perfect," he told her and then slowly parted from her body. She grabbed at him, wanting him to remain inside of her, never wanting these sensations and this strong connection to break. She felt so safe and perfect when one of her men were inside of her.

My men? Oh my heavens, I'm losing it.

* * * *

Hank stood up and Millie began to close her legs when she felt strong, rough hands against her thighs.

She opened her eyes and locked gazes with Dalton.

Oh my good heavens, does he look determined and needy?

He was still wearing his black shirt but no pants. Why was he wearing his shirt?

She swallowed hard as she absorbed the sensation of warm, large hands against her thighs. His green eyes sparkled, his pupils nearly dilated. They were mesmerizing and so was he. She couldn't help but shiver with anticipation.

Dalton was complicated, mysterious, and suspenseful. These words were what came to mind instantly. Did he really want her or was he just along for the ride with his brothers? Her heart ached a moment at the thought, but then she focused on his face, his scar, and his aura surrounding her.

"Dalton."

"Shh." He spoke so deeply and with such power she stared at him.

Then she wondered if he needed her to make the first move. She reached up to remove his shirt or at least press her fingertips against his skin. She knew he would be taut and muscular beneath the clothing.

He shook his head and she didn't understand what was giving him such a difficult time.

"Dalton?" she whispered again then reached for him. This time he grabbed her wrists, placed them above her head, and leaned forward. The move caused her breasts to push up and toward his face as he descended upon her and his eyes sparkled. He seemed to be going through some inner struggle. Either that or he didn't like being touched. What the heck?

Before she could question him he leaned down and ran his tongue across one nipple. *Fuck does that feel good.*

Millie was on fire again. She didn't care what he did just as long as he touched her. He lapped at one nipple then nibbled on the tender flesh, causing her to feel the tightness from her breast to her pussy. She tilted her hips up against him, but his thick frame didn't allow for much room.

She gave in to his demands for control. It seemed to be the way he wanted it and she wasn't complaining. Dalton hadn't hurt her or appeared as if he ever would. Instead, she relished in the foreplay he was initiating.

He feasted on her for several long minutes before he moved to the other breast. It was getting to the point where she wanted to grab his face and make him lick, suck, and nibble where she needed it most. But Dalton wouldn't budge. He was taking his time. Every so often she would try to move her arms from his hold to touch him, but he would squeeze a little tighter. She couldn't touch him and for some wild reason it turned her on but also made her feel frustrated.

She could feel his thick cock against her mound as he rubbed back and forth ever so softly. Between that and the brush of cloth from his shirt against her mound, she was turning nearly insane with need.

"Dalton, I want to touch you," she began to say, but he cut her off by kissing her hard on the mouth. She could feel the tip of his cock at her entrance as she lifted her legs, placing her feet on the comforter for leverage. She would make him push inside of her. She needed it and she needed it badly.

She thrust her pelvis up, but he wasn't ready. Dalton made love to her mouth, exploring every bit of it as he held her hands above her head. Her body began to quake and tighten with need as she whimpered into his mouth. He released her lips then licked along her collarbone to her neck. He nibbled, causing tiny goose bumps to travel along her skin.

"Please, Dalton, I need."

"I'm going to give it to you, Millie. Please be patient with me." She was suddenly shocked at his plea. *I was right. He is struggling. Is it another woman? The bitch! Did she hurt him? I'll wring her neck.*

"Keep your hands above your head." He pressed them down in a show of added seriousness to his command. It wasn't a request.

She watched him as he absorbed her body. She focused on the scar by his neck and shoulder that disappeared beneath his T-shirt. She wanted to kiss it, to kiss him, touch him, and hold him tight.

"Dalton."

"Shh."

He played with her breasts, pulling and squeezing them before leaning down to kiss each nipple.

She moved her hands and he sat up, staring at her in warning.

She absorbed his expression and the fact that his shirt was still on. It didn't sit right with her, but she obeyed his pleas. Perhaps now wasn't the time to analyze him.

When he reached down to play with her clit, she closed her eyes and lifted her pelvis. Her hands remained above her head as she gripped some material between her fingers, holding on so she wouldn't mess up and touch him. This position of compliance and submission aroused her fully. *God, I want him so badly it hurts.*

When he lined his cock up with her entrance and lightly moved the tip back and forth across her sensitive flesh, she felt her pussy tighten then leak again.

"Oh please, Dalton. I need you inside of me."

He took her plea seriously and slowly, torturously pushed into her.

She tried to thrust up into him so his thick, hard cock would penetrate her faster, but he reached up to hold her upper arms then pushed in.

She gasped at the fullness and opened her eyes to look down. Dalton wasn't fully inside of her.

"Oh, God," she panted and he eased into her.

"Easy, baby. Don't tighten up. You can take all of me."

And she did want all of him. She wanted every part of him.

He released her arms, grabbed her thighs, and shoved fully into her, making Millie scream. Over and over again he would pull out then thrust back in. She kept her arms above her head and that added to her desires. She was wet again, very wet as the sloshing sound seemed to echo in the room. She was in tune to every sensation. With every thrust, she watched her breasts bounce. She felt her nipples tighten and her belly muscles squeezed tight. Dalton grunted with every in-and-out movement of penetration.

"So tight and so fucking sweet," he yelled as his thrusts intensified and Millie fought to touch him.

"Oh God, Dalton!" She screamed her release and then exploded with Dalton still pumping into her. Her breath caught in her throat and then Dalton roared her name as he came.

He pulled her into his arms and rolled to his back with his cock still deep inside of her. He hugged her tight. She could hardly breathe but snuggled against him.

"Incredible," he whispered and she closed her eyes and absorbed the feeling of safety and contentedness of being in his arms.

Chapter 15

Dalton sat up, causing Millie to straddle his waist and hold his shoulders. She snuggled against him and he tightened his hold. She scattered kisses along his jaw and then to his neck. As she made contact with the scar while pressing her hands against his chest he grabbed her hips and pushed her away.

She was shocked.

"Don't."

"Don't what?" she asked as she held his gaze.

She swallowed a bit of fear. She knew that Dalton wouldn't hurt her, but she also sensed his strength and was aware of his training as ex-military.

He wouldn't answer her as he turned away.

Millie began to ease off of him and he gripped her hard and held her ass in place on his lap by gripping her hip bones.

"Don't push, Millie."

"Really? Don't push, huh? Just like how you didn't push me at the dojo for answers as to why I quit training, or just like you didn't push me to try harder when we were sparring. Sure, Dalton, no problem."

She tried to get up but he squeezed her hips.

"You never did tell us why you quit before earning your black belt."

"My boyfriend at the time made me quit," she blurted out before thinking her statement through.

"What?" he responded with an expression that showed his disappointment in her. She didn't need him feeling that way about her, too. It was bad enough that she allowed asshole Stewart to take from her what she loved most.

"I don't want to talk about it."

"Was this the Frank guy?" he asked.

She shook her head.

"Another guy? Why would he ask that of you?"

"Because he was a control freak. He thought that it wasn't ladylike. But ya know what? After he got me fired from my job, I wish I had the opportunity to use some martial arts moves on him. The jerk."

"He got you fired from your job?"

"Yeah, because he dumped me and then got mad at me for wearing a sexy dress to the gala event and getting attention. He insulted me, told me men would only want me for a quick fuck. Things like that," she rambled on then tried to get off of him.

"What the hell! My God, Millie, that's terrible."

"Hey, it is what it is. My track record with men isn't really good."

"Well, my brothers and I aren't like that. We would never put you down or hurt you like that."

"Really?" She crossed her arms in front of her chest and stared at him.

"Yeah, really," he stated firmly and as if he were surprised that she could question their sincerity or respect of women or of her.

"Oh, so then why can't I touch you when we're making love? How come you kept this T-shirt on?" she pushed, and he appeared shocked.

"That's different."

"How so?"

"I'm not ready to discuss it."

"Well, I didn't want to hang out all of my dirty laundry but oops…it's too late now, isn't it? Fess up, Dalton."

"You are a pushy little thing."

"And you're trying to avoid this conversation."

"I need some time, Millie. It's been a long time since I've been with a woman."

"Some woman hurt you? She cheat on you or something?"

"No. It's nothing like that. I have some issues to work out."

She was silent a moment as she sensed his upset with her. He really had some personal struggles going on. Well, that fact made her feel like less of the odd one out.

"Okay. I'll give you some time, but know that I want to touch you. I like you. I like the attraction I feel for you and your brothers. I feel safe in your arms. Ah, forget it. I don't want you to think I'm crazy or clingy."

He pulled her against him and hugged her tight.

"Never feel that way. You feel great in my arms, too, sweetness." He kissed her shoulder then stood with her still in his arms.

"Ready for some supper?"

"I think I need some clothes first."

"What for? You won't be wearing them long," he teased, and she gave him a light slap on his arm.

He lowered her to her feet and smiled.

"You get dressed. The bathroom is that way if you need to freshen up and I'll meet you downstairs."

"Okay," she stated as he grabbed his clothes and headed out of the room.

Millie took a deep breath and smiled. That was some serious lovemaking. She would never be the same again.

* * * *

"I hope you like your steak rare, darling, 'cause that's the only way Anthony knows how to cook them," Jeremy told Millie as they gathered around the table on the screened-in back porch. She had watched Jeremy and Anthony cooking on the outdoor kitchen grill while she, Hank, and Dalton set the table. Marco was getting the beers and lighting some candles.

Anthony placed the platter onto the table.

"What the hell is up with the candles, Marco?" Anthony asked.

"Hey, it's romantic," he replied.

Anthony was about to say something, but then he looked at Millie and she smiled as she lowered her head to stifle her laugh. Marco took a seat next to her as he placed a platter of roasted potatoes onto the table.

Anthony blew out the candles. "Save the romance for one on one. I'm not sitting by candlelight with all of you in a romantic setting," he snapped.

She looked up wide eyed and surprised at his macho, male attitude toward the candles. But before she could say anything, she felt Marco's hand on her knee slowly moving up her thigh and under her dress. He leaned into her neck and kissed along her skin. "Candlelight is good ambience for making out with my woman at the dinner table."

She closed her eyes, absorbing the scent of his cologne and the feel of his fingertips that were about to reach her mound. When his fingertips touched her bare pussy, he paused and pulled slightly away so he could look into her eyes. At that same moment Dalton sat beside her.

"What's wrong?" Hank asked from across the table.

Dalton held her gaze and Millie felt her cheeks warm.

"Baby, you're not wearing any panties," Marco stated.

Millie heard forks drop and then Dalton chuckle. She glanced around the table and all the men stared at her, looking very sexy.

"I couldn't find them. They seemed to have disappeared," she told them. She had a feeling one of the men hid them from her on purpose. She just wasn't sure who because they were all more than capable of such a trick.

Anthony nibbled his bottom lip then picked his fork back up to slice into one very thick, large, juicy steak.

"I think I like where this is going. As a matter of fact, I think we should start setting some rules for our woman, what do y'all think?" Anthony asked then brought a piece of steak up to his mouth and took a bite. The others began to do the same and she felt Marco press a finger to her clit then pull her earlobe into his mouth. His warm breath and firm touch to her most sensitive flesh had her pussy weeping for more.

"First rule, baby, is never wear panties around us."

Oh Lord, he didn't just say that.

Dalton leaned over to caress her other thigh then slowly move his hand between her legs where Marco now vacated so he could eat his steak.

"We want this pussy accessible at all times. It belongs to us. Every part of you does," Dalton told her then brushed his finger across her already swollen clit. His Texas accent added magnetism to his demand.

Millie moaned.

"I think you should eat up, Millie. You're going to need your energy," Jeremy chimed in and Dalton pulled his hand slowly from under her dress.

Millie was strung tight as a bow and these five men sat there looking smug and content as they ate their monstrous-looking steaks. She wouldn't beg for another one of their fingers to press up into her needy cunt. No. She was stronger than this. Instead, she shrugged her shoulders, picked up her fork and knife, and began to eat her steak even though all she wanted to do was come.

* * * *

Anthony listened as his brothers talked about their family and establishing their individual businesses. He was impressed with how ladylike and sweet Millie was. Every so often she would dab her napkin against her mouth or smile shyly toward one of his brothers' comments. She was listening intently and adding her thoughts here and there. Conversation ran smoothly and as if they had known her for a long time. It interested him that she could be so feminine and delicate, yet she was practically a black belt in martial arts.

"So, Millie, what did you do when you worked in New York?" Jeremy asked her.

"I was a fundraising coordinator for a large firm."

"What kind of projects did you work on?" Hank asked.

"I was working on one to raise money for a women's shelter. I actually succeeded and we were celebrating a few nights before I had to leave. It is going to be a great shelter where women can go for a fresh start. They can even get help with training and education so they can work and support their families if they have any."

"That sounds wonderful," Dalton added.

"What made you get into that?" Marco asked.

"I needed a better job. I make my own jewelry and worked in a jewelry store for a while, hoping that the owner would come through on his promise to display my stuff, but it never happened. It was frustrating and I needed a better-paying job. I was doing the self-defense classes at the time and they were costly. I had volunteered a lot at the local women's shelter and then met a woman who worked for the company that financially supported them. One thing led to another and I got a job interview."

"So you've always volunteered?" Anthony asked, and he watched as Millie placed her hands on her lap and took a deep breath. When she looked up he thought she looked like an angel.

"I started volunteering at the family shelter to offer support to women who were battered or raped. It was difficult, but I felt I could offer some sort of support since I was a survivor. You see, after the attack by Frank, I was hospitalized for some time and that time alone, healing made me see that I was given a second chance at life. I wanted to continue to help, but I wanted to make that help more accessible, and I also wanted to follow my dream of selling my homemade jewelry."

"That's great, Millie. I bet the boutique in town would display your stuff and sell it for you on commission," Jeremy added.

She smiled.

"I should go in to talk with them. I brought a lot of my things, but some of my tools are still in New York. I guess eventually I'll have to go back there to gather my stuff."

"No. You're not going back there. Not until Frank is captured," Marco stated firmly. She turned toward him and Anthony felt the same words on his lips. He wouldn't let her leave Pearl. He wasn't going to take a chance of losing her nor letting that psycho ex-boyfriend of hers find her.

"Marco, I left in a hurry. I had no choice and I'll need my things."

"You'll work it out another way. Don't think about that now. You're staying here and that's not up for discussion," Marco replied.

"Don't do that."

Marco stared at her. "Don't do what?"

"Tell me what to do or not to do."

"I will tell you what to do because you're part of me now and part of us," he replied.

Millie stared at Marco and Anthony thought she was going to hit him or cry. He wasn't sure.

"Don't say things like that," she whispered and it made him wonder just how badly those two men from her past had hurt her.

"I speak the truth. You belong to the Lewis brothers now. We're going to take care of you and protect you. That includes guiding you in decisions that threaten what we're trying to protect."

"Marco, please. This is going so fast. I mean the sex was incredible. Really, *incredible*." She took a deep breath. Anthony had to hide his chuckle, but he felt a little tinge of fear. He hoped it meant more to her than just sex. It sure as hell did to him and his brothers. He'd never seen Marco so forward like this, or Dalton, for that matter.

"Glad you enjoyed it, baby, because it's only gonna get better," Marco replied and Millie smiled then lowered her eyes. They were all silent a moment.

* * * *

Hey, Millie, were you looking for these?" Jeremy asked with a smile as he pushed his chair back and sat there holding her sexy black thong with one finger in the air twirling it.

"Jeremy!"

He winked. Damn, she made him so fucking hot. Her attitude, her desire for a better life, and the need to be protected turned him on like nothing ever had before.

"Come here and get them if ya want them."

Millie took a deep breath but rose to the occasion.

That's my girl.

She sashayed that lovely body of hers around the table to where he sat with his legs wide and her thong on his finger. When she reached for it, he pulled it away.

"How much do you like these here panties, baby?"

She smiled at him as if she knew where he was headed. Damn, he was filled with erotic fantasies about Millie. One was going to be achieved right now.

"I like them a lot."

He could see out of the corner of his eye his brothers moving dishes and items off of the table and out of the way. Perhaps he wasn't the only one with this fantasy of spreading Millie over the table and fucking her from behind. She had an ass that was to die for. Jeremy reigned in his excitement and pulled Millie in.

"I think you should give me something I really like so you can get back what you really like."

"And that would be?" she asked.

"That pretty little pink pussy you're hiding under that blue dress, darling."

Her cheeks turned a shade of pink and he knew she wanted it, too.

"Just for my panties?" she asked.

"And of course for your pleasure."

"My pleasure?" she questioned, and he reached for her, pulling her between his legs. His hand went immediately up her dress and squeezed her ass to him.

"Fuck yeah, your pleasure. All of ours, baby. I want you and I want you now."

Millie closed her eyes and squeezed his shoulders. He kneaded her ass cheeks with his hands then ran a finger over the crevice of her ass. Millie's cheeks tightened and then he moved farther down to press a digit to her already wet cunt.

"Fuck yeah, you're wet already. Do you know how I want you?" he asked as he rotated his finger and thrust in and out of her pussy. She parted her legs to give him better access and his dick swelled up in his jeans.

"How?" she asked in a somewhat quivering voice. Her vaginal muscles gripped his finger. She was ready to come.

"I want to bend you over that table and fuck this sweet, wet pussy from behind while my brothers watch."

She was silent, her breathing rapid as she began to move her hips against his hand.

"Can't they join in?" she asked, shocking them all.

"Hell yeah!" Marco stated and the sound of chairs moving filled the air.

Jeremy pulled his fingers from her then lifted her dress up over her head. She was completely bare to them. He stood up, towering over her small frame, and drew her body against his own. He leaned down to cover her mouth as she moaned against him.

It was a rush to try and devour her with his kisses and let her know how hot and turned on she made him.

He pulled her mouth from his, turned her around, and pressed her body over the table.

"Spread your legs," he ordered, and she did.

There she was, bent over the handmade mahogany table with her ass in the air, her thighs spread, juices dripping down from her pussy and her palms flat on the table.

He unzipped his pants and pushed them down, whipping out his cock. One look at his brothers and he saw they were doing the same thing.

Millie's face was by the right edge of the table where Marco now stood just a few inches from her.

Jeremy ran the show and he was all fired up about it.

He pressed the palm of his hands on Millie's ass and began to massage her cheeks.

"Open that mouth up wide, baby, I think Marco has something for you."

Millie did as she was told and opened her mouth, causing her breasts to fully lay out on the table. Dalton, Anthony, and Hank sat there looking stunned.

"Fuck, baby, that's it. You can take it all," Marco whispered as his cock disappeared inside her mouth.

"I love this ass, Millie. One day real soon we're all going to fuck this ass," Jeremy told her as he rubbed the tip of his penis over her pussy, wetting it with her cum before pushing slightly against the puckered hole.

"Oh, sweet Jesus!" Anthony stated holding his cock in his hand. Jeremy smiled.

"Would you like that, baby? Maybe a little taste right now?" he asked and she pushed her ass back against his cock as she moaned against Marco's cock.

"Shit, her mouth is amazing. I'm about to come already," Marco stated.

Jeremy proceeded to rub the tip of his cock against her pussy. The sounds she was making were killing his intention to go slow. She was moving back and forth over Marco's cock and Jeremy couldn't take it.

"Fuck, baby, you are something else."

He lined his cock up with her pussy from behind and pushed in, filling her to the hilt. The table rocked with every thrust and stroke he took banging into her from behind. Marco screamed his release, calling Millie's name, but Jeremy was lost in a rhythm and his own desire to claim his woman.

Jeremy saw Marco move and then Anthony take his place, but he wasn't certain. He was beginning to lose his own focus with each thrust as he tried to hold off exploding.

"Fuck, baby, I can't take it. I'm coming, Millie!" Jeremy thrust into her, grabbing her hips hard. In and out he stroked her multiple times then exploded, pouring into her then pressing his body against hers.

When she moaned, he quickly stood up, pulling his cock from her in the process. She was eagerly sucking on Anthony's cock and now Hank took Jeremy's position.

* * * *

Hank knew he wasn't going to last long. Staring at Millie's breasts pressed hard against the table while she sucked on Marco then Anthony as Jeremy fucked her from behind was too damn amazing. Quickly, he leaned down to kiss her spine, but his cock was ready to explode.

"Damn!" He hurriedly pressed into her pussy from behind and thrust into her. She pushed her ass back and actually countered each of his thrusts while she sucked on Anthony.

Anthony held her hair with his hand and began to thrust his hips slowly against her mouth.

"Oh, for crying out loud, I can't take her mouth." Anthony moaned then thrust again and again before he exploded.

It was too much for Hank and he followed suit, thrusting into Millie then losing his fight to hold off any longer. He exploded, pouring into her then hugging her tight.

* * * *

Millie was out of breath and she felt satiated. She never felt like this before. She was in love with these men, absolutely in love.

Then suddenly, she felt herself being turned around. It was Dalton and he looked fierce.

"I know you're probably tired," he began to say and she jumped up into his arms, wrapped her arms around his shoulders, and kissed him. He pressed her to the table again and ravaged her mouth. Her pussy clenched then moistened, ready for another round of sex. Dalton didn't have any pants on, but his shirt remained in place. She thought she could possibly touch him this time, but as if he read her mind he instantly grabbed her wrists and placed them above her head.

Her breasts pushed forward as he pulled his mouth from hers and began to suck on her right nipple.

He ass was over the edge of the table, her back flat on the hard surface of the table, and for crying out loud all she could think about was Dalton's thick, hard cock fucking her hard.

"Please, Dalton," she begged and then he began to lick and suck her left nipple, pulling and teasing her mercilessly.

"Oh!" she moaned and rolled her head side to side, but she kept her hands above her head as she was told to do.

His tongue moved along her cleavage to her belly as he used his hands to spread her thighs wider.

"So delicious. Eating on this table will never be the same again."

She felt the tip of his cock against her clit and then he pressed into her. She gasped, knowing how thick and large he was and that her poor pussy would certainly be sore tomorrow, but she didn't care. She was entirely turned on right now.

"Mine," he stated then thrust deeply into her. He held himself there a moment, his hands on her hips, his thumbs slightly pressing into her flesh.

"Fuck me, Dalton. Don't go slow. I need fast and hard," she told him, and he growled then pulled back and thrust in hard like she asked for. He was relentless with his strokes. She was finding it too difficult to keep her hands back and away from him.

"Oh God, Dalton, please let me touch you."

"No. Stay still, Millie, I'm almost there, baby, please." He increased his thrusts until the table squeaked and he no longer could hold back.

"Millie!" he yelled then poured himself into her, thrusting three more times until he couldn't move. He clung to her and she wanted so desperately to touch him. She felt tears in her eyes.

"Please, Dalton," she whispered, and he looked up toward her from her chest and nodded his head.

She ran her hands along his blond hair then to his shoulders. She wished he wasn't wearing the shirt. But she wouldn't push. He said he had his reasons and one day he would share them with her.

"So perfect," he said then kissed her sweetly on the lips before helping her to sit up.

Marco walked closer to her and helped her put on her dress. When she was standing before all five of them, she felt content and alive.

"You're a dream come true, Millie. The Lewis brothers' prayers have been answered," Marco whispered then took her hand and led her out of the room.

* * * *

Millie woke up feeling content and a bit sore. She had a wonderful time with Dalton, Hank, Anthony, Jeremy, and Marco last night. The dinner was excellent, the conversation fun, and dessert had been just as good the second time around as it had been the first. She smiled as she thought about them. Never in her wildest imagination did she think that she would end up in a ménage relationship. It was funny how she pushed Stacy when she first arrived in Pearl. Now she understood Stacy's reservations when she had first come to Pearl just like Anna's and, of course, Lena's.

Slowly, she got out of bed and stretched her muscles. Parts that hadn't been used so thoroughly in a long time ached, but she couldn't help but feel content. She also couldn't wait to see the guys, starting with Jeremy and Anthony over at the Triple C this morning. As a matter of fact, she never did get those panties back.

She chuckled.

She also wanted to meet the two new women that arrived yesterday. She hadn't met them yet and wanted them to feel welcome. Millie made her way to the bathroom and started the water in the shower.

* * * *

"Good morning, sexy," Jeremy whispered, sneaking up behind Millie and wrapping an arm around her waist. Millie gasped as she was caught off guard.

"Jeremy, quit sneaking up on me."

"Hey, now why would I do that when I get such a pleasant reaction from you?" he teased as he gave her breast a squeeze, and she felt her cheeks warm with embarrassment. She quickly glanced around to be sure no one had seen and there stood Anthony, arms crossed and a huge smile on his face.

"Quit teasing her, Jeremy. Can't you see she's embarrassed by your show of public affection?" Anthony approached them.

"Hey, I am not. I don't mind a kiss or hug, but to cop a feel in public is a different story."

Jeremy squeezed the arm around her midsection tighter and kissed her neck.

"As I recall, you kind of enjoyed a little public exhibition last night." He thrust his cock slightly against her rear and Millie gasped.

"She sure did, didn't ya, sweetness?" Anthony asked as he cupped her cheeks then leaned down to kiss her deeply on the lips. Of course she weakened in their arms, and before long, Jeremy was reaching between her and Anthony to pull and tease her nipples. She pulled her mouth from Anthony.

"Someone might see. Stop, Jeremy. It isn't fair." She practically moaned.

"No one is coming into the rec center now. They're all meeting by the main office."

"Oh God, I was supposed to be there, too. What time is it?" she blurted out and tried to get out of Jeremy's hold.

"Oh, about time we check to make sure you're following rule number one."

"What?" she asked and then she felt Jeremy's hands caress over her breast, down her belly, to the button on her jeans.

She pretended to be concerned, but the truth was she decided that not wearing underwear, as the men demanded, turned her on. So much that just thinking about it had her rubbing her finger over the V between her legs, liking the sensation the jeans caused.

"Hot damn, baby. Anthony, she isn't wearing any panties."

Anthony cupped her cheeks again as Jeremy worked the button and zipper to her jeans.

"Good girls get rewarded, darling," Anthony whispered and his dark brown eyes sparkled with mischief.

"What are you—"

Before she could ask, Anthony was kissing her again as Jeremy pressed his fingers down her jeans to her pussy. He hummed against her ear and she tightened her body, trying to hold off from coming like this. But Jeremy was on a mission. A single digit turned into two and soon she was begging for release. Anthony devoured her moans while Jeremy brought her to release. Two more pumps and then he pressed hard on her clit and Millie moaned against Anthony's mouth. Jeremy didn't stop despite the fact that Millie just came so hard from his ministrations. Her hips were still rocking against his fingers and his cock felt awfully hard and thick against her ass.

"Oh fuck, Millie."

She couldn't believe it. Jeremy was going to come. She helped him get there by reaching back as she thrust her ass back against his cock and leaned forward a little. The move caused Anthony to release her lips, but it also got the results she was looking for.

"You naughty little witch." Jeremy grunted then came in his pants with his hand still cupping her mound and a digit still inserted in her.

"Now that was fucking hot. I can't wait to tell the others that Millie made you come in your pants," Anthony teased and Jeremy released his hold on Millie then tried to shift his legs.

"Ah hell, give me the keys to the truck."

"What for?" Anthony asked as Millie fixed her jeans.

"I need to go back home real quick."

Anthony laughed as he tossed the truck keys to Jeremy.

Jeremy kissed Millie then headed out. As Millie began to head out, too, Anthony wrapped an arm around her waist and held her against him, her back to his chest.

He whispered softly against her ear, "You're amazing, Millie. I'll see you tonight."

He tapped her on the ass then sent her on the way.

She turned and winked at him. "You betcha, cowboy."

* * * *

"Marco, I need you in here," Wyatt yelled as he was walking back to the desk in the sheriff's department. Marco was in a damn good mood this morning and it had everything to do with a certain brown-haired bombshell.

"What's going on, Wyatt?" Marco asked as he approached the sheriff by his office door.

"I need to speak with you. Come on in and take a seat."

Marco didn't like the feeling he had. Something was up. Wyatt had been on the phone for quite some time this morning.

He watched as Wyatt closed the office door, ran a hand through his hair, then leaned against the front of his desk. Wyatt stared at Marco.

"You and your brothers making some progress with Millie?"

Marco hadn't expected that and he gave Wyatt a strange look.

"Well, what I mean to ask is that is she learning to trust y'all? Will she let one of you or whoever stay with her at her cottage?"

"Wyatt, what the hell are you asking this for?"

Wyatt took a deep breath then released it.

"I just got an update from New York."

"And?"

"And I'm concerned about Millie's safety even more. I think she shouldn't be staying alone in that cottage."

"Why not? What happened in the case to make you feel this way, Wyatt?"

"Did she tell you about her boyfriend, Stewart Thomas?"

"A little bit. From what she said he was a real asshole. He made her quit martial arts and he put her down all the time. Sounded more like verbal abuse than physical, but I still gathered him to be an asshole."

"Yeah, well, he also got her fired from her job. Plus Anna and Stacy said he told Millie some nasty things. Anyway, it appeared that Frank found out about Stewart."

Marco sat forward in his seat.

"And what?"

"Stewart Thomas was found murdered early this morning around 3:00 a.m."

"What? They think Frank did it?"

"They know Frank did it. He taped it with Dr. Perkin's cell phone. Detective Flynn received a copy of the video along with shots of Perkins tied to a chair, beaten and bloody."

"Holy shit, Wyatt. How did they find the body? What about the doctor?"

"Stewart Thomas was found in a motel on the outskirts of Alabama."

"Alabama! Damn it, Wyatt, he's headed here. He knows where she's at."

"It seems so. They've got detectives following the trail, but now the FBI is involved, too. Thomas sent them a copy of the video and apparently he killed a retired agent who happened to be staying in the motel. The investigators believe that the retired agent became suspicious of Frank and went to check him out by asking some questions. Frank must have convinced him that things were fine and the agent believed him. Then Frank returned later, snuck into the guy's motel room, and killed him. It was really gruesome, Marco." Wyatt ran his hand over his mouth as if talking about it made him feel sick.

"What? I want to know everything, Wyatt. My brothers and I will need to protect her."

"Frank tortured Stewart in front of the doctor then cut his heart out. He did the same thing to the retired agent."

"Holy fuck. This guy is really sick in the head."

"Which is why I'm very concerned. He's evaded capture. He's headed this way. He has to be because even on the video he talks about Millie."

"I want to see the video."

"No, you don't."

"I sure do. I want to know everything. You can't keep me out of the loop here just because she's my woman."

Wyatt smiled.

"I'm glad that you and your brothers found your woman, but I think knowing all the details and actually seeing the murder on tape will make things worse for you and for Millie. Take this seriously, but also let the woman live her life. We'll be stepping up security around the ranch. I suggest we go over to Millie right now and break the news then explain the new sleeping arrangements."

"Oh God, Wyatt. She's going to take this hard."

"I'm sure. We'll explain together."

* * * *

Millie had been speaking with one of the social workers, Cindy, in the main office. She had expressed concern over one of the new women that arrived last night named Sally.

"So, I think she really doesn't understand why we have this place. She seems to think that she can kick back for a while, get everything for free, and then leave whenever she wants to. She was also flirting with some of the ranch hands earlier. She shouldn't even be over toward that side of the ranch," Cindy stated.

"I'll go talk to her and explain the rules. If she's not interested in accepting the terms of the shelter, then she's gone. Rules are set for a reason."

"I appreciate it, Millie."

Millie headed out toward one of the cottages. She noticed Sally leaning over the fence, trying to gain Jeremy's attention. That just immediately pissed her off, but she pushed those initial feelings aside and went on over to speak with Sally.

"Sally?"

The redhead turned around and gave Millie the once-over.

"Who are you?"

"The name is Millie. I'm one of the main people involved with the shelter. I'd like to talk to you."

"What about? Can't you see I'm busy checking out the local attractions?"

Millie swallowed her annoyance.

"First of all, you aren't supposed to be over here flirting with any men. Secondly, I think you and I need to go over the rules."

"What, are you jealous? Afraid I'll gather me up a handful of good-looking cowboys and you'll be left a fat old maid?"

"Now you listen here, Sally. This is not a place for women who are looking to fool around and end up in trouble again. This is a place for women in need of support and shelter after sustaining abuse and neglect."

"I heard what this place is all about. I can stay if I want to. It's government-funded anyway. It's not like you own the place."

"Actually, it's not government-funded, and I do own the place along with my sisters. If you can't abide by our rules, then you're out of here. Take it or leave it."

"Hey, Millie. We gonna get together for lunch?" Jeremy asked as he tipped his hat toward Millie then Sally.

Millie felt her cheeks redden as Sally gave her a smirk that said it all. She was busted and now Sally would purposely flirt with Jeremy to get at Millie. Millie needed to talk with Anna and Stacy and get Sally out of there.

"Sure, Jeremy. I was headed back now. I just want to remind Sally that she needs to remain in the designated area of the facility."

Jeremy must have picked up on Millie's attitude because he gave Sally the once-over then nodded his head at Millie.

"I'll meet you out front by the office."

"So, that's your boyfriend, huh? How about the other one? You got ahold of him, too? Because if ya don't, I sure would like to sink my teeth into him. Anthony, I think his name is."

Millie felt her blood boiling. Damn it, why did this bitch have to come here looking for trouble?

"They're both mine, and by the way you're acting, I don't expect you to be around here for much longer. I'll send one of the deputies to explain the rules then, honey." Millie walked away. She could hear Sally cursing her out, but at least she got the last word in.

She also figured maybe Sally was acting so tough and trying to cause a fight because of the trouble she was in. Maybe she would have Cindy speak with her one-on-one again and get to the bottom of things. She personally knew how difficult it was to talk about certain experiences in life. It had taken Millie so long to confide in Anna and Stacy about Frank's abuse, so long that it nearly cost her her life. As if that hadn't been enough, Millie didn't even tell her best friends about Stewart. If she had, she may have wound up in Pearl after Frank's assault. Millie shook her head as Stewart entered her mind. He was a mean, self-centered, egotistical jerk who didn't deserve to be respected. People like him destroyed innocent lives on a daily basis.

Millie felt herself getting angry again. She didn't know why, considering he was thousands of miles away and she would never see him again. It was surprising that she even got involved with him to begin with. Good looks and charm could only go so far before personality kicked in.

She laughed. At least she could chuckle about it now. Weeks ago, she cried her eyes out in despair pathetically when he dumped her. His angry, hurtful words were clear in her mind, yet the weak, foolish woman she was allowed that, him, to get inside of her mind. Never again. She was done being weak. She was finished feeling worthless and out of control of her life and her destiny. She was a good person who loved people. Especially people who needed some extra help.

Millie glanced back over her shoulder and saw Cindy opening the front office door. Millie smiled at her. She was going to ask Cindy to please talk with Sally again. Maybe she was just having a difficult time telling her or anyone else how she wound up in Pearl and the shelter.

"Millie, I just got a call from Deputy Lewis. He needs to meet you up at the main house."

Millie instantly smiled. She was dating a deputy of Pearl now. Damn, did that do something to her insides.

Millie waved.

"I'll head back there now," she said, and instantly thoughts of last night with the Lewis brothers filled her mind. She was living in a fantasy world. Like something from a storybook except erotic romance style, with several handsome, sexy princes and one not-so-perfect princess.

She giggled to herself. *I wonder what Anthony, Jeremy, Dalton, Hank, or even Marco would think about that?*

Chapter 16

Marco stood alongside Wyatt as Millie approached from the side of the house. As soon as his eyes locked with hers he felt a little better now that she was in his sight and safe. He wasn't sure how he was going to handle this situation. He cared for her. In fact, if he wasn't mistaken, he was in love for the first time in his life.

"Hi, Wyatt. Hi, Marco." Millie waved as she approached the steps, made her way to Wyatt first, and kissed his cheek. Then she blushed as she smiled toward Marco.

He immediately reached out his hand for her to take it. She did, shyly, and he pulled her closer to him. "Hey, beautiful," he whispered then leaned down to kiss her softly on the mouth. He made it quick because of Wyatt and the situation, but he sure as hell wasn't happy about it. He'd like nothing more than to take his woman back to the Lewis ranch and protect her from the world. It was selfish and also unacceptable. Millie would never allow that. He and his brothers had work to do in convincing her she needed their protection now.

"So what's going on?" she asked.

"Let's go inside and sit. I think Max is pouring us some sweet tea," Wyatt stated then opened the screen door. Millie's facial expression changed as she glanced at both Wyatt and Marco.

She pulled her bottom lip between her teeth and took a deep breath. "Okay."

When they walked inside and through to the kitchen, sure enough, Max was pouring ice-cold tea into glasses. He was in uniform and no one else was around.

Millie sat down and Marco sat down beside her despite the fact that his hands shook in anger. Millie was gorgeous with her long brown hair and dark blue eyes. She didn't deserve this situation. No one did.

"Millie, there's been an update in the investigation back in New York," Wyatt began to explain and Millie nodded her head then looked at Marco. He reached over to take her hand and squeezed it before laying it on his thigh. He hoped that she didn't feel his body shaking. He feared for her life.

"Your facial expression is telling me this is bad. Let's get on with it," she whispered, and Wyatt nodded his head.

He began to explain about Stewart disappearing and then turning up murdered.

She pulled her hand away from Marco's and covered a gasp with her hand. As Wyatt explained the situation without giving too many gory details, yet indicating the danger and seriousness of the situation, Millie began to shake her head, and then she looked at Marco.

"We're going to protect you. He won't be able to find you here."

Millie stood up and walked toward the counter. She gripped the surface and Marco waited for her to do something like cry or scream in frustration, but instead she shocked him as well as Max and Wyatt.

She turned toward them.

"Frank killed Stewart because of me?"

* * * *

Millie felt almost numb. She stared at the three men in the room, not really seeing them at all but instead, images of Stewart. Every good thing he ever did crossed her mind. When they first met, his compliments, his attention to every detail about her appearance and style of clothing. She couldn't think of any of the insulting, verbally abusive comments at the moment. She felt like shit. She had said such hurtful, mean things about him in her mind. She had hoped that he would suffer. She had said that. She wanted others to know how much of an asshole he was, and now this? Frank found out about Stewart. He killed him because they were lovers and Frank wanted Millie all to himself.

You're mine and we belong together for eternity.

Frank's words came crashing into her mind.

She felt someone grab her by the shoulders. Opening her eyes, she looked up and up until she locked gazes with blue eyes. *Marco.*

"I don't know what thoughts are running through that head of yours, Millie, but this is not your fault. This guy, Frank, is one crazy bastard. He is going to get caught."

She shook her head. Frank was conniving, slick, and manipulative. When she thought of him in the past, she thought of the song "Bad to the Bone," and he was out of his mind.

"He's in Alabama and obviously headed this way. He knows where I'm staying. I won't bring danger here to the Triple C. I won't put the family at risk, baby Hope, or anyone else, for that matter."

"You're not leaving here," Marco stated firmly. "The FBI are involved now, Millie. They'll get to him before he steps foot here, and if not, we've got your back."

"The FBI?"

"He killed a retired agent." Wyatt began to explain what happened. All she could imagine was poor Stewart being tortured and then killed. He was probably scared out of his mind.

"Poor Stewart," she whispered.

Marco gripped her shoulders.

"Poor Stewart? He was an asshole to you. He hurt you almost as badly as Frank. Don't feel sorry for hating him and think that you're a bad person."

The tears hit her eyes. How the hell did Marco do that? How could he read her mind?

"I do feel bad. I can't help it, Marco. I feel terrible that Frank killed him. What about Clare and now this innocent FBI agent? It's all because of me. It's my fault. Frank told me things. He swore that we would always be together. Oh, God!" Millie pulled out of Marco's arms, getting away from him far across the room. She squeezed her arms around herself and all three men stared at her.

"Millie?" Marco whispered, taking a step toward her, but she shook her head.

"Honey, what is it?" Wyatt asked.

"I can't see you and your brothers anymore, Marco. He'll come here and he'll kill all five of you."

* * * *

"Marco, calm down. She's upset."

"I can't calm down. Her thinking this way is asinine. This fucking piece of shit will not come here and kill me or my brothers nor will we let him lay a hand on Millie."

"I understand you're upset and angry, but think about where Millie is coming from."

"I get it. I do, Wyatt, and she has to see that she's not alone and we will protect her. We love her."

"Have you told her that?"

"No."

"Well, start there. Make her see that what you have between the six of you is real and forever. Make her understand that you're part of her life. Get to it and convince her to keep each of you by her side. Max, Eric, myself, Charlie, Ben, and the other deputies will watch over the women and children. You guys watch over Millie. I'll call Detective Flynn when I get back to the department. I promise to keep you abreast of any updates."

"I appreciate that, Wyatt." Marco shook Wyatt's hand.

"It will work out. She's being stubborn just like her two best friends. Remember that she's hurting inside. It's tough to put aside the jealousy and anger of the situation, but you need to for Millie's sake and for your own control. Handling this professionally will help you keep a clear head and protect her," Max offered and Marco nodded his head then shook Ben's hand.

Marco pulled out his cell phone. He was going to need reinforcements.

* * * *

Anna and Stacy walked Millie out toward Marco's truck. It had taken some convincing, but Millie accepted their insight and decided she needed some time alone, but not necessarily completely alone, in the cottage. Marco would stay with her until the others arrived after work.

She gave them each a hug and prayed that they would be fine and that Frank wouldn't make it to Pearl, never mind the Triple C ranch.

"Oh, what about my truck?" Millie asked.

"No worries, darling, Jeremy will drive it to your place later," Marco said as he closed the door to the sheriff's patrol truck.

She clasped her hands on her lap and remained quiet as Marco drove her back to the cottage. When they arrived at the cottage, some of her Aunt Marie's workhands were walking around the cottage, holding shotguns. She swallowed hard.

"What's that all about?"

"They're just keeping the area secure. You'll be protected at all times, Millie. Don't you worry about a thing."

"They're going to guard like that for how long? This is crazy. They're ranch hands and are supposed to be looking after the land and the horses. They have work to do."

"They offered to help out and the work around here won't be ignored. You'll have round-the-clock protection with me and my brothers."

"Oh, for crying out loud!" Millie opened the door to get out of the truck. She stomped up the steps and the cowboys waved to her. She waved back then pulled out her house key to unlock the door.

Once inside, she fisted her hands together and grunted angrily.

"Why? Why is this happening? How could he keep doing these things? I can't believe that Stewart is dead. No matter how much of an asshole he was to me, no one deserves to die like that. I can't live in fear, Marco. I can't do this. I'm going to lose my mind!" she ranted on and on, feeling so frustrated and angry, and then Marco pulled her into his arms and hugged her.

"Oh God, I'm sorry I'm being such a bitch. I don't know what I'm doing. He's got me crazy."

"Shh, honey, it's a normal reaction to all of this. You're handling it quite well, actually."

She pulled back ever so slightly, looking up and up until her eyes locked with his gorgeous blue ones.

"Kiss me, Marco," she whispered, and instantly he swooped down and covered her mouth with his own. He kissed her thoroughly and then released her lips, lifted her up against him, and hugged her to him. Millie wrapped her legs around his waist and held on tight.

"I love you, sweetness, and I'm going to take care of you."

She sniffled then kissed his neck.

"It's crazy, but I love you, too, and your brothers." Then she chuckled.

He pulled back a little, holding her up against him. She was half crying and half laughing.

"What is it?"

"That statement just sounded so odd and funny, yet perfectly sane."

"That's because it's real and we all love you very much."

Millie leaned forward and kissed Marco again.

"I'd better start making some coffee and pulling out food for dinner. I have the feeling this little cottage is going to be crowded very shortly."

"Don't bother. Just go pack some clothes for the next few days and anything else you might need."

"What? Why would I do that?" she asked.

"Because you're going to the Lewis estate."

Millie placed her hands on her hips. "No, I'm not. You all have jobs to do and babysitting me is not one of them."

"This is not up for discussion. You either come willingly or I'll handcuff you and take you as my prisoner. Either way, I don't care." She was shocked. He stalked toward her, holding out a pair of metal handcuffs he retrieved from his waist.

"You know, I think I might like handcuffing you then bending you over that table of yours while I fuck you."

Millie felt her cheeks warm and, damn it, her pussy flex with anticipation. He strode closer to her, gently using the handcuffs to caress along her arm and then her breast, tickling her nipple.

"As a matter of fact, I think when we get over to my place, I'm going to handcuff you to the bed and keep you there, spread open wide for my pleasure."

"Oh God, Marco."

"Yeah, baby, you, naked and bound with this pretty pink pussy dripping with your cream would drive me fucking insane."

Marco rubbed the handcuffs gently between her thighs against the V of her legs. His other hand grabbed her left hip and he pressed against her.

"You feel how fucking hard I am? I'd keep you bound and aroused every fucking minute of every fucking day, Millie."

He leaned in and kissed her hard on the mouth. She weakened in his embrace as she grabbed on to his shoulders and held on to him. He released her lips to suck along her neck. Millie rubbed her mound against his cock. She gyrated against him until he held her hips in place.

"You ain't gonna make me come in my pants like you did to Jeremy." His Texas accent was extra thick, making her blush.

She shook her head and felt her cheeks heat. She was the one coming in her panties. If she were wearing any.

"You know about that?"

"Honey, there aren't any secrets between us brothers. Plus, I saw Jeremy back at the house this morning while I was leaving. I asked him what he was doing back home and he carried on about some wild sexual fantasy come true. Anthony called me and told me what happened. You are some piece of work, darling, and tonight, we're going to see just how wild and wet we can make you."

He kissed her again, lifting her up so she straddled his waist. He was thorough and she felt on fire with need. Then he set her feet down onto the rug. As she turned toward the kitchen, he gave a light smack to her ass.

"Damn, woman, you sure can fill out a pair of blue jeans."

That made her smile and forget for a moment that danger wasn't too far from her doorstep.

Chapter 17

"Why are you making me do this? I don't want to. I can't take it anymore. Just kill me!" Dr. Perkins screamed as Frank held her face with one hand while he shoved the recorder near her mouth.

"Say it, bitch! Say it or I swear I'm going to cut you up in pieces."

She cried out in pain and fear.

He squeezed her face tighter. He wanted to kill her. He didn't need her anymore but for this one last thing to ensure his plan worked. She knew that, but what choice did she have?

"Now! Say the fucking words I told you to."

She sobbed, her voice shaking as he hit the record button.

"This…this is Dr. Sheila Perkins. Oh, please, he's going to kill me. He's just outside the door. Please!" she screamed, and he pressed stop on the recorder then shoved her face away from him.

"Good girl. Now I can get everything ready."

He stepped away from her, leaving the knife on the bedside table. She glanced at him. He was so lost in his vengeance and desire to get Millie that he felt invincible and didn't even believe Sheila had it in her to defend herself.

Her arm was broken, her body bruised and battered, but she wasn't going to die weak. Sheila knew she was as good as dead. She wished she could have helped Millie, but the poor woman wouldn't have a chance.

Sheila reached for the knife.

"I hate you and you deserve to die. You'll never have Millie. Ever!" she yelled as Frank turned toward her and laughed.

"You're weak, woman. You don't have it in you to kill. Put down the knife and shut the fuck up."

Sheila felt the anger tear through her body. She shoved herself off the bed and lunged toward Frank. She knew the knife hit his side, but barely scraped it. He didn't even flinch and now he was on top of her on the motel room floor with the blade at her throat.

"Now I get to say your line, doc, since I'm running this session."

"What?"

"Time's up, doc."

* * * *

Marco pulled the cruiser up in front of his house thirty minutes later. There was Anthony, standing on the front driveway, talking with some other men. They weren't familiar looking at all.

Marco gave a nod in their direction as he rounded the front of the car to open Millie's door.

He placed an arm around her waist and led her toward the men.

Anthony immediately pulled her into his arms and hugged her to him.

"You doing okay, darling?" he asked in a husky voice, and she squeezed him back then tried to pull away a little. She wasn't sure who these other men were.

As if reading her mind, Anthony introduced them.

"These are friends of ours. Kevin and Mathew Lawkins."

"Howdy, ma'am." Both men reached their hands out for her to shake. She did. They were very tall. Almost as tall as Marco.

"This is Jimmy and his brother, Taylor Morris," Anthony introduced the other two men.

"Nice to meet you, Millie," Jimmy stated.

"Nice to meet you all as well," she replied, but she still wondered who they were.

"Dalton called them so we could go over some security measures." Marco offered the information. Anthony didn't seem to want to tell her what was going on.

"Security measures?" she inquired then thought about Dalton. He had wanted to leave the dojo with Hank, but she had insisted that they remain working. She appreciated their concern and desire to be with her, but they had work, businesses, and lives, too. This threat from Frank shouldn't make them have to change their routines.

"Yes, ma'am. We were in the service with Hank, Dalton, and Marco. We're back home on some R & R and stopped by to talk with Dalton when he told us about the situation. We're offering our time and services for when your men can't be present," Jimmy stated and he looked her over, as did the other three men. Then they smiled.

"I really don't think that will be necessary," Millie replied, feeling that she would need to discuss a few things with Marco and Anthony as well as Dalton, Hank, and Jeremy.

Then she felt Anthony squeeze her waist. He began to turn her toward the house.

"I appreciate you coming by. We'll talk more later."

Anthony reached to shake the men's hands, and as Marco escorted them to their trucks, Anthony walked her into the house.

She was feeling a bit on edge. She didn't like being told what to do or patronized. She thought she was handling the situation pretty damn well. As a matter of fact, she hadn't had any time alone to think about what Frank had done and the fact that he could very well be headed here. If she thought on that too much, she would begin to panic.

The moment Anthony had her inside the house, he pulled her into his arms again and hugged her to him. She was surprised.

"Damn, Millie, I was so concerned. I couldn't wait to hold you in my arms, too…"

He spoke against her neck then chin before covering her mouth, unable to finish his sentence. He ravaged her as he lifted her by her thighs and pressed her against the wall. She kissed him back, wrapping her legs around his waist, running her fingers through his hair, and absorbing his take-charge attitude.

In some distant part of her mind, she thought she heard the door open then close. Then Anthony slowly pulled his lips from her mouth while he cupped her right breast with one hand, while his other hand held her under her left ass cheek and against the wall.

"I'm not letting you out of my sight," he told her, his brown eyes looking so damn dark they almost appeared black. He clenched his teeth. She could tell as his facial expression hardened. Millie caressed his shoulders and then his chest.

"You need to calm down," she whispered.

He looked to the right, to where Marco stood with a similar expression.

"Calm down? How the hell could you ask me to calm down? I was worried sick about you. I can't get the thoughts out of my head, Millie. He's out there. He's brutally murdered multiple people."

"Put me down, Anthony," she whispered to him. He grabbed her tighter, his hands on her hips, the bulge between his legs snug against her mound.

"No, I'm not letting you down. You look at me, woman, when I'm speaking to you."

She was shocked by his tone, but she looked at him. Their gazes locked.

"You belong to me and my brothers. We are going to protect you and be here for you at all times. I am not going to take any chances."

He was so dominant and bossy, but she wasn't afraid of him. She knew that he cared for her deeply, just as she cared for him.

Millie reached toward his cheeks and cupped his face.

"You can't let him get to you, Ant. You can't give him that kind of control of you. It will eat you up and it will put a wall between the two of us. Please, baby, please listen to me. I love you." She pressed her lips to his.

Anthony hugged her tighter then she caressed his cheeks as she slowly pulled her lips from his. She leaned her forehead against his forehead and he shook his head.

"Stubborn woman."

"Stubborn man," she countered, and he chuckled, then pulled her away from the wall and lowered her feet to the floor.

Marco approached with a smile on his face.

"I have to head back into town for a few hours. Anthony is staying with you. Jeremy will be home later as well as Hank and Dalton. We'll work out a schedule."

"We'll discuss that together later, Marco. Your jobs come first," Millie stated.

Marco wrapped an arm around her waist and hoisted her up against him. "You come first." He quickly kissed her before he released her to Anthony and gave her a light smack on her backside. There would be no talking to Marco right now. Later on, when all the men were together, she would set them straight.

* * * *

Anthony locked the door then he grabbed her bag with one hand and her hand with the other as he led her through the living room to the stairs.

"Since I'm here to welcome you into our home for your stay, you get to sleep in my bed tonight."

Millie chuckled. Anthony seemed quite pleased with the idea and she wondered if his brothers knew yet.

"How do you think the others might feel about that?"

"Oh, who cares? I've got you and that's all that matters right now."

Millie tightened her hold on his hand, making him pause at his bedroom door.

"They won't get upset, will they?" she asked, worried about jealousy. Although they hadn't minded sharing her one bit and were knowledgeable about ménage relationships, she wasn't sure. This was the first and, God willing, the last time she would be in a relationship with five men.

He pulled her against his chest and stared down into her eyes.

"We enjoy sharing you and loving you. If we couldn't handle it, we wouldn't have started this relationship. Got it?" he asked in the firm, boss-like tone she was getting used to with Anthony.

"Got it, boss," she retorted, and he chuckled as he pulled her into the bedroom.

"I think I like the sound of that."

He tossed her bag to the side then grabbed for her, pressing her body hard against his own.

"As a matter of fact, I think you need some bossing around, especially here in my bedroom."

Oh Lord, what have I just unleashed by calling Anthony boss?

He made quick work with his hands, divesting her of her clothing. She attempted to unbutton his shirt, but he was in charge and she couldn't get a move in edgewise.

When he pushed her jeans down and saw she had no panties on, he tore his shirt from his chest.

"Fuck, baby, just knowing that you're obeying our rules, especially this one, makes me so fucking horny right now. I can't wait to be inside of you."

She placed her hands on his shoulders for support as she stepped out of her jeans. Running her hands over his wide, muscular chest made her just as horny as he proclaimed. The manly dusting of brown hair along his pectoral muscles that led straight to his jeans made her lick her lips. She undid the button just as he reached between her legs to cup her sex.

Before she could get the zipper down, he was inserting a finger and stroking her.

Millie tilted her head back and tried to discard the jeans from Anthony. He helped her with his other hand then stepped out of his pants, all while he used his other hand to stroke her folds.

"So wet and hot for me, aren't you, baby?" he asked, stepping forward to lick along her neck then jaw. He cupped her breast, massaging and pulling the mound to his liking.

"Oh please, Anthony, I want."

"You want what?"

"This."

She gripped his cock with both hands. One hand squeezed his balls while the other encircled his long, thick penis.

He moaned this time and added a second digit to her cunt, making her squirm and lift her pelvis toward him.

"I see you and I are going to be battling over who's boss here, huh?" he teased.

"What makes you say that?" she asked in a shaky breath while she continued to stroke him as diligently as he was stroking her.

"Enough."

He pulled from her body, turned her around, and pressed her over the edge of the high mattress. Her belly muscles tightened as she hit the thick, fluffy comforter.

He used his legs to spread her thighs then gripped her hips.

"Get ready, baby, the boss is going to fuck you long and hard so you know who's in charge."

She was on fire with lust and desire for this man. His words heightened her arousal and she felt her pussy drip with cream.

"Oh yeah, you like being told what to do in bed, huh, baby?" He caressed her hair, gripped it, then released it, making her heart rate increase as she wondered how rough he would be. She had the feeling he was testing the ground to see what she would allow. So much for him being a boss and more so for him being her passionate, caring lover.

"I like that," she whispered.

He leaned his body over hers, she felt him rub the tip of his engorged penis back and forth against her wet pussy from behind.

"You like what, sexy?" His warm breath collided with her neck, sending goose bumps along her spine. But she couldn't answer him. She was nervous. She didn't know if he would like it or love the fact that she wanted him to be a little rough. She needed it that way.

He grabbed hold of her hair and yanked it back just enough so she could see his facial expression. "You like it when I do this?" he asked, and she nodded. His brown eyes glazed over.

"I want you to tell me everything you like, Millie. I want you to tell me when something is too much or if I go too far. You hear me?" He yanked her hair again. She nodded.

"Say it."

"Yes."

"Good girl."

He released her hair and stepped back slightly. She was disappointed. She needed him more than ever right now. She was so turned on just a stroke of his fingers would set her off. She was about to complain when she felt both hands glide along her thighs and up to her ass. He kneaded her flesh with his big, strong hands. Damn, were Anthony's hands huge. He massaged her body all the way up to her shoulders then back down, reaching under her to pinch a nipple, surprising her.

She parted her legs wider, rubbing her pubic bone against the bed in an attempt to allow the friction to ease the ache inside of her.

Smack.

She hadn't expected the smack to her ass and she jerked.

"Don't you try to get off by yourself, woman. I'll be the one to make you come."

He reprimanded her and, damn it, did she just leak some more cream. Holy shit. He spanked her, and she loved it.

She jerked when the palm of his hand came down softly instead of harshly.

"You have a beautiful ass, Millie. While you're staying with us, we're going to get this ass good and ready for cock." He pressed a finger to her pussy.

"Oh!" she screamed then lifted her hips and thrust against the bed again trying to find release.

Smack.

"Damn!" she yelled, not expecting that smack again.

"I warned you."

She pressed her mouth against the comforter, moaning into the fabric.

His cock was at her pussy.

"Such a fine ass indeed. I think I'm going to fuck this sweet, wet pussy and then I'm going to play with this ass." She felt his finger swipe against her thigh and then against the puckered hole. She was strung so tight, she didn't care what he did to her as long as Anthony helped her come.

"Oh God, yes. Yes, I want that."

Anthony shoved into her to the hilt.

Millie screamed then clutched the comforter again, moaning into it.

He began to ease out only to press back into her with long, slow strokes.

He was going to kill her.

"Please, Ant. Please, I need to come."

He pulled out and shoved back in as he pressed a finger to her puckered hole. With the digit inserted, she screamed her release as he began a series of fast, hard strokes.

"Your ass is so fucking tight it sucked my finger right in. Hot damn, woman, I can't wait to fuck this ass." He pulled his finger from her ass and continued to pump into her pussy repeatedly.

He yelled as he thrust two more times before pouring into her. She felt his body shake and then the slap to her ass.

"Hey."

"Hey, yourself. Your ass is too irresistible to not play with."

"It looks that way from here, too," Jeremy stated as he stood in the doorway. Millie looked over her shoulder and felt her cheeks blush.

Anthony pulled from her body as he massaged her ass cheeks. He leaned down and kissed her cheek.

"See, baby. I'm not the only one who's been fantasizing about your ass."

* * * *

Jeremy pulled off his shirt and tossed it onto the rug as he approached the bed. He pulled Millie up into his arms and kissed her. She wrapped her arms around his neck and kissed him back.

Carrying her back toward the bed, he lowered her to her back.

"I couldn't wait to see you," he admitted, and she smiled.

"I hope you didn't leave work too early for me."

"Baby, don't you worry about anything. We have a great crew of workers. You're my number-one priority." He leaned down to kiss her again then cupped her breasts.

"You look so beautiful. Your hair wild, your cheeks rosy, and lips swollen like a woman well loved. I want to make love to you now, Millie."

"I want you, too," she whispered, and he quickly removed his jeans.

He lay over her, supporting his weight with his forearms, and he stared into her eyes.

He began to scatter kisses along her face, her chin, and neck then back up again. Millie wiggled below him then adjusted her legs so she could wrap them around his waist. He lifted up, reached down to align his cock with her entrance, then slowly pressed into her.

He closed his eyes, absorbing the feeling of warmth as her vaginal muscles gripped him tight. He held himself there a moment, lost in his own selfish need to feel her so intimately and to know that here, in his arms with his cock buried deep within her, she was safe from any harm.

She tilted her hips up toward him and he chuckled.

"Someone feeling needy?" he asked, and she nodded her head.

"Make me come, Jeremy. Please make love to me."

His heart soared and he lifted up so he could gain better access to her body.

"Yes, ma'am," he replied in a thick Texan accent, and she smiled while reaching for his chest. He simultaneously reached for her breasts, and when she brazenly pinched his nipples, he returned the gesture.

"Oh!" Millie screamed.

"Serves you right, woman."

"She has a problem with authority," Anthony chimed in, "but I've got something that should tame our little wildcat." Jeremy and Millie looked up at Anthony. He held a tube of lube in his hand and tapped it over his open palm.

"That's right, our little woman wants a cock in her ass. She told me so."

"Fuck, Anthony. I'm gonna come just thinking that." Jeremy began to thrust into Millie as he pulled her thighs higher against his side. He reached under her to play with the puckered hole and she screamed then bucked against him.

"Fuck, she sure does want it. I say we give it to her now." Jeremy rolled to his back with Millie still wrapped around him.

Millie gasped then tried to lift up as Jeremy scooted lower on the bed. Now Millie's ass was hanging over the side, and his legs were spread wide.

* * * *

"Oh God, I don't know if I can," she panted, feeling very excited about trying anal sex. Thank God she never did that before and the Lewis brothers would be her firsts.

She felt Anthony's warm hands caress her back.

"We'll go nice and easy, baby. I'll get this ass good and ready before I fuck it."

"Oh, shit," she blurted out, totally turned on by Anthony's dirty mouth.

He pressed her shoulders lower onto Jeremy.

"Ride him, baby," Anthony ordered, and she did without hesitation. Jeremy cupped her breasts, pinched her nipples as she rode his cock, feeling his thick rod push deeper. She tried to move faster, needed to reach orgasm, but Jeremy grabbed her hips to slow her down.

"Don't move so fast, baby. I don't want to come until Anthony is inside that tight ass of yours. The feeling of fullness will be worth the wait." He pulled her down by her neck so he could kiss her. The move stilled her body, her breasts pressed to Jeremy's chest.

Then she felt the cool, thick liquid on her hole and Anthony push a finger into her.

She moaned into Jeremy's mouth and he devoured her cries of pleasure. She did feel full and tight. How the hell could she handle two cocks in her at once? She felt panicked, but then instincts or something kicked in because as Anthony stroked her hole with his finger she began to push back against him, wanting more.

Anthony caressed her back.

"That's it, baby. It feels so good, don't it?"

Jeremy released her lips. She panted against his shoulder.

"Yes, oh God, it burns, but it feels so good and so naughty."

"That's right, baby, you're our naughty girl," Anthony told her then smacked her on the ass.

Millie shook then felt her pussy cream.

"Oh hell, Anthony, get in her already, neither of us are going to last."

Anthony pulled out his finger. She moaned and Jeremy held her tight against him.

"Nice and easy, baby," Anthony whispered in a strange voice. It sounded like he was hurting.

Then she felt the tip of his cock at her back entrance. He pushed a little farther, and she felt the tightness then pop before he pushed in deeper.

"Breathe, Mill," Anthony whispered, and she did. Anthony shoved the rest of the way inside of her, cutting off her breath for a second.

"Oh," she moaned.

"That's it, sweetness, nice and easy now. Fuck, this looks so beautiful. My dick pushing into your ass, buried deep inside of you." Anthony caressed her ass cheeks while he began slow strokes. He would pull a little bit out then press back in.

"Please, Anthony, go faster. Please. Too slow." She pressed her ass back as she lifted up onto Jeremy.

Jeremy thrust upward and then pulled back. Anthony thrust into her then pulled back. They began an in-and-out motion, leaving her swaying recklessly between them. She reached for Jeremy as she held back a hand to touch Anthony.

"Fuck, her tits look hot bouncing and swaying every time you thrust into her," Jeremy told Anthony.

Anthony pulled back then thrust back into her.

"You should see her ass sucking in my cock. Fucking incredible."

"Oh, damn!" Millie screamed then began to push back and forth against the two cocks. They got her hint and picked up speed, stroking over and over again until they both shoved in three times simultaneously and exploded together. Millie screamed her release then collapsed against Jeremy. Anthony fell against her and together they lay there trying to catch their breath.

"Incredible, baby. Absolutely incredible," Jeremy told her then kissed her mouth.

She felt Anthony pull from her then kiss her shoulder. "Thank you, sweetness. Thank you for trusting us with that."

Jeremy pulled from her then squeezed her into his arms as they lay entwined on the bed.

Anthony took position behind her and placed his hand on her hip bone.

"Get some rest. You'll need it when Marco, Dalton, and Hank get home."

* * * *

Jeremy slipped quietly from the bed. He glanced over his shoulder to take another look at Millie, who was wrapped tightly in Anthony's arms. He had heard his brothers enter the house a while ago and he wanted to get updated by Marco before Millie woke.

He pulled on his jeans, grabbed his shirt, and headed downstairs. As he approached the kitchen he heard his brothers talking.

"She wasn't too happy about us getting the Lawkins and Morris brothers for extra security. As a matter of fact, she gave Anthony an attitude about it," Marco stated as Jeremy entered the kitchen. He overheard them talking.

"Hey, how is she doing?" Hank asked Jeremy.

Jeremy smiled wide. "She's really good. Sound asleep right now along with Anthony."

"We figured as much," Marco stated with a smile.

"She's amazing," Jeremy added as he reached into the refrigerator to grab a bottle of water. He guzzled it down as his brothers continued to talk about the case.

"So what can you tell us about the murders? I mean, Wyatt gave you details, right?" Hank asked. Dalton remained quiet and he looked pissed off.

"Wyatt didn't want to give me too many details. He knows how important Millie has become to us. He's trying to protect us, too."

"That fucking bad, huh?" Dalton mumbled with his arms crossed in front of his chest.

"The guy cut their fucking hearts out after beating them to near death," Marco told them and mumbled curses went through the room.

"She's not allowed to be alone. Ever," Dalton raised his voice.

"That is not going to fly with her," Marco stated.

"Tough shit," Jeremy said.

"I've been giving this some thought since hearing the news, leaving her here this afternoon, and speaking with Wyatt. When she's at the Triple C there are plenty of people around, including Anthony and you, Jeremy. Plus we have the extra security right now with the shelter in operation. When she's here, she'll have us and of course the guys. We'll protect her," Marco told them.

"Sounds like a good plan," Hank replied.

"The shelter means a lot to her. We can't make her stay here and not work there with Anna and Stacy," Hank added.

"That is definitely not an option. She wouldn't go for that, and as long as she has one of us or security around her, she should be okay. Maybe the police or FBI will have better luck tracking Frank down."

"I sure as hell hope so, because right now, I want to place her in hiding and go hunt that asshole," Dalton stated to everyone.

"Speaking of the asshole, I got a picture of the guy from Wyatt. We figured all the security guys and law enforcement should know about him and what he looks like. That way if he does get into town, we'll have a better chance of recognizing him." Marco sifted through a couple of folders and books in a pile on the table he had brought home from the department. He pulled out a yellow envelope and handed the picture to Hank first.

"Damn, he's a big boy."

"Not any bigger than us," Dalton added as he looked over Hank's shoulder.

"He's a good-looking guy," Jeremy stated, and his brothers all looked at him. "Hey, don't read into that statement. What I mean is that he doesn't look like some psycho killer. He looks like a guy who wouldn't have problems getting a date."

"He's right. It's not what I expected at all," Hank stated.

"Well, take a good look. I also can send it to your cell phones so you have it on hand just in case." Marco pressed a bunch of keys on his cell phone. A few seconds later, several cell phones went off around the room.

"So the FBI is involved, too, now? That should help, right?" Hank asked.

"It should. In the meantime, we do what we do best and protect what's ours," Marco stated, and everyone agreed.

* * * *

Millie awoke to warm, soft kisses against her neck. She snuggled in tighter against the large, solid body and inhaled. It was Anthony, she was certain. His cologne was fresh and light where Jeremy's was spicy.

"Wake up, woman," Anthony whispered against her neck as his hands caressed her hip.

"Are you always this bossy?" she asked, her voice sounding tired and rough.

He pressed his hand over her backside and squeezed. "I thought we went over that already."

She giggled as he pressed his thigh between her legs so his erection hit her pussy, causing her to awake more fully.

She opened her eyes. His face and head were now even with her breasts. She watched in fascination as he licked her nipple, rolling his tongue over the areola before sucking some of her breast into his hot, wet mouth.

Millie grabbed his shoulders, and then rocked her hips against his erection.

"Mmm," he moaned, his mouth full with her breast and his cock pressing deeper against her thigh.

She reached between them and cupped his balls. An instant later he was on top of her, using his thigh to spread her legs.

"You're a naughty little thing who needs discipline." He sat up and pressed her hands up over her head. The move caused her breasts to lift upward and her thighs to spread wider over his thighs.

"You really are very bossy all the time, huh? You like this with your brothers?" she challenged, and he raised one eyebrow at her in a show of intimidation, maybe, but she chuckled instead.

He leaned down, making his cock brush up against her pussy, then returned to his position. He was teasing her.

"It's in my nature to be in charge. Always been and always will. My brothers accept it."

She thrust her pussy up toward his cock. "Well, you're not the boss of me," she teased.

"I say otherwise and the faster you realize that and accept it, the better," he responded firmly and she widened her eyes in shock then he chuckled.

Son of a gun, serious, bossy Anthony just played a trick on me. Well, let's see how he likes this.

"Bossy men turn me off." She turned away.

He gripped her wrists with one hand then used his free hand to reach underneath her and press a finger against her puckered hole. She screamed.

"That's not how it was this afternoon. As a matter of fact, you like being bossed around in the bedroom, darling. You liked it so much I got to fuck this hot, tight ass of yours," he told her, and she felt her pussy clench and cream drip from her. She closed her eyes and moaned.

"Oh God, Anthony, that's not fair."

She panted and moaned as he pressed his finger through the tight ring. His thumb teased her pussy, and then pressed between the folds.

"What are you doing to me?"

"Loving you, baby, and showing you that you like being bossed around by me. Don't you?" he asked as he leaned up and licked across her nipple. How the hell was he doing so much to her at the same time?

"Please, Anthony."

"Please what, darling? Tell me that you like me being your boss."

"Oh damn, you know I like it. Can't you feel how wet I am? Please, do something."

"Oh, I'm going to do something."

He abruptly released her wrists then lifted her thighs over his thighs so her hips were lifted up and he had better access to her pussy and her ass.

He thrust his cock between her folds, making her gasp then moan in pleasure. Before she knew his intentions, he pulled out, reached for a nipple and pinched it. She thrust her hips upward and the tip of his cock hit her anus. Grabbing her hips to steady her, he pressed his cock through the tight ring. She relaxed her muscles and he was fully inside her ass. Millie threw her head back and grabbed on to the comforter. Her pussy clenched and swelled with such need she wanted to scream for him to do something. Instead, Anthony began to press slowly in and out of her ass. She was slick and wet for him.

"Oh, Anthony, please, I can't take it I need more."

"I know exactly what you need, baby. Your pussy's so tight and needy right now, isn't it?"

She nodded her head then turned it side to side. She couldn't take how hot and aroused she was. His thick, hard cock was in her ass, her thighs stretched over his thighs and her nipples taut and needy. Just one touch to her pussy, just one finger or stroke of something…

"Please, Anthony, touch me, please," she begged, and he thrust his cock into her ass again and again in slow, torturous strokes. He pressed a thumb to her clit and she shook.

"Oh God, more. More, damn you!" she yelled, and he chuckled then pressed a digit up into her pussy. In and out he alternated thrusting into her ass and adding a second digit to her pussy, thrusting his fingers up into her. She tightened up like a spring. *Just a few more strokes.*

"What the hell is all that yelling about?"

Millie opened her eyes to find Hank and Marco standing in the doorway. Hank approached the bed and Anthony rocked his hips into her.

"Just proving a point." Anthony continued to stroke her and fuck her in the ass while his brothers watched.

"Oh," she moaned, not caring about anything but finding her release.

The thought that Hank and Marco watched her right now was just what she needed. She rocked her hips and Anthony called her name as they both exploded together.

As she tried to catch her breath, she opened her eyes to see Hank completely naked, and Anthony pinched a nipple again.

"Hey."

"Hey yourself," he replied then slowly pulled from her. He got up off the bed, and then lifted her up. He passed her to Hank then caressed a hand over her ass cheek.

"Later, sweetness."

She smiled.

"What was it he was proving?" Hank asked as he carried her toward the bathroom.

"How bossy he thinks he can be!" she yelled over Hank's shoulder and Anthony pointed at her in warning. She giggled against Hank's shoulder, feeling so carefree and alive.

* * * *

Dalton was in the kitchen looking out the window and toward the fields that surrounded their home.

"Hey, whatcha doing down here all alone?" Anthony asked as he entered the kitchen wearing only his jeans.

Dalton glanced at him then turned back.

"Not much. Just thinking."

"I'm going to take a quick shower then start dinner." Anthony grabbed his phone from the counter and looked at his messages.

"Shit." He ran his hand through his hair. Dalton watched him. His brother more than likely got the text message from Marco with Frank's mug on it. Jeremy was right. The guy was good looking and appeared charming and everything a woman would want. Perfection, actually.

"Marco wanted us to know what the asshole looks like," Dalton stated.

"I wasn't expecting this," Anthony replied, and Dalton wondered if he wasn't the only one feeling strange.

"He's good looking, as Jeremy described after looking at his picture."

"He is. I expected a monster. I guess this is why he's gotten away with his crimes. It's how he manipulated the doctor to help get him released."

"Millie's a beautiful woman. Her skin is soft and feminine. Her dark blue eyes give away her emotions and it's fun to watch," Dalton said as he continued to look out the window.

"Why are you holding back from her?"

"What?"

"She'll love you, scars and all, Dalton," Anthony offered, but Dalton didn't want to hear it. He was scared that she would see his war scars and be disgusted. It's why he wore the shirt. His brothers were perfect, even the fucking psycho ex-boyfriend was perfect, but not Dalton.

"Give her some credit, Dalton. She's not superficial. She's sweet, she's empathetic, and she already loves you despite you hiding part of yourself from her."

"I never felt like this about anyone before," Dalton admitted.

Anthony chuckled. "Join the fucking club."

Dalton looked at him and Anthony smiled.

"She'll love you no matter what. It's just the way Millie is. I'm going to take that shower now so I can start supper. Do me a favor and tell Jeremy to get his ass out of the shower and help me."

Dalton pushed away from the counter and went in search of Jeremy with a still very heavy heart.

* * * *

Millie kissed Hank's skin as the water from the shower flowed over and between their bodies. She kissed his arm muscles then took in the sight of his tattoo. Placing her finger over the bright colors, she asked him about it.

"So you were in the army, too?"

"I was and so were Marco and Dalton."

"Where is Marco?" she asked.

"Showering then probably waiting on Anthony's bed for us to return there," he teased as he cupped her breasts, massaging them then squeezing then together.

"What's this tattoo all about? I noticed part of one on Dalton's arm, but his shirt covered it." An uneasy feeling filled her belly. Why was Dalton hiding from her?

Hank sighed. "His is different. Don't worry, honey, he'll come around. He loves you but he has difficulty letting his emotions show and baring everything to the world. I'm sure if you ask him to see his tattoo he'll show you."

"I guess so." She picked up the soap and began to lather it in her hands before caressing it over Hank's skin.

"So explain the tattoo," she whispered, absorbing the feel of muscle beneath her fingertips and how his cock tapped against her belly and chest. He was way taller than her. They all were.

"I chose it in memory of my fallen soldiers and, of course, out of respect for our country."

"I see that. The American flag and the word *army* over it. It's really nice," she told him as she absorbed the rest of the tattoo. In front of the American flag and word *ARMY* were a pair of empty combat boots with a large gun sitting straight up in one of them and an empty helmet laying over the top of the gun. Along with that was a pair of dog tags. She swallowed hard, thinking how dangerous of a job he had and how lucky she was that he and his brothers survived.

Suddenly overwhelmed with emotions, she hugged his arm to her chest and kissed his shoulder.

A strong, solid arm wrapped around her waist and pulled her in front of him.

"Aww, baby, come here," he whispered then leaned down to cover her mouth with his. He kissed her deeply as he caressed along her body, lifting her so that she straddled his waist.

He pulled his lips from hers and touched foreheads.

"You're a dream come true, Millie." He trailed his hand between them and over her belly to her pussy. He pressed a finger up into her pussy, making her moan then thrust her hips against his hand. He pumped into her and she felt his cock tap underneath her.

"Please, Hank, make love to me."

He smiled then kissed her chin. "You don't have to beg, baby. I want you, too."

He removed his fingers, grabbed hold of his penis, and lined up the tip with her opening. She held on to him and slowly he pushed between her folds.

"Ahhh, like heaven," he whispered then stroked against her, thrusting his hips down and up as she stretched back against the wall.

She held on to his shoulders, nibbling and biting his skin harder with every stroke of his cock.

"So good and so tight," he grunted then increased his speed. "I love you, Millie. I love you so damn much," he confessed, and she moaned again as her muscles tightened.

"I love you, too." Then they both exploded together. He rocked his hips a few more times then covered her mouth, kissing her deeply.

They remained there, connected so intimately for a few more minutes until the water began to turn cold.

* * * *

Hank stepped out of the shower and saw Marco standing there naked.

"The water's gone cold," he told him as he wrapped a towel around himself. Marco smiled just as Millie began to step out.

"Stay in there, sweetness. I'm next," he told her, and she placed her hands on her hips.

"It's kind of cold."

"I'm on fucking fire waiting out here listening to my brother make love to you in there. Get back in." She stepped back into the shower. Hank laughed as Marco stepped around him.

Marco placed Millie under the cold spray of water. She shivered then grabbed on to him, trying to find warmth in his embrace.

"Don't worry, baby, you won't feel so cold in a second." He lowered to the shower floor and lifted one of her legs. He placed it on his knee and opened her to his viewing. "Fuck, baby, your pussy looks so good. I thought about eating your cream all day." She moaned then placed her hands palm down against the wall of the shower, giving his mouth full access to her cunt.

A swipe of his tongue and Millie was shaking.

"See, baby, not so cold now, huh?" he asked, and she shook her head. He licked across her pussy lips then pressed his tongue between the folds. Instantly, Millie was grabbing his head, running her fingers through his hair, and then caressed his shoulder. He nipped her lightly, surprising her.

"Be a good girl and lean back so I can get me a nice, long taste of what's mine." She did as she was told. She leaned back but moved her hips forward. He took a moment to press a finger up into her, making her immediately ride his digit.

"That's it, baby. So wet and needy for cock, aren't you?"

"Yes, oh please, Marco, please."

Marco chuckled then pulled his finger from her folds. She lost her balance and he caught her by her hips.

"Time to fulfill one of my fantasies, sweetness."

He turned her around, placed her hands palm up against the wall, then pulled her hips back a little so she was bent over. Millie gasped and he used his thigh to spread her thighs then lined his cock up to her pussy from behind.

"I love this ass. Tonight, I'm going to fuck it."

He thrust into her in one smooth stroke and Millie moaned. In and out he stroked his cock between her tight vaginal muscles, loving the feel of them gripping him. It was pure torture and he was so incredibly aroused and needy for her just as his brothers were. He didn't want to think about the danger she was in. It made him angry and possessive. As the thoughts filled his mind he increased his thrusts, grabbed her hips, and plunged into her repeatedly until he could no longer take the exquisite tightness.

"Fuck, baby, I love you. I love you," he blurted out, and Millie said something. He thought she said "I love you, too," but his ears were ringing. He felt deaf as he wrapped his arm around her waist and leaned against her and the wall. His breathing calmed as he caressed her body, slowly pulling apart from her. Her cheek was pressed against the wall of the shower, her eyes closed.

"I can't move. My legs feel like jelly," Millie stated.

Marco chuckled.

"I'll take care of you, sweetness. Come here."

He turned her around and hugged her to him. The water was really cold now, practically ice cold, and she began to shiver.

"Let's get out of here," he said, turning off the water.

"Good idea," she replied, teeth chattering. He quickly wrapped her in a towel and carried out to the bedroom.

* * * *

Millie was so tired she was practically falling asleep at the kitchen table. Her men took complete advantage of her condition and explained the schedule for the next week in regards to her protection, where she could go, and who would be watching over her. She took a deep breath as they began to clear the table of the wonderfully cooked meal by Anthony. The chicken was tender and the corn sweet and she complimented him on a job well done. Meanwhile, she glanced at Dalton, who looked so sad and angry it bothered her. Why was he keeping his distance? He was the only one to not make love to her today and she needed him. It was odd, but even though she made love with Anthony, Jeremy, Hank, and Marco, she felt incomplete not having Dalton. That fact sure did freak her out. Instead of focusing on that, she figured they had spoken enough and it was time to stand her ground on some changes to their well thought out schedule.

She dabbed her mouth with her napkin and pushed slowly away from the table. She stood up on shaky, tired legs and began to carry her plate to the sink when Hank took it from her.

"Sit down, baby. You look like you're about to fall over."

She released an annoyed sigh as he took the dish from her and Dalton pulled out a chair for her to sit.

"I'm fine. In regards to this little schedule you all came up with, there are some much-needed changes." That statement seemed to get their attention as all action stopped and the room fell silent.

Dalton had his arms crossed in front of his chest as he leaned against the counter. The others just looked ready as if they expected her challenge. Good. Maybe they didn't think she was such a pushover after all.

"Tomorrow morning I will not be leaving with Jeremy and Anthony for the Triple C. Hank and Dalton will be giving me a ride to the dojo for my training session. Also, I will need to be at the shelter for the day, helping out some of the new women and finishing decorating the rec center. One of you can pick me up at seven if you think it's necessary and you're unwilling to let me drive, that is. Then the following week—" She stopped midsentence as Dalton stalked toward her. The look in his eyes did wonders to her insides. He was not a man to reckon with and she knew it, but she wouldn't back down. It's not like she was telling anyone to not protect her, it was just that she still needed to work, to train so she felt confident and had some control.

"There's no need for training when you've got us. You're not going around without an escort and you're not pushing us away so you can try to act tough and confident when you're scared inside. We won't accept that." Dalton stood a few feet in front of her. She looked up into his face.

"Who said that I'm trying to act tough? I need to have some control here, Dalton. If I relinquish everything I've fought for, then Frank wins. I'm tired of being weak. I want my life. I want to do what makes me happy and that's martial arts and working at the shelter."

"You can do any of the regular classes we offer," Hank chimed in and she shook her head.

"I don't want those classes. I want the ones I discussed with you. I need to feel confident that I can defend myself. I need this."

"You don't know what you need," Dalton barked at her and she widened her eyes in shock.

"Oh, really? And you know what I need, Dalton?" she asked, taking a step toward him.

"Yeah, you need to know that we're here to protect you. You're not hiding from anything. You have us."

"Well, you're the expert on hiding, aren't you?"

"What?" he asked.

"It's okay for you to hide behind that T-shirt of yours and not allow me access to you for your good reasons, but I can't try to do things that make me feel confident?" she challenged him.

"That's different."

"How so?"

He shook his head. "How the hell did this conversation wind up about me?" he asked in frustration. The others backed away, allowing this much-needed confrontation to take place.

"It wound up about you because you're the one causing the situation. How come I have to relinquish everything I have, my life, my freedom, my heart, but you get to keep your secrets and hide things from me?" She turned, about to walk out of the room. Dalton grabbed her arm and turned her back toward him.

"Damn it, Millie, this is different. I'm not keeping secrets. I'm not lying about anything or holding back. I love you. I've told you this."

"Really? Because the way I see it, if you truly loved me and trusted me than you'd stop hiding behind your shirt." She crossed her arms in front of her chest and stared at him.

Dalton looked utterly angry and kind of scared. What did he have to be scared of and how the hell did this conversation wind up about his need to keep his shirt on during sex?

He stepped back from her, glancing at his brothers, who looked on expectantly.

Dalton placed his hands on the seam of his shirt and began to lift it up and over his head. All she saw were scars, long, pink lines from knife wounds or something that caused deep gashes at one time. The one from his neck crossed along his shoulder then down. She covered her mouth. Not out of disgust but sadness. He was afraid of her response. In that moment, he turned from her and began to walk out of the room.

"Dalton!" she called.

"Forget it. Now you know. Satisfied?"

"No, I'm not satisfied. Look at me."

He slowly turned toward her.

"This doesn't change anything between us."

"Don't pretend that these don't bother you." He stuck out his chest.

"They don't bother me. It saddens me that you would think that."

"How could you not be bothered by them? I can't stand to see them, to remember." He ran a hand through his hair.

Millie took that moment to open the robe she wore and point out the scar from her groin to her hip.

"Look at me, Dalton. Look at the scar I have. I know exactly how you feel. Don't you think that every time I glance at this damn scar it reminds me of him, of what he did to me and how I almost died?"

"Don't!" He stomped toward her, lifted her up into his arms, and hugged her to him. "Don't talk about it. Don't relive that. You understand, I know you do. Fucking forget it." He pulled back and covered her mouth with his own. The robe hung off her shoulders, and he walked her out of the kitchen after he released her lips and carried her down a different hallway to the left of the house. Using his foot, he kicked open the door and laid her on the bed. This was his room, far on the other side of the house.

He pulled the robe from her body and knelt on the floor. His hands parted her thighs, and her ass hung off the bed. He stared at her pussy then ran a finger gently over the scar.

It was his way of dealing with his own pain, his own memories. She wouldn't push him further. He gave in, he shared his secret with her.

"Dalton?"

He looked up as he used his thumbs to part her pussy lips.

"I love you, scars or no scars. I love you just as much as I love your brothers."

"I know," he whispered.

"Do you know, Dalton? Do you really know and feel it, too?"

"Yes, baby. I'm gonna show you."

Dalton lowered his mouth to her pussy and began to feast on her. She swallowed hard, spreading her legs wider, placing the heels on the edge of the bed. He alternated between finger then tongue, and she moaned with every stroke.

"Oh, Dalton, so good, that feels so good."

"I want to go slow, Millie. I need slow and perfect."

"I know, Dalton. I need it, too."

He kissed and licked along her inner thigh, making her squirm and wiggle. He chuckled, and when his warm breath collided with her pussy, she thrust her hips forward.

He released her and stood up. He began to pull off his jeans and she watched him, never letting her eyes leave his. He discarded his clothing and she waited in anticipation.

He stood there, stroking his cock, making her mouth water to taste him. She absorbed his taut muscles, the ridges and dips, and of course his tattoo across his arm and one down his side.

"I want to taste you," she whispered, and she slid from the bed onto the rug in front of him. She knelt before him, her mouth a few inches below where his cock bobbed against his belly.

Slowly, she licked the tip, tasting pre-cum and rolling her tongue around the bulbous head.

"Aww hell, baby, that feels good."

"You taste good," she stated in a mumble because her lips hit the tip of his cock. He tightened his legs and chuckled.

"That tickled," he admitted, and she knew exactly how that felt. His warm breath had collided with her pussy and it drove her insane before.

She took more of his cock down her throat, working it slowly deeper. He was thick and long and there was no way she could take him fully, but she would try her best. He reached down and held her hair and head with his hand. She moaned and so did he.

His hold tightened and then he gave a little tug of aggression. Her pussy wept and he chuckled. "Anthony said you like to be controlled in the bedroom. He wasn't kidding."

She sucked harder and cupped his balls at the same time and he gasped.

"I like that, baby, and I like control just as much as my brothers do."

Millie began to move faster, taking his cock deep then pulling almost all the way out when suddenly, Dalton pulled her from him. He lifted her up and covered her mouth with his own. He was hungry and she tasted her own juices on his tongue as they battled for control. They fell to the bed, him landing between her legs. Their lips parted.

"So much for going slow," Dalton said then reached down, lifted up slightly, and lined up his cock with her pussy. A moment later he penetrated her and began a thrusting rhythm that sent her through wave upon wave of tiny combustions. She kissed his neck along the scars there and then back to his face. He thrust into her, pulling her thighs higher against his sides until he lifted up to gain deeper penetration. Suddenly, her legs were up over his shoulders, her breasts pressed to her slightly swelled belly until he was balls deep inside of her. In and out he stroked her, trying to scratch an itch that was feeding her hunger for more of his cock.

"Harder, Dalton. Harder!" she screamed, and he gave her what she wanted. His thrusts were wild and deep. The bed shook, he growled over and over again, and suddenly she exploded, closing her eyes and feeling as though she were out of her body. He called her name then thrust three more times until he came inside of her, pouring his seed into her womb, and she wrapped her arms around him best she could as they recovered from their lovemaking.

He pulled from her slowly, then dragged her farther onto the bed and pulled her into his arms and snuggled close.

"That was incredible, baby. I love you."

"I love you, too."

He kissed her forehead and they closed their eyes as the darkness of evening filled the room.

Chapter 18

"It's nice to meet you, Jessie." Millie reached her hand out to greet a young woman that arrived just that morning. It was Friday. Millie had survived the week despite her men trying their hardest to stick to their version of a schedule for her. She chuckled just thinking about them. Their lovemaking got better and better every time. She had nearly passed out with excitement when Marco handcuffed her to the bedpost.

She cleared her mind. Now was not the time to be thinking about that.

"It's nice to meet you, too. This place is great." Jessie looked around them. She fidgeted with her hands and looked kind of scared. It had only been a few days since Jessie had arrived. Of course she would still be a bit nervous.

"Well, you let me know if you need anything. I can introduce you to some of the other women or help you with just about anything around here."

"Sure. I appreciate that. I guess I should get going. I think dinner is going to be served soon."

"Millie!" Millie heard her name being called, and when she turned, Marco was standing there along with Anthony.

"You ready to go?" Anthony asked.

She waved. "Yep."

"Are those your boyfriends?" Jessie asked, and Millie felt her belly quiver. The women that showed up at the shelter and in Pearl learned quickly about the multiple relationships. Especially with Anna and her men as well as Stacy and her men around the ranch.

"Two of them," Millie replied.

Jessie looked at her strangely then recovered and smiled.

"How many boyfriends do you have?"

"Five. I'd better get going. I'll see you tomorrow."

"You bet. Goodnight." Jessie walked away as Millie headed toward Marco and Anthony.

Marco pulled her into an embrace.

"Have a good day, sweetness?"

"Yep."

"Good, Anthony's going to take you home to the ranch. I forgot something at the department. I'll meet you there in a bit."

"Okay. See you later." Millie said, and Marco headed toward his police cruiser while Anthony took Millie's hand and led her toward his truck. Jeremy was leaning against it, talking with Eric Cantrell.

* * * *

Jessie snuck out that night, which wasn't too difficult. One guard patrolled near the cottages and as soon as he passed hers Jessie headed out of there. She took the bike that was leaning against the main house and headed out of town toward Turbank. She hoped that her hair looked good after the long ride. Not that she was interested in the guy, but he was really good looking and muscular. He had sex appeal, that was for sure. Jessie pedaled faster as she thought about him. Maybe once he found out that that woman, Millie, was fucking five men, he'd reconsider caring about finding her? Then Jessie might actually have a chance.

Twenty minutes later, she pedaled up toward the small motel. She hid the bike in the back as she had three nights before, but before she could get around the front, he was standing there.

"Hey, beautiful. No one followed you?" he asked. She felt her belly tighten. Damn was he sexy and his voice to die for.

"No one followed me. Like I told you, I've snuck out of shelters before and even private school when I was a kid."

He walked closer, and his dark-gray, nearly black eyes sparkled. He reached out and caressed his knuckles against her cheek.

"You are far from some little kid, honey. What info do you have for me?"

Jessie blushed. "Well, I don't think it's what you expected to find out. I think you should forget about the bitch."

He took a step toward her then stopped himself. *What the hell was that all about?*

"Why would you say that?"

"For starters, she's fucking five men." His eyes widened and his hands were in fists at his sides.

"What?" he asked through clenched teeth. Obviously, she needed to spell it out for him. She hoped that he didn't back out of his promise of paying her five hundred dollars for doing this shit.

"The town of Pearl, where the shelter is, is filled with multiple-partner relationships. There's, like, one woman to two, three, four, and even more men. It's wild and it's acceptable. Your little girlfriend has five of her own and one is a deputy."

"Interesting. I need you to do something else for me."

"No. You said five hundred for this, just info. Now what?"

"I need you to bring her here. I need you to get her off the ranch without anyone knowing."

"How the hell am I supposed to do that? There are cowboys everywhere and two of her men come to pick her up every night."

"Then get her here during the day. I don't care how you do it, just do it."

"Where's my five hundred?"

"I'll make it five thousand if you get her here."

"Are you serious? You're not going to stiff me and take her anyway?"

"No, honey. If you get her here and no one follows, you get the five g's and I'll take care of the rest."

She thought about that. Five thousand was a lot of money.

"Okay. I'll do it."

"Good. Now get back there before you get caught."

Jessie hurried back to her bike. As she made her way to Pearl and the shelter, she thought she had gotten away with sneaking out, but one of the other girls, Sally, busted her as she entered the shared cottage.

"Where the hell did you go to? We're not supposed to leave the grounds."

"Says you, the one with the attitude that keeps breaking the rules."

"That was before. It's nice here and these women aren't trying to hurt me."

Jessie didn't want to make it obvious that she was helping some guy find his girlfriend. *Maybe that's how Millie wound up here in the first place. Maybe that guy beat her.*

"I didn't want to tell anyone," she began to say as her mind made up the lies.

"Tell anyone what?" Sally asked.

"Tell anyone about my friend. She's only fourteen. She's been abused and she fears everyone. I mean I couldn't even talk her into sneaking in here and staying in the cottage for the night. I've been bringing her food and stuff. Please don't tell anyone. She'll be so upset."

Sally nodded her head in agreement.

"Good. Now can we get some rest? I'm really tired."

"Sure, but you may want to talk with Cindy or even Millie. They're both really nice and can be trusted."

Jessie thought about that. It was what she was counting on.

"Maybe. I'll see. I'm going to meet my friend tomorrow."

"During the day?"

"Yep. She said some guys saw her and started harassing her so she had to run through woods to hide. It's not safe out there."

"Oh no, you better tell Millie. She'll help you tomorrow."

"We'll see." Jessie walked toward her bed. It was a really nice place and she wouldn't mind staying there a while, but after tomorrow she would have no choice but to leave.

* * * *

"Dalton, be serious, will you? I mean it now." Millie yelled at Dalton as he grabbed her around the waist and kissed her. Hank chuckled, but Millie was getting fed up. Just as they began to move around the mats and work on some moves, Dalton wouldn't keep his hands off of her.

She wasn't really getting annoyed with him, but she did want her training to be taken more seriously. After all, he was supposed to be her instructor.

"Okay, I'm sorry, baby, but you smell so damn good. It's hard to concentrate."

She twisted out of his hold and stood in a ready stance with her fists a few inches apart as well as her legs. She was ready for his next move.

Dalton stepped toward her and made her circle back. He took a few shots, which she countered or ducked. Then Hank came at her from behind. She grabbed his arm and flipped him onto his back. Dalton laughed as he pointed down at his brother. Hank looked shocked.

"Holy shit, baby, that was hot," Hank told her as he jumped up from his position without using his hands.

They continued this until Dalton went in for the kill. He grabbed Millie around the waist and hoisted her up over his shoulder. She screamed. She hadn't expected that or the smacks to her ass. She wiggled furiously until he lost his hold nearly completely. She made her way like a snake down his back, between his legs, and made him fall.

"She got you good," Hank teased and Dalton rolled her to her back, straddled her waist, then held her arms above her head.

"Looks like I got her good."

She couldn't fight him nor did she want to. He thrust his cock against her body and she moaned.

"That isn't fair," she stated, out of breath.

"Now was that a slick move, climbing over my back between my legs," Dalton replied.

"You told me to improvise, overcome, and adapt. That's exactly what I was doing. Aren't you proud of me?"

"I'll show you how proud I am," he whispered then rubbed his erection against her mound. He leaned down and kissed her, releasing her hands from confinement. Millie wrapped her arms around his neck and kissed him back.

"Mmm. Sweet," he stated after releasing her lips.

"Is this what goes on in these private combat training sessions?" Marco asked as he stood in the doorway. Hank was hiding his chuckle. Millie felt her cheeks blush and Dalton just shook his head.

"Haven't you ever heard of knocking?" Dalton asked as he stood up, offered a hand to Millie, and then pulled her up to him.

"Sure have, but then that defeats the whole point of sneaking up on you," Marco replied with a smile.

"I heard him come in, but you two were having too much fun," Hank stated as he took Millie's hand and pulled her toward him. He kissed her softly.

"You did good, even though Dalton began to fool around at the end," Hank told her, and she gave him a squeeze.

"You ready to go, honey? I have to be back in town in thirty minutes," Marco said.

"Definitely," Millie replied as she grabbed her water bottle and bag. As she approached Marco, he pulled her against him and gave her a kiss.

"Where are you going to be?" Dalton asked her.

"Your place, taking a quick shower, then Marco's going to drop me off at the shelter."

"Okay. Are we still on for lunch?" Dalton asked.

"Of course. I'll be by Anna's and Stacy's waiting for you."

"Okay. See you then," Dalton replied then Hank and him walked Marco and Millie out.

* * * *

"So things have been going extra great with the Lewis brothers?" Anna asked Millie as they talked in the main office at the shelter. Cindy was in session with one of the girls and a few others were beginning to settle in and ask about work schedules. Stacy was organizing the tasks, the pay, and the locations.

"It's been fantastic. I can't believe I'm in love with five men." Millie smiled. Anna touched her shoulder and squeezed.

"You deserve great men to love you and protect you. I'm so glad you came back to Pearl," Anna replied then smiled.

"Me, too."

"Hey, have either of you seen Jessie?" Cindy asked as she came out of her office.

"No, why?" Anna asked.

"I just stepped inside to speak with Mary and I was supposed to meet with Jessie two hours ago. No one has seen her," Cindy replied.

"We should go look around the cottages," Anna stated then began to head out.

"I'll look over near the rec center. I know sometimes Sally hangs out on the benches near the fields. Perhaps she told Jessie about them since they're sharing a cottage."

"Okay, I'll call the stables and see if she's over there," Cindy told them and the women split up.

* * * *

Millie was walking by the side of the cottages and to the pathway leading to the rec center. Along the way she spotted Sally.

"Hey, Sally," Millie called to her, and Sally waved back. Millie was glad that the young woman was coming out of her shell and got rid of her bad attitude. She was already working and pulling her weight around the shelter.

"What's going on, Millie?"

"Have you seen Jessie? She was supposed to meet Cindy two hours ago and hasn't been seen."

Sally shook her head, but she turned away.

"Are you sure?" Millie pushed, feeling that perhaps Sally knew where Jessie was but didn't want to snitch. "You won't get in trouble for telling me. I just want to make sure that she's okay and not in some kind of trouble."

"She's okay. She may have gone to see this other girl. She mentioned her last night."

"Another girl? Who?"

"She wouldn't say. She told me that the girl is scared and doesn't trust anyone. She's been hiding out and Jessie's been bringing her food and stuff."

"Why wouldn't she just bring her here to the shelter?" Millie asked, feeling concerned for the girl.

"Jessie said some guys went after her friend and she hid in the woods. The girl is afraid of everyone. Maybe Jessie is with her now? I can help you look," Sally offered and Millie agreed. They both headed toward the wooded area behind the rec center.

"I'll go this way if you want to check down the path that leads off the property and toward Turbank," Sally stated.

"You know where this path leads?"

"Sure. We all want to know a quick escape in case we're in danger. We've lived in some shitty shelters, Millie. This place is the lap of luxury."

Millie smiled in understanding. It was a reminder of how desperate these women had become and how untrusting they were of others.

"Okay. You go that way and I'll go this way," Millie stated, and they separated.

It was a beautiful, sunny day and the temperature warmer than usual. Millie felt the perspiration reach her brow. She was nervous, concerned for Jessie's well-being as well as the friend Sally mentioned. It would make sense as to why Jessie would disappear sometimes. Millie, Cindy, and the others felt it was her way of dealing with her emotions. Jessie wanted to be alone and that was acceptable. As the social worker assigned to each woman who came to the shelter, it was her responsibility to get through to the women and help them with whatever they needed. Cindy was doing well getting the women to share their stories of struggles and then providing what they needed to heal and put their pasts behind them. Millie, Anna, and Stacy recently connected with businesses in Turbank where the women could work if they didn't feel comfortable working for the bed and breakfast or on the ranch. There were delis, clothing stores, shopping centers, and other much larger stores that Pearl didn't have.

As Millie entered the thicker area of fields right before the dirt path that led out of town, she spotted Jesse's green shirt.

"Jessie!" she called, and sure enough Jessie came out of the pathway and began walking to her.

"Millie, what are you doing out here?" she asked, looking rather surprised and a bit nervous. Millie had that uneasy feeling in her gut. Something seemed off and the best thing to do was to walk back to the ranch and call one of the men for help. She began to turn.

"Come on, let's head back and you can tell me why you're out here and why you missed your meeting with Cindy."

Millie felt Jessie grab her arm.

"Wait, I can't go back yet," Jessie stated, and Millie turned toward her.

"Why not?"

Jessie looked back toward the fields and then to the ground.

"I can't say, but I can't go back yet."

"What is it, Jessie? Tell me what's really going on." Millie didn't want to let Jessie know that she knew about the girl. She was afraid that Jessie might get angry with Sally for confiding in Millie about her friend.

"I just need to go over there, at the end of the trail. I'll come back later."

"Who are you meeting, Jessie? Are you in some kind of trouble?" Millie asked.

"It's just a friend of mine. You see, she's scared. Really scared, Millie, and I've been bringing her things."

"Why won't she come to the shelter? You see how we are there? We'd be more than willing to help your friend if she needs it."

"Like I said, Millie, she's scared. Some guys chased her through the woods in Turbank. She got away, but it frightened her. She won't go far, but today I got her to meet me closer to Pearl. I think if I can convince her that it's a nice, safe place then she'll come and you can meet her."

"What if I talk with her? Do you think she'll run if she sees you coming with someone?"

"I'm not sure." Jessie looked back toward the path as if deciding what to do. Millie reached over to touch her arm. She understood her fear and Millie wanted to help.

"I won't upset her. Why don't you let me try?"

Jessie smiled then swallowed hard before nodding her head.

"It's just a little ways past the end of the trail," Jessie told Millie, and they headed that way.

The farther they walked the more uneasy Millie was becoming. She didn't know what made her turn back to take a look at how far they walked, but when she did she sure as hell wasn't expecting to see Frank sneaking up behind them with a knife in his hand. Millie lost her breath and her ability to scream. She looked quickly toward Jessie, concerned for her life, but Jessie didn't look scared. She looked relieved.

* * * *

Wyatt pulled up to the Triple C by the main house. He was going to have lunch with Anna, but just as he made it up the drive, his cell phone rang. He placed the truck in park and pulled out his cell phone. In the rearview mirror he noticed Dalton's truck approaching. *He must be meeting Millie for lunch, too.*

"Sheriff Wyatt Cantrell," he answered his cell.

"Wyatt, it's Detective Flynn. I'm glad I caught you. I just received a call from FBI Agent Michael Benz. They got a lead on Frank."

"That's great news. Where's he at?" Wyatt asked.

"He's somewhere in Turbank by now, perhaps in Pearl. They received a frantic call from the psychologist. She claims to be hiding from Frank and that he's right outside her hotel door. They've got people on their way to the scene."

"What? What the hell do you mean? He's here somewhere?" Wyatt asked as he looked out across the fields and around the house. He was immediately concerned for everyone's safety. That's when he saw Anna running toward his vehicle. She looked upset.

"I'm on my way. I'll be there in less than thirty minutes. The FBI should arrive at the ranch any time now. Wyatt, they found Dr. Sheila Perkin's body. She's dead."

"Son of a bitch!" Wyatt exclaimed then looked at Anna. "Hold on one moment, detective." He covered the phone.

"Millie is missing. She went to look for Jessie because she was missing and then Sally came back saying she saw them with some really big guy near the end of the fields."

"What's going on?" Dalton asked as he approached.

"Tell him, Anna," Wyatt stated then he spoke into the phone.

"Did you hear that, detective?" Wyatt asked.

"Yes. Find her, or she's as good as dead."

Wyatt hung up the phone.

"Let's take the truck, Dalton."

"Fuck!" Dalton yelled then jumped into Wyatt's vehicle.

As they skidded out of the driveway, Wyatt called into the station and Dalton called Hank. As they drove out, Wyatt could see Anthony and Jeremy jumping into their truck along with two more ranch hands.

Wyatt sped toward the location where Millie was last seen.

* * * *

"Give me my money and you can have your little reunion," Jessie told Frank as Millie tried to keep a distance from Frank. She wondered what the hell was going on that Jessie was asking for payment. Did he set this up? He must have found Jessie and convinced her to help him. That was just like Frank. He was manipulative and used his looks, his charms to get what he wanted. Millie took a step back, slowly trying to inch away. Maybe she could make a run for it. Her heart was pounding in her chest.

"Don't move, Millie," Frank stated firmly, and she froze.

"What do you want, Frank? You know I'm not interested in anything you have to say."

He was in her face in a flash. The hit was quick and right to her belly. She hung over, gasping for air.

"Hold on to that thought, honey, while I tie up some loose ends," he stated calmly and before Millie could look up Jessie fell to the ground screaming.

Millie was shocked and she wasn't sure if she was imagining it, but blood gushed from Jessie's belly.

Millie screamed then stumbled toward the ground as she attempted to run.

The large hand grabbed her hair, pulling her back up. She felt the slice to her arm, the sting of pain as she turned and pulled from Frank's grasp.

He stood before her, arms wide, the hunting knife in one hand and the most evil, dark expression on his face. She wouldn't pull her eyes from him to look at the gash to her forearm. She knew it was deep and she knew she would need stitches if she made it out alive.

"Don't run, Millie. I really want to spend some time with you before I kill you."

"You're sick, Frank. You need help."

"I need you, Millie. You're my one and only lover and we belong together."

She had to keep him talking. By now, Sally would have gotten back to the ranch and they would all be looking for her and Jessie.

"That's not what I hear."

"What?" he asked as he slowly walked toward her and she sidestepped. They were circling one another and he was about to pounce.

"I heard you were sleeping with your doctor, Frank. You cheated on me," she stated, not knowing why she said that. She was rambling and trying her hardest to not reveal her fear of him. Her voice chattered no matter how hard she tried to calm herself. She was going to die. He just stabbed Jessie, he killed Clare and Stewart and who knew who else.

"I had to do that so I could get to you, don't you see that, baby?" Frank replied.

She shook her head. "It's not right."

"No! What you're doing isn't right. You fucking five men, Millie. I heard about them. I know about them and they're as good as dead. One of them already is."

Her eyes widened in shock. *Dalton, Anthony, Jeremy, Hank, and Marco? Oh God, he killed one of them?*

First she was filled with fear, but then anger arose inside of her.

"You're a fucking liar. They're better than you and you wouldn't ever be able to get to them."

He lunged for her and she struck her injured arm out, banging him over the neck.

He faltered then quickly turned around to come back at her with the knife.

She remembered what Dalton and Hank had taught her. She would tire him out. She had been training and could do this. Her life and their lives depended upon it.

He lunged the knife at her and she kicked at his wrist.

"You're going to come with me. We can do this the hard way if we have to," he told her.

"I'm not going anywhere with you, Frank. This ends here and now." She was so scared she felt as if she weren't even in her own body. Frank was here. He had killed one of her lovers and she didn't know which one. It hurt so badly inside she didn't care if she lived or died.

"You're mine, bitch, and your men are going to die one by one. Only four to go."

He lunged again and again. She countered then struck him hard in the face. Her knuckles burned and her arm dripped with blood. He caught her leg with the knife. She stumbled back and he came toward her. Quickly she sidekicked, knocking the knife from his hands but losing her balance as he fell on top of her. Immediately, she wrapped her arms around his neck and her legs around his ribs and squeezed. He reeked of sweat and cologne. He growled and yelled in her ear as he pounded his body against hers, making her lose her breath with every pounce against the hard ground. She screamed and tightened her hold and he lost his breath for a moment. She did it again and he rolled her to the side. They rolled and rolled and he was crushing her. Before she knew what he was doing, she caught the reflection of the metal blade in the sun. He was trying to get to the knife. She wiggled and squirmed as he got to all fours with her still wrapped around him like some winter scarf.

"I was hoping to fuck you first, but I guess I can kill you then fuck you."

She fell to the ground and he reached for the knife. She swung at his arms, scrambled to her feet, and kicked him in the face. She turned to reach for the knife and her legs came out from under her. She screamed as Frank pulled her ankle and calf. Her belly scraped against the ground and she wiggled her body to roll to her back. He was crawling up over her, his mind now set on raping her instead of slicing her.

Her eyes darted around. She got her bearings, saw the knife, and reached for it.

He tore her shirt open. Her arms were raised above her head, her fingers on the handle of the hunting knife.

He was so out of it. His focus was on her body, her breasts. The bastard thought she was still weak, a victim ready to falter from her attacker's assault.

"Mine." He yelled as he squeezed her ribs with his hands on either side of her waist. The move hoisted her up and she gripped the knife tighter.

"No. Don't!" she screamed. She could feel the bruising where his fingers dug into her flesh. Then he let go and began to rip the button of her jeans open.

She kicked her legs and he grabbed her and shook her.

"Lay still and take what you deserve. You'll never be with another man. You're mine, bitch, and then you're dead."

"No. Never again!" she screamed.

"Stop, police!"

Millie lunged the knife forward with all her might as Frank turned toward the loud male voice.

The blade slammed into his neck and he froze above her as blood shot from where the blade stuck out.

She shoved him over and scrambled backward, crying in fear.

When she felt strong arms touch her shoulders, she screamed and fell backward onto the ground.

"It's okay, baby, it's me." She looked up toward Dalton. He had tears in his eyes and he looked as white as a ghost.

"Oh God, Dalton!" She jumped up into his arms and he held her against him, rubbing her back as she sobbed.

She could hear sirens, lots of voices, and Wyatt's voice. "He's dead, the piece of shit."

She lifted her head off of Dalton's shoulder to look back to where Wyatt was and to see for herself that Frank was dead.

"Don't, baby," Dalton whispered with his hand against her cheek.

"Millie, my God, are you okay?" Jeremy asked as he knelt down on the ground next to her. He brushed the hair from her cheeks and she nodded.

"You're bleeding, baby. You need medical attention," Anthony stated as he joined them.

They were all concerned.

Marco now stood above them. He was out of breath and looked madder than hell.

"Holy shit, Millie. He could have killed you," Marco stated as Dalton stood up and helped Millie to stand. They looked her over. Her body throbbed, but mostly her arms stung and her legs were shaking.

"Is he dead?" she asked, still in a fog from the events that took place.

"Don't look, Mill," Marco whispered to her as he cupped her cheek while Anthony pulled her shirt closed so no one could see her breasts. She was so numb with fear she didn't even care. One of them zipped up her jeans.

She saw Wyatt standing over Frank's body. To the right, she saw other men in suits. They were looking over at another body.

"Jessie?" Millie gasped then covered her mouth.

"She's dead, Millie."

"Oh God."

"She helped him find you and get to you. I wouldn't think twice about her, either," Anthony stated firmly.

"Millie, let's get you to the hospital, honey," Wyatt said.

"Is he dead, Wyatt? Is he really dead?" she asked, and he nodded his head. "You did real good, Millie. You fought hard to survive and he won't be able to hurt another human being ever again."

Dalton lifted her up and carried her out of the fields and to the awaiting ambulance.

Chapter 19

Millie was lying on the bed, sleeping. Her bandaged arm lay across her belly. She moaned a lot in her sleep and Marco, Dalton, Anthony, Jeremy, and Hank took turns lying around her, keeping her from rolling onto her arm. Right now Hank and Dalton lay with her while Anthony, Jeremy, and Marco cooked breakfast.

Dalton stared at the bandage on her thigh. She didn't need any stitches there, so she shouldn't have a scar. Her arm was a different story. Over three hundred stitches and a lot of healing to do, but she was alive. Her ribs were bruised, her belly scraped up from her struggle. Dalton took a deep breath then leaned down to kiss her skin.

"It will all heal, Dalton. She's tough and she survived," Hank whispered then pulled the sheets up higher so her breasts were covered. Millie moved and the sheets fell down. Hank re-covered her again. This went on a few more times until Dalton chuckled. "I think our little angel is awake."

Millie smiled then opened her eyes.

"How can I sleep when you two are staring at me and kissing my belly?"

Hank ran the palm of his hand down under the sheets to her belly. The sheet went down with his hand and revealed her beautiful breasts.

Both Hank and Dalton leaned forward and licked a nipple.

"Oh, now, you are so going to have to give me more than that," she stated, and they continued to feast on her breasts. Both men lifted their heads and blew warm breath against her nipples.

"Please touch me," she begged.

"Doctor Jones said to take it easy. We don't want to open up those stitches or make you feel any pain from the bruising on your body," Dalton reprimanded then cupped her breast.

She turned toward him. "You better do something or I'm going to get very angry."

"What's going on in here?" Marco asked as he entered the room.

His eyes zeroed in on her breasts and Dalton smiled.

"Seems our little woman is quite horny."

"Fuck, baby, we're all fucking horny," Marco stated.

"I need you guys and you're not being fair." She pouted.

"Doc said to take it easy so the stitches don't open up," Marco said.

Millie lifted her arms above her head, causing her breasts to lift up toward them and the sheets to fall lower, almost revealing her mound.

"I promise to keep my arms above my head."

"Fuck, that just ain't fair," Dalton stated then cupped her breast. Hank ran the palm of his hand from her breast down her belly to her pussy.

Millie moaned and then Marco pulled the sheets down as he climbed up between her legs while Hank pressed a digit up into her pussy.

"Oh!" she moaned.

Dalton swallowed hard as he watched Hank finger Millie. He looked toward Marco, who had somehow removed his jeans in a flash and now sat back between Millie's thighs.

Marco ran the palms of his hand up her thighs, his fingers expanding over her skin.

"So sexy and hot," he whispered.

"So needy," she chimed in, and they chuckled.

Hank pulled his fingers from her to help Dalton spread her thighs a little wider as Marco lowered to his belly. Marco smiled up at Millie.

"You keep those arms above your head, Millie, and if we hear a sound of pain coming from you, we're stopping. Understand?" Marco asked, and Millie nodded.

He swiped his tongue over her pussy then latched on to her clit. Dalton and Hank kept a hand on her thighs so she couldn't close them and she thrust her hips upward in frustration.

"Please, more. I need more," Millie told them.

"More you'll get, sweetness," Dalton whispered then leaned up to kiss her mouth.

* * * *

It was exquisite torture being spread like this in front of her men. Now all she needed was for Anthony and Jeremy to join them and she would be very happy.

Marco moved his mouth and sucked along her inner thighs. The aches and pains in her body subsided with every touch, caress, and stroke from her lovers. Even if she felt some pain, she sure as hell wasn't going to tell these men. They had willpower beyond hers.

Marco lifted up and she was momentarily disappointed until he replaced his tongue with his cock. Slowly, he pressed his engorged penis into her while Dalton and Hank held her thighs wide open. In this position, he felt full and completely ready to come. These men of hers were good. They knew how they could pleasure her without moving her body so much that it may cause her pain.

"Feel good, baby?" Marco asked as he pumped his hips slowly in and out of her.

"Faster, Marco."

"Not too fast, baby, I may hurt you."

She locked gazes with him and when she went to reach for him with her injured, bandaged arm he stopped and gave her his "don't mess with me" look.

She immediately pulled back. "I just wanted to tell you that you could never hurt me. I love you, damn it, now make love to me or else!"

"Or else what?"

Millie looked toward the doorway where Anthony and Jeremy stood wearing only blue jeans. Their muscles looked enticing and she had the urge to lick every inch of them all.

Marco took that moment to shove into her to the hilt then pull back and do the same thing three more times.

She gasped and moaned while he increased his thrusts and both Hank and Dalton pinched and suckled her breasts. She was ready to explode when Marco beat her to it. He filled her with his essence and then leaned over her to kiss her mouth and ravage her. When he pulled his mouth from hers he also pulled his cock from her pussy, making her moan.

"No worries, baby, this pussy will be filled with cock momentarily," he teased then pinched her clit as he moved off the bed. She squirmed and tried wiggling, but Hank and Dalton remained holding her thighs wide. It turned her on and kept her so high strung and ready to catapult off the bed it was exhilarating.

Dalton slid off the bed and Jeremy took his place holding her thigh, except now he was naked. He smiled at her.

"Love you, sweetness," Jeremy told her then leaned down to kiss her mouth.

The bed dipped and Dalton sat between her legs. He leaned over her and licked her lips, kissed them, then licked a trail from her mouth, over her breasts, to her belly.

Jeremy and Hank held her thighs wide as Dalton pressed his cock into her pussy.

Millie moaned. This was sensational and she felt so loved and safe here with her men.

"I love you, baby," Dalton stated then began to stroke her slowly, eliciting moans from her and causing tiny quakes of release within her body.

"I love you, too, Dalton, but please move faster. I need to come."

He pulled out and thrust hard and fast into her. His speed rocked the bed and apparently turned on his brothers, because Jeremy began making love to her mouth while Hank licked and kissed her breast. She felt the tap to her cheek and there was Jeremy, holding his cock for her to taste. He awkwardly knelt up on the pillow and she reached her tongue out to taste him. She took him as deeply as she could in such a position and with her arms still raised above her head.

Dalton screamed her name and came as he thrust hard against her. Jeremy pulled from her mouth.

"Dalton," he called, and the men exchanged looks. Dalton pulled from her body and Jeremy took his place. Just as Jeremy slowly pushed into her pussy, he rolled to his back, taking her along with him.

She was laying over Jeremy, his legs and her ass over the edge of the bed.

His cock was hard inside of her as he gyrated his hips up into her but kept her locked against him so she couldn't move. His cock felt incredibly hard and his eyes were glazed over. She started to rise up, wanting to rock her hips against Jeremy's cock, but he hugged her to him as Hank pressed her down.

"Lie against him with your arms over his shoulders so you can't hurt your arm," Hank told her.

She wasn't certain what they had in mind, but she was so aroused she really didn't care. She could hear the dresser drawers opening and closing and Jeremy kissed her mouth, drawing her attention completely on him.

Behind her, large hands adjusted her ass, then she felt the cool liquid and her heart rate increased. She pulled her mouth from Jeremy's just as the tip of a penis pressed against her puckered hole.

She tried to sit up a little, wanting that cock to penetrate now and go fast and hard into her, but Jeremy held her down.

"We don't want to hurt you, but if you sit up you could injure your arm. Let us take care of everything," Jeremy whispered then kissed her forehead.

God, she loved these men. They put her first always.

"I'm going in, baby. I've been dreaming of this tight, sexy ass for days now," Anthony told her, and she smiled then slightly lifted her ass.

The smack came out of nowhere.

"Hey."

"Hey yourself," Dalton replied, and she hadn't suspected him, but then it didn't matter as Anthony began to press his cock through the tight ring of her ass.

He used his hands to spread her ass cheeks then pushed forward until he was fully seated in her ass. She cried out her first small orgasm and began to rub her pussy onto Jeremy's cock. Jeremy thrust up into her as Anthony pressed into her ass. She felt amazingly full and the fact that she couldn't move excited her even more. She felt her pussy explode in pleasure as liquid lubricated both her pussy and ass.

The men began to move one in then one out, over and over again. She was so incredibly wet. They surely were slick and could move faster than usual.

"Damn, baby, this pussy is soaking wet. I fucking love it. Don't you love it, Ant?" Jeremy asked. His dirty talk turned her on and her body began to coil up tight.

Anthony was thrusting into her faster and harder. The bed was rocking, her thighs were shaking, and then both men slammed into her at once. She began to scream her orgasm and felt Jeremy's cock harden then pulsate within her, indicating that he was coming, too. She screamed her release that seemed to go on and on and Anthony pulled out then slammed back into her two more times as he came calling her name.

They were gasping for air. Her cheek was wet against Jeremy's chest as he brushed her hair from her face.

"Love you, sweetness," he whispered.

"Love you, too," she panted.

She felt Anthony's hands on her ass then caressing up her back. When he leaned down to kiss her shoulder and cheek, his cock bumped inside her ass, making her moan. He chuckled then slowly pulled from her ass and kissed along her spine then stroked her ass cheeks again. He seemed obsessed with her ass and she loved it.

"Fucking beautiful."

"Are you okay, baby?" Hank asked.

"Definitely okay," she whispered and closed her eyes as Jeremy rolled her to her back, pulling from her body. She felt hands moving the sheets over her then lift and place her arms over her belly.

"Rest, sweetness. We'll watch over you," Dalton whispered and as she closed her eyes, she embraced the feelings of completion, knowing that with her men she would always feel protected and loved. This was a new beginning, and the fears and mistakes from her past were finally behind her.

Epilogue

Millie, Anna, Stacy, Lena, Sage, Cindy, and Sally were standing in front of the main office along with the other twelve women now living at the women's shelter.

Anthony and Hank were hammering in the hand-carved sign that was currently covered with a sheet so no one could see the name Millie had chosen. The women were waiting to plant some flats of flowers and bushes to decorate the area.

A feeling of triumph filled Millie's heart and she was certain that Anna, Stacy, Lena, and the other women were having similar feelings as they finalized their establishment with a name. It had taken some time, but finally Millie had come up with something perfect.

The sign was burgundy and the letters bold and carved then painted in gold by Anthony and Jeremy themselves. Millie had seen it yesterday and it brought tears to her eyes. The men had made it themselves and she loved them for it.

"Well, Millie, don't keep us in suspense," Stacy stated, and Millie walked over to the sign that was covered with a sheet.

Millie smiled then removed the sheet.

"Welcome to Second Chances."

Everyone began to clap and cheer and the women gathered around to hug one another.

Millie felt the hand on her shoulder and leaned back against Marco.

"It's a great name for the women's shelter, Millie," Dalton whispered to her.

"It sure is. I knew you would come up with something perfect," Anna stated.

"Well, it was hard trying to come up with one or two words to describe everything we're trying to do here at the shelter. When I started to think about the stories everyone has shared and about what brought them here, I realized that coming up with a name wasn't so difficult after all. This is what we're all about. This is why we wanted to create this shelter," Millie explained.

"You're right about that. Perhaps if other women had this kind of place, they could have survived or made a better life for themselves," Lena added, and everyone agreed.

"This is only the beginning, Millie. Together we're going to help so many women have a second chance at a better life," Anna stated.

"To Second Chances!" Lena cheered, and everyone else clapped and cheered for the women's shelter.

Millie smiled wide. She was a survivor just as many of the women standing around her were. With help, support, and love, anything was possible, especially in an amazing town like Pearl. She turned toward her men and smiled wide. She was in love with five men, she was back home where she belonged, and things were only going to get better because this was her second chance at life.

THE END

WWW.DIXIELYNNDWYER.COM

ABOUT THE AUTHOR

People seem to be more interested in my name than where I get my ideas for my stories from. So I might as well share the story behind my name with all my readers.

My momma was born and raised in New Orleans. At the age of twenty, she met and fell in love with an Irishman named Patrick Riley Dwyer. Needless to say, the family was a bit taken aback by this as they hoped she would marry a family friend. It was a modern-day arranged marriage kind of thing and my momma downright refused.

Being that my momma's families were descendents of the original English-speaking Southerners, they wanted the family bloodline to stay pure. They were wealthy, and my father's family was poor.

Despite attempts by my grandpapa to make Patrick leave and destroy the love between them, my parents married. They recently celebrated their sixtieth wedding anniversary.

I am one of six children born to Patrick and Lynn Dwyer. I am a combination of both Irish and a true Southern belle. With a name like Dixie Lynn Dwyer it's no wonder why people are curious about my name.

Just as my parents had a love story of their own, I grew up intrigued by the lifestyles of others. My imagination as well as my need to stray from the straight and narrow made me into the woman I am today.

For all titles by Dixie Lynn Dwyer, please visit
www.bookstrand.com/dixie-lynn-dwyer

Siren Publishing, Inc.
www.SirenPublishing.com

Lightning Source UK Ltd.
Milton Keynes UK
UKHW02f1907140818
327243UK00011B/476/P